'Once outside, he took a step, then another and another. The drones swarmed back and forth. Some were camera drones no doubt taking footage, some were personal drones out spying. What if someone realized he was outside and came to attack him? Despite the armor, he walked faster, rifle extended out before him, index finger on the trigger. The factory was only five blocks away but even if it was one block, venturing beyond one's secure apartment dwelling was a foolish endeavor.'

(From Prisoners of War by J. Saler Drees)

The characters in these short stories are influenced by their environment whether they live in the present, future or past. Some are victims of the dangers surrounding them. Others find safety in unexpected places. The city clashes with the countryside. Nature attacks humans. Buildings harbour secrets. This anthology will take you on a journey through a variety of Selected Places.

More Books from Simone Press

Paranormal Horror - An Anthology of Short Stories

Paranormal Horror Two- An Anthology of Short Stories

Indie - Trigger Short Stories

Offbeat Summer Poems

Facebook- www.facebook.com/simone.press.1

Website- www.simonepress.com

Selected Places

An Anthology of Short Stories

From

Simone Press

Contents

Find Out Where the Train is Going by Allen Kopp

We're in a long room that was once used for something else. There are thirty beds in two rows. These are accommodations for guests of the state: check bouncers, bigamists, shoplifters, pickpockets, prostitutes. You could go on and on calling out their misdeeds, but why bother? They are the morally bankrupt repeat offenders who are not beyond being redeemed or reformed. Give them two years, or four or five, and they'll be out if they're lucky. Redeemed? Not very likely. The really bad ones, the hardened criminals, the murderers, the ones that would throw acid in your face and enjoy doing it, are in another part.

Juniper Tarrant has only been in residence for a few days. She didn't do anything. She is innocent. She was left with some hash or blow or something—she wasn't even sure what it was called—that belonged to her boyfriend, a man named Ed King. He disappeared and she went to jail, no matter how many times she told them it wasn't her fault. Her one hope is that he comes back and tells them what really happened. Of course, she's going to stick a knife in his ribs if she ever gets the chance, but that's something that is going to have to wait.

On her fifth or sixth day (she has lost count already), her lawyer, an elderly man named Arthur Lux, comes to see her. She meets with him in a tiny room with a table and two chairs. A blank-faced guard stands against the wall, a silent observer. As she tells the lawyer again everything that happened, he writes it all down.

"When I woke up," she says, "he was gone."

"*Who* was gone?" the lawyer asks. "You have to be specific in your answers."

"Ed King."

"Was that his real name?"

"It's the name he gave me."

"Did he use any other names?"

"I don't know. Why would he do that?"

"How long had you known him?"

"I don't know. A few months."

"How many months?"

"About six."

"You didn't know he was involved in the selling and distribution of drugs?"

"No! And if *he* was, I wasn't!"

"Do you have any reason to believe he deliberately framed you?"

"No! Why would he do that?"

"So, the two of you were living in this hotel together. What was it called?"

"The Excelsior. And I wouldn't say we were living there. We were staying there for a few days."

"For what purpose?"

"Why does anybody stay in a hotel?"

"Hotel records show the room was registered in your name alone."

"Ed always took the room in my name."

"Why is that?"

"He always had the feeling that somebody was following him. Watching him."

"And you suspected nothing?"

"No. I stayed out of his business."

"After the Excelsior Hotel, where were you planning on going?"

"I don't know. If Ed knew what our next move was, he hadn't told me."

"So, you traveled around with him from place to place and you didn't know what kind of activities he was involved in?"

"He told me he was a salesman."

"What did he tell you he sold?"

"In his day he sold cars, washing machines, life insurance policies and other things, too. He didn't like to talk about it."

"And you didn't question him?"

"Why should I?"

"And you thought he was a perfectly legitimate salesman?"

"I had no reason to believe otherwise."

Arthur Lux closes his notebook, puts his pen away and places one hand on top of the other. "Would you be able to identify him if you saw him again?" he asks.

"Of course!" she says.

"Were you in love with him?"

"I thought I was but right now I hate him so much I could kill him."

"Did you give him money?"

She shrugs and pushes her hair back out of her face. "All I had," she says.

"How much?"

"Five thousand dollars and some change."

"It seems he did you a dirty deed."

"If he would only come back and square me with the police," she says. "Tell them the truth about what really happened. That's all I ask. I would never bother him again."

"Maybe you should be more prudent in your associations in the future," Arthur Lux says with a sad smile.

"Thanks for the advice. It's a little late."

"We're doing all we can but, in spite of our best efforts, we haven't been able to locate him."

"You've got to find him!"

"There's no indication that he even exists."

"What are you saying? Do you think I made him up?"

"I'm not saying that at all. I'm saying that he probably gave you a false name and that he planned on running out on you from the very beginning."

"I fell for his line. I was such a fool."

"We're all fools."

"Can't you pull some strings to get me out of here? Some writ of habeas corpus or something? I don't belong in prison."

Arthur Lux reaches across the table and pats her arm. "Don't despair, my dear. Something is bound to turn up."

Now, every night at nine-ten, just before lights out, a passenger train goes by the prison. For fifteen or twenty seconds the long room with the thirty beds is filled with the clatter and excitement of

9

a train on its way to some undisclosed location. Some of the prisoners cover their heads with their pillows to try to drown it out, while others wait to catch a glimpse of it and, if the light is just right, to catch a glimpse of some of the people riding on it. The train goes by so fast that it is just a blur, but some of the prisoners claim to have seen passengers on the train that they recognized. One woman said she saw her husband who was supposed to be in a mental institution but was obviously out having a good time. Another claimed to see the daughter and son, twins, that she gave up for adoption at the time of their birth twenty-seven years earlier.

Juniper Tarrant falls into the habit of watching the train every night. She is one of those, who, for a few seconds at least, feels a curious sense of release and possibility as the train goes by in the night. As long as trains carry happy people from city to city, the world cannot be all terrible and bad. Some day I'll be free and I'll be the one on the train.

After a week or so of watching the train, she sees Ed King, looking out at her from one of the sleek passenger cars that glides through the night like a bullet. She sees his face so clearly she cannot be mistaken: the dark hair with a little gray mixed in, the brown-green eyes, the little scar above the right eyebrow, the commanding chin. He is wearing a gray suit with a light-blue shirt and a red tie. She remembers the tie. It was the one tie of his that he liked the best.

She turns away from the window, lets out a little cry and is sick. Lying on the floor, she has a kind of seizure. The prisoner in the bed next to her calls for help and she is taken to the infirmary. When the doctor examines her, he tells her she is going to be a mother in about seven months time.

She is given a sedative and kept in the infirmary overnight for observation. In the morning she is desperate to talk to Arthur Lux, her lawyer. When she asks to call him, she is denied. ("What do you think this is, a finishing school?") One of the matrons will try to get a message to him if she can. The message is simple: *I saw Ed*

King on the train. Find out where the train is going and there you will find Ed King.

Betrayal by Melodie Corrigall

Drifting in and out of consciousness, his raw face pricked by the coarse grass Evan's sense of betrayal burned through the pain. His first tears in over sixty years spilled down his bleeding cheeks. His cowardly attempt, to escape witnessing her anguish, had failed.

He had made many promises in his life, some of which he had not kept. His "till death do us part" to his wife Willow had been cut short by divorce. His "Count on me to be there for grad night," to his son was preempted by an emergency board meeting.

But although he was not always reliable, Evan prided himself that in his most essential commitment, he remained true. Together to the end had been his youthful commitment the first time he sensed her splendor although, even then, he had known that he was one among many.

After seventy years, sight of her still made his heart lurch. However extended their separation, nothing diminished his devotion, nothing challenged his surety that without her, he was as air, and that, in turn, he was embedded in her. Nothing, so he had thought, until violently, minutes earlier, sliced between the moment of falling and the sight of his own mortality, he acknowledged his duplicity.

As he hurtled to the rocks below, the raw terror of the impending pain had ripped the screen from his eyes. Flashing like pin ball lights, the many times he had chosen poorly: opportunities ignored, actions put on hold, and inexcusably gullible to promises that his vulnerable lover wouldn't be harmed through his actions.

Thanks to the forgiving cliff side bushes, he had survived the fall.

When he regained consciousness, first at his side was his son Tim who had hurled himself down the hill, after his father, when he saw him slip.

This was to have been the day Evan was to demonstrate to Tim that as CEO of Canadian Wood Industries he had been a wise steward.

"Betrayal," Evan slurred through his bleeding lips.

"Did you say portrayal, Dad?"

"All right, sir, the ambulance is here. You'll soon be safe in hospital."

"Safe?" Evan scoffed. He'd never be safe again.

"It's Evan Williams," someone shouted. "Christ, do the media know?"

They'd know soon enough, the old man thought.

"Are you worried how they'll portray you, Dad? Daran will deal with that."

Daran, the bugger, had dealt with too much. In his smoke and mirrors dips and dives, he had convinced Evan that all was well. He would have prevented his boss' visit to the site today had he known. For the first time in years, Evan had slipped behind the P.R. Screen and was appalled by what he saw.

When they arrived at the hospital, unknown forces jerked the stretcher out of the ambulance. Evan was bumped along as harshly as a cart rumbling over Roman cobblestones: swirls of lights flashed overhead, anxious grey faces swooped down at him.

He needed it to stop. He needed a minute, a silence, a chance to reconnoiter.

"Get the Director," a voice hissed.

"Find him a bed. Now. We'll move someone."

A profound melancholy crushed his chest.

He was sinking.

"Evan," he called to himself, leaning forward to catch his outstretched hand, and then he watched helplessly as his body was sucked into a black whirlpool. It's the shot, he assured himself, grabbing onto the possibility of resurfacing.

The irony was that he had discovered the betrayal on a day of celebration. Back, after forty years, to the paradise of his youth with his long estranged son roped in for the occasion. Evan smug that his son, Tim would be forced to acknowledge that, however it had appeared over the years, his father had been true to his roots. As CEO, he had ensured that Wood Industries addressed environmental concerns when they developed property. Moreover, he had involved young people in the project, so that they would have, as he had, the experience of living with nature.

He had relished the idea of witnessing Tim's amazement when he saw the *Youth At It* project.

Time then for some apologies from a son who learned the phase "Show me" at 11 and never passed up reading a company press release without strutting around asking for proof.

The decision to come had been last minute. Evan had challenged his son to come and witness what the company was doing and, as it was his father's 70th birthday, Tim had relented.

The struggle to keep profits up, to respond to community concerns, and to convince the Board to take on the youth project had been difficult but as the press release six months earlier had shown, it paid off. He had succeeded; profits were up and the environment was protected.

On the drive to the mountain, Evan had taken the opportunity to send a few last messages, and instructed his staff what to do in response to the pipeline proposal. It was only when he left the parking lot with his son and the guide, that Evan noticed the changes: peeking out from behind forested openings, the haggard face of abuse.

Where once there had been the strong forest, now a violent clear-cut, the brook's banks eroded wounds. This was where bears scooped salmon from the stream, but there was no salmon now.

"You're the only bear left around here, sir," joked the young guide.

Evan, puffing and in pain, hurried his pace as they mounted the hill, they would soon come upon the youth project. It showed that, if a CEO kept the faith, business could benefit. From the photos, he envisioned the camp just down from the mine. The project used the water from the stream for electricity and recycled by-products from the excavation.

Around the corner and there it was. But no, no it wasn't. What had happened? Instead of the old stream, there was a dry bed. The forest had been roughly clear-cut and a pile of rusting metal equipment collapsed against a sagging lean-to.

"What happened to the Youth Camp?" he asked the guide.

"The PR thing? All gone."

A disheveled young man crept out of a transit hut, blinking against the sharp sun. "You want something?"

"What's up?" Evan cried angrily. He pointed to a faded *Youth At It Project* sign swinging from a post. "Where is the camp?"

"Kaput. The PR moment for Wood Industries has passed." Then, with a hopeful grin, "Are you with the media?"

"I am not," Evan said. "Wasn't there a camp here?"

"Yeah, but they dammed upstream for the mine and then there was a slide because of the cut above. Ask them down below what happened."

"And the kids?"

"Long gone. I'm here 'til the end of the month to watch over the Company's assets," he laughed, pointing at the pile of rusting equipment.

"What's this eyesore?" his son asked.

Daran had known, damn him. Known that the celebrated youth camp promoted at the stockholders meeting was a bust. He'd put the bugger out to dry when he got back.

His anger pushing him, Evan struggled up the hill to view the site from the summit. When they finally stopped, his heart was jumping. He was too old for this. She was weeping, her dress was shredded and torn, a victim of rape, gang rape. "How could you do this?" she cried, reaching her arms out to him.

"Watch out, Dad. It's slippery," his son called.

Evan leaned cautiously over the crumbling ledge to witness the winding river below. From that height, even the murky waters appeared pristine. He marveled at the tiny figures moving purposefully, oblivious to his watchful eyes. Behind him, he heard her cries but he hadn't the courage to turn and face her. And then, he flew.

In Winter, The Snow by SP Hannaway

A starveling in the winter sky – it's high up, on the wing. It darts about the eaves and the slates, slipping on the roof. It races through the icy air; it wheels and dips. Then it circles back, circles round. A ball of speckled feathers, a gaping yellow bill; it's desperate.

And all around it, frozen, still.

Knot idles on the path. He can't take his eyes off it; his worn face riveted. He can feel its belly aching for a berry. He knows its heart. He sees it climb, soar above the crumbling chimneys of the house, then swoop down in a panic, flit about the farmyard. For a moment, a breath, it stops. It hangs weightless in the heavy evening air. Then it's off, up towards the window where it sees the sky and fell reflected – a way out, another world. It rushes headlong. It cracks into the pane of glass, bounces off. It falls down, limp, to the cold ground.

Knot edges closer, keeping one eye on the house. He longs to be near the bird, to be with it. He loves to see the little things – everything there is, is in the little things – its glassy eye, the twitch in its craggy foot. It's crumpled up among the stones, its heart failing, blood popping from its beak. A herald: a sign of death to the living. To Knot.

•

It's night in his dream. He is Knot, looking dapper in his slightly crumpled tweeds. And he is flying. He is high above the valley, the deep tumbling hills. He's fleeing to the fell – Death on his tail. But the wind is against him. It tosses him. It tries to force him back. And the more he fights, the stronger it becomes. Until it throws him, head over heels, his long arms dangling by his sides. And he falls.

He jumps awake, gasps. He's alive.

A stone crashes into his shed door. He struggles up in the murk and cold, his long johns sagging at the knees. He hunkers down behind the door. He loves to watch Miss Racket throw a stone. It's her sign, her way to bring him to the house. Through a crack, he can see her scout around the yard for another stone, one with a bit of life. She doesn't know he's got his eye on her, the way she lifts her apron as she skirts the puddles, her greying hair pulled back, pinned. Purple shadow pasted round her eyes; the way she hides. He sees her falter as she lifts one – it isn't small – takes aim.

–Do it! Knot mouths.

And she does. The rock clatters against his door. And Miss Racket grins like a little girl. Knot coughs. He sees Miss Racket tilt her head, light up inside. Then she does her morning dance. In the dim light, she sets about it. She scoots round the yard. Circles it.

Sometimes, she slips, slides in her sensible shoes. She sticks her arms out as she picks up speed, as if she could take to the air. But she's startled. Noises from the house – muttering. It flusters her. She puts on her best face, vanishes inside.

•

The orange sun spills over into day. Knot is at the door, hovering. He knocks. Knocks again – an echo of the first. He feels awkward in his suit, shuffles, tries to slough off the panic. He turns away. The house behind him hunches down under lanky trees. He looks to the land- the rough-sewn fields, tired hills, the broken line of mountain.

There's a mouse-under-the-floorboard cough. He looks back. And Miss Racket is behind the door. In the small square window at the top, her painted eyes are caught in the light. They seem to tremble as she looks at him.

–Are you psychic, Mr. Knot?

This is Miss Racket's little game- to know and to seem to not: to not know and to seem to. She witters on.

–How did you know I was looking for you? Was it in your head, Mr. Knot, in your heart of hearts?

This tickles Knot. He glows.

–The thing is, Mr. Knot ... if you're looking for Snuff, he's gone. The young master took him, pushed him in the van. I could hear his nails clawing, scraping on the metal in the back. Off down the lane. In the night.

Knot is beside himself. The young master, take the dog, the life of the farm, Knot's strength?

–Miss Racket?

Miss Racket's eyes circle to the clouds.

–It's his dog, Mr. Knot, not yours. He doesn't want you having it, petting it. He doesn't love the dog, or the farm. The old master died when he was little. You and I were here. And he's still young. Still lost.

Knot is seething. He feels thwarted.

–I have to take them, Miss Racket, before the sky closes in, before the snow. I need the dog.

Miss Racket's eyes flutter.

–Shh, Mr. Knot! He's asleep. He doesn't like to be disturbed.

–The ewes, they have to go to the fell, to the heft. There's nothing here. We're down to the bone.

But Miss Racket disappears, the window empty. Knot slips to the side of the house where the van is dumped. Its ice-grey paint's chipped. He tries the van's back door. But it's tight. The engine clicks as it cools. And Snuff stuck in the back, freezing, slowly.

•

It's a last supper. He rips the bag open with his faithful knife, empties the pellets. The ewes charge, knock him sideways. He loves the way they barge and scrum, their dripping fleeces trailing in the muck. It's hunger. He has to wrestle them from one trough, shove them to another. They're headstrong. They're hard to shift. And there isn't much feed: a bag, two. The young master doesn't care. And so: a last supper. What else is there?

•

Knot twists on his mattress on the floor. He can't sleep. He misses Snuff lying at his feet, keeping them warm. The wind rages and the leaves are aflutter. A spatter of hailstones strikes the window. Soon, the snow will come.

He hears the van – the young master barreling through the night, tearing up the windy lane. Knot huddles by the door in his blanket, has to see. The headlights arc through the air. The van hurtles into the yard, screeching. Its lights stay on. Its engine rumbles. Then the gears shift; the van reverses, fast, whining as it backs away. Knot can see it stop. Rev. Then it takes off. He can't believe it. The van is headed straight for the house – to ram it – the door where Miss Racket lingers, the spot where Knot sometimes stands.

•

It wracks his heart. It kills Knot. His door stirs in the morning wind but no stone comes. He clambers up, trailing the blanket at his bony feet. Through the door, he scans the yard for a pair of skipping shoes. It's empty. The air is cold, cutting– a sliver of daylight.

At the house, Miss Racket is behind the door. He can hear her shoes scuff the concrete floor. But no eyes appear. The little window is a mirror for the sky. A feather duster pops up, waves at him. It's pink. And ruffled.

–Are you ready, Mr. Knot?

Her voice is quivery.

–Will you cope with the sheep? They're hefted.

She seems distracted.

–It's a thankless task, birthing. You can't keep them, Mr. Knot. You can't save them from themselves.

Knot would like to see her eyes, tell her he knows them better than he knows himself. She babbles on.

–The young master does what he likes. I promised his father I'd take care of him, and I can't. I love him like a son.

Miss Racket's voice tails off.

–I didn't call you this morning, Mr. Knot. I couldn't.

– ...

–Mr. Knot, the young master doesn't want you here. He says you interfere, turn my head. He says you won't see another winter.

Knot looks down at his polished shoes. He'd like to die. He has no choice, no clout: he's just a hand. He looks up, sees a snowflake falling. It idles, drifts.

–Winter, he says. –It's time.

He turns from Miss Racket, the house. But down the path he stops: there's a voice trailing him.

−Mr. Knot? He's shut me in.

●

He unties the gate, winds the blue twine round his reddened fingers. The gate falls away from the sheep. They don't know what it means. They huddle in the corner of the field, facing the gap. They stare at Knot. They sniff the air as if it's new.

−Come by!

He says it without thinking. He looks around for Snuff, for the shape of him. The ewes trickle into the lane – in their memory a panting dog, a black shadow lurking in the grass. They spill out from the field, on their way, hundreds of them. When they reach the end, they could go either way.

−Get down, he urges.

The ewes heed the gruffness in his voice, veer away from the dog not lying in their path. They head for the fell. Their hooves patter on the ice, mud scattering.

They make good time on the bending road, in the dead hush of winter. Knot buries himself in his heavy coat, feels the air nip his face. He clutches the twine bundled in his pocket. It tortures him, what he's left behind. Snuff, Miss Racket; in the master's grip.

Before he realises, it's open ground. The upland unravels. The fell pushes up to the sky. The ewes rush forward and Knot struggles to stay with them. His boots sink in bog. Bracken slows him; it's thicker this year. A rock gives way, slides beneath his tiring feet. The hillside is steep, the ground uneven. His legs burn but he digs in.

On the upper fell, the land is closer to the sky. The high wind nearly knocks him off his feet. And Knot remembers his dream: flying. The sheep scatter to find fresh shoots of heather. Knot digs in his pocket for a sweet, puts it in his mouth. It's sharp like a berry bursting on his tongue. He's landed.

●

He drops down on his knees at the hawthorn. It lies prone on the hillside, sculpted by the wind. But it still has life. And power. Knot's in awe of it, the way it grips the earth; bowed down, unbroken. He tears a thorn from the tip of a twig – it's razor sharp –

tears off another, a third. He invokes the tree. He whispers to the thorns: Snuff, Miss Racket, the young master. He binds them in the twine, makes a knot. Then he digs a hole with his knife. And he buries the knot under the twisted trunk.

It's strange. It feels warm. A bead of sweat trickles down his nose. The air is different. And then the snow comes. It falls like a gift from another world. On little frozen wings, a ghostly flock.

•

The light skulks away behind the hills. The dark descends. It folds around Knot like a swirling cloak.

He climbs further, higher. He has to bow his head to stand in the unforgiving gale. He finds the place. He beds down in the heather, on a shelf of rock. He looks up at the snow rushing toward him, without end. And he surrenders to it, accepts it.

His eyes close under the cold white blanket. He lets the snow cover him, the winter take him.

•

And the wild plants burst from the earth, grow up through his bones, are born: yellow stars, sundew, a sea of wavy-hair-grass. Knot's in them. Somewhere.

A starling flies up with a cloudberry in its beak. It seems giddy, it dances; it's madly alive. Then something compels it, it sweeps away. It hurtles across the awakening land.

Sole Survivor by Tom Larsen

I came around to a slap of salt water and a sea level view of nothing but blue. The boat, the Ballesteros, the Brandy Alexanders, gone, all of it, lone survivor spared for worse. The smart money would have been on Ballesteros, all that brawn and blather, but BB's gone and gone means dead. Her too, though it's hard to believe it. She was telling me something when we hit the reef, a loud crack and we both pitched forward. That's all. Two dead, one yet to die.

Alone in the purest sense.

Only one thing to do so I do it, pick a direction and start swimming. Lose the shoes, lose the pants, don't think just focus. But even on its last track the mind feeds back images, the final flailing, the tortured breath, the drowned man's surrender to stillness. I've read the books, against all odds. I know what it takes and I don't have it.

But for now, swim, toward or away from, no marking progress, no gap to close. What's left is to stop swimming and that time will come.

Regrets, aw Jesus. Vienna for New Year's, a dream turned to dust even as I dream it. To see Angie again, if just for a moment, last time drunk with love and lemoncello. The old demons raring up, my dog, my dad, my chosen path. What you don't miss until it's gone, a stiff drink and a chance to redeem yourself.

The life vest was no safety measure. I wore it for bulk, to fill space as BB did. I liked the way it looked, vanity as a survival skill. How I won't wear a seatbelt in fear of a wrinkle.

"I will not die," to test the effect, a human voice if only my own.

Then, on impulse;

"I will not say anything vapid."

The shoulders will go soon enough, stomach and thighs from treading water, taking longer to rest. Good shape for my age but not long for this shit. Cold now and getting colder, give up time before things get worse, muscle cramps, sharks and whatnot. Die in daylight, the little left of it.

Fuck me.

BB was a dick. The ocean always spooked me. She was the reason. Not to love but to even the score, put the horns on BB as he did me. Late one night over too much wine, she told me the tale of Doctor Sardonicus. Her voice gave me pleasure, nothing more.

I stop to rest but there is no rest, straining for the surface, huffing in ragged gasps. Oh shit. Fucking shit. My Art Tatum records, the new bag of weed, oh sweet Jesus. My time ticking down in a groan of sorrow, wracked with grief, missing myself. Bye mom ... bye ...

My eyes squeeze shut, but it's there when I look, a pale light ahead. And it's real all right, but I'll never reach it.Kill me, God, only don't make me laugh.

I know now rage saved those never say die boys. Nothing else can push us that far, no other force will prevail beyond pain to a zone of madness. Sink your teeth in the hand of fate, kill what would see you die, and even that's not enough. Luck draws last so you have it or you don't, way of the world, nothing personal.

I'm not thinking this. I'm not thinking anything. The light shines low on the water, lost to the swells again. Choking now every few minutes, the vest straps rubbing raw. Can't move but can't sink either. Turned around in the tug of tide then back again and the light looks closer. I watch then don't watch, could be the charm, too cold to function, too weak to form intent.

Closer still.

I end up curled into a sand dune, barely breathing and better off dead. First and worst of the castaway's fears; live through it to die anyway. Crazy with thirst I stagger into the bushes, naked, shoeless, both feet bloody in twenty yards. Back to my dune, as if to get something, cell phone, shoes, my dune, as if I could find it. Cross the beach at a wobble, down wind and into the sun. Water somewhere but how to find it? Fast.

Desert island, right?

Inland slopes uphill. Water runs down, I know that. Keep walking, my one shot and the most I can manage. Sure enough it's not even far. A freaking lagoon and its wade right in, drink my fill, soak up strength and chase down my senses. The squeal of gulls like nothing's amiss, a rush traced to a waterfall, picture perfect and me with no camera. A laugh, like I've got this knocked, buck naked and ranting like a fool.

So, immediate need duly met. I won't die of thirst, which is no great shakes but gives weight to the moment. First bullet dodged. One nothing, me.

The rest is academic with no shoes. Mid afternoon by the sun, four hours of light left, maybe less. Food would be top priority, or is it shelter? No clouds as yet, but this is the tropics. Face the night wet or hungry, probably both if I don't think of something. Wrapping my feet in leaves? Some guys, maybe, but not me in a million years. What then? Sit here when I can still move? Skirt the island, if nothing else. Keep to the sand, maybe stumble on something, a cave or culvert, an all night bodega. My snicker dissolves in waves of despair.

Now it's getting dark and I haven't done anything, walked a little, dozed on a rock. Fuck it, I'm not up for this. Rain on the far horizon. Let it come. Go mad. Think candy bars, taco chips, beer pretzels crusted in salt. Think burgers and baked potatoes. Think of
...

... the light!

Lost in the long day's coming to terms. The light was real.

Someone's here.

I scan the hillside but there's nothing, a darker hump in the darkness. Do they know I'm here? You could hardly miss me all day naked on the beach. Either they're coming or they're hiding. If they're coming it may be to kill me. If they're hiding it may be to kill me. If they meant to save me they'd be here by now, but they choose to wait. Or they didn't see me or something's blocking the light. A cliff or overhang, a bad angle, maybe I'm too close. Or there wasn't any light just to cover everything.

If someone's here they must have food. I think of Catherine Street, the pepper and egg sandwich I'd get on my way to work. I made a point to commit it to memory and there it is. And I could use a shirt, now the breeze has picked up. Shoes, of course, and anything you can think of, really, the correct time, a freaking match. What I need is help. What I don't need is a psycho in the bushes.

If someone's here they'd leave footprints. Tomorrow I will circle the island, or as much as I can of it, find a way to get myself out of this. Of course, that will mean leaving *my* footprints all over, but it can't be helped.

I sleep buried in the sand with a club in my hand.

So hungry it makes me nauseous, hollow inside, my stomach busy digesting itself. I eat some grass, just to see, grinds up into shards, maybe a molecule of nourishment. I trap a bug but can't eat it. Not alive. So I smash it and forget the whole thing.

But I can stand up. And except for a million bruises and scabs on my feet, I'm all right. What I know from the binge years. I can go three days without eating a thing. Day Two, the same as Day One weatherwise, my only break but nothing to scoff at. So then … off I go and I'm OK, almost upbeat. The day I give it my all. Let the chips fall etc.

But my feet can't take it and I stall in the shade and stare morosely out to sea. My tan parts bronzed, the rest cherry red, lunchtime by the clock in my stomach, roast pork sandwich on the brain, ballpark franks, T-bone, thick and smothered in onions. Or a banana how about it? I read somewhere you can sustain life on bananas. Not much of a plug but something you remember when you have no bananas. Or coconuts, the other staple my desert island doesn't feature. Spear a fish. Think Tom Hanks in Castaway … except he was alone. Think violent death when I least expect it, which won't be any time soon.

That night I see it, the light. Midway up the hill, a fire looks like, maybe a mile off. Someone's up there, doing God knows what. Saving himself, a fellow survivor, or something else entirely. I try to think what to do, but it just goes in circles. Crazy to try anything in the dark, but crazier to wait, and I'm fucking starved, so I just go.

And it's agony, feet sliced to ribbons but making a dent and stoking myself. Fuck it, do what it takes, let adrenaline kick in. An hour later I'm halfway there.

God damn!

It's daybreak when I reach the ledge. I follow the smoke to a guy hunched at a campfire, big guy in a trance of some sort. He's bearded and bald with a blue kerchief headband. Not much of a campsite, roasting spit, stacks of wood, a bed of grass tucked in the rocks. Hasn't been here long, from the look of it. Clothes in fair shape, and he's wearing shoes. The fire dwindles, a mist settles over. I watch through the leaves but he doesn't move.

Then he does, rocking slowly side to side, drunk maybe, who knows. Then he's singing, softy at first then louder, the tune lost to volume, no language I've ever heard. Then he's quiet again, stone still, sensing my presence or sound asleep. Either way I stay where I am.

No food that I can see.

So while getting here seemed so urgent, what to do is not so clear. Is he crazy? No way do I stroll out of the jungle and chum up a great big crazy man. And you would go crazy here if you didn't starve first, though he's not too crazy to feed himself. Still he comes across wacko. To me, crouched naked in the woods. Glued to the spot no less, thinking what would BB do? Ex-marine by way of a washout, windbag by trade, though BB always had a plan. Half-baked to lame brained but a course of action, a move to make. I need some of that.

This guy's story … whatever it is he brought stuff with him. The blanket strung on a line for one, the line for another. That box by the bed didn't wash up on the beach. He had a boat. Or someone left him here.

And this trance and the singing, maybe it's a cultural thing, a rescue rite … or just a guy by himself blowing off steam. Who doesn't act the fool when there's no one to see? No way for me to know so I just watch. Him. The box. I just know there's food in it. Twinkies and Mars bars, chips and dip, I don't care. Head cheese, anything, Tic Tacs.

… Who would leave him here, and why? Some score settled or worse. He did something, killed somebody … or worse, a maniac with survival skills, and shoes, and that box of burgers. What else could explain him being here? My only hope is he'll go

26

someplace so I can find the food. But where would he go? And what if he doesn't? Hunger, and now, of course, thirst will soon force my hand. How I can't imagine.

It gets worse. He spends an hour throwing a knife at a tree and not missing once. Big, nasty knife and the last thing I wanted to see. Later he slips off when I'm not looking and I lock up in panic. Knives! ... With me it's a phobia. And I don't even breathe but the surf blocks the silence. I feel around for a rock, anything.

But then he's back again. With three squirrels by the tail and I don't have to guess how he came by them. I watch him work the knife then fit the critters to the spit and it takes a while but the first whiff brings me to my knees. Meat sizzle not ten yards away and I hug my knees, squeeze hard as I can. What to do? What? But with his knife and my footprints the conclusion is foregone. This place isn't big enough for two sole survivors.

He works the spit and I creep in inches, centimeters. Do it while he's distracted. Kill him now with this rock. Don't waffle, my only chance. He's got a weapon and a hundred pounds on me. And he will kill me if only not to worry. Then my mind goes blank. I leap from behind and cave his head in.

Two years ago, would be my guess, and not a day goes by where I don't miss him, American, from Ohio. There were letters, a book of crossword puzzles, nothing to say why he was here.

Stevenson his name was. I knew a guy once named Stevenson.

Fourth of July in Maine by William Doreski

Brett hated the Independence Day parade. Kids in silly costumes pretending to be patriots and rebels, when they'd all grow up to be right-wing, self-enslaved Republicans. He watched his six-year-old daughter march past in her Betsy Ross frilled dress, a firetrap if anyone ever wore one. "I hate this parade," he said to the couple beside him.

The man looked startled, but the woman replied, "I do too, but we have to pretend to enjoy it, so smile and look proud of your daughter."

How did she know that was his daughter? Everyone in Castine seemed to know Brett by name, but he couldn't even remember what to call his next-door neighbors, the ones in the brick Federalist house with the gold eagle above the door. The eagle looked tacky, but the house was a beauty, an imitation Samuel McIntyre, authentic enough to shame everything built after 1830. Brett's own house wasn't bad—a Greek Revival from the 1850s—but lacking house-pride, he would have sold it in an instant and never come back to this tourist-trap town if Becky hadn't convinced herself that the twins had to summer among the yacht-club swells.

Now Brett's son passed in his blue Revolutionary soldier-coat with a toy musket dragging on the pavement. "Pick up your musket," Brett whispered as the boy passed without hearing him. The child looked drugged.

The woman observed, "He looks just like you."

Brett supposed she meant that the child looked like he was having about as much fun as his father. If only we could ignore these silly holidays: Memorial Day, in honor of war dead no one remembered or cared about; Fourth of July, commemorating a rebellion that would gain no traction in today's timid middle-class America; Labor Day, truly pointless for people who equate union membership with joining the Communist Party. Brett wasn't especially fond of Maine, but it was mostly the holidays that irked him; he didn't really mind the rest of the summer. He liked looking from his back yard over the bay at the islands drifting here and there, and he enjoyed sailing when he could find someone from the yacht club sober enough to crew for him. Becky hated sailing, and resented every cent Brett spent on his boat, which was pretty ironic considering how she worshipped the yacht club set.

As he turned to slip through the crowd the woman caught his arm. He looked at her. A sleek blonde, about his age but nicely preserved. Her figure would stop traffic if this rich town weren't full of her type. He remembered her name: Priscilla. Priscilla Muld. He remembered that name because Becky had joked about how Priscilla's husband, whose name was Rick and was a lawyer, should have belonged to a law firm named "Muld, Slime, and Mildew." Since Becky hardly ever made jokes Brett had carefully filed that one away.

"Nice seeing you," Priscilla said and let go of his arm. Her smile looked more sheepish than flirtatious.

"You too, Priscilla," Brett said, and she looked so pleased that he realized that she thought he had lost her name beyond recovery. Rick turned and nodded, his doughy lawyer-face a vague abstraction. He apparently was enjoying himself as much as Brett was.

Brett cut across the village common where a few older kids were tossing a Frisbee. The girls looked almost naked in their halter tops and tiny shorts, and the boys looked childish with their backwards baseball caps and heavy metal-band T-shirts. Brett's house loomed over the common like a giant tombstone. It felt that way, too, chilly inside even in the hottest weather, and impossible to heat in the winter. His great-aunt had left it to him out of spite. He had almost reached the door when he remembered that he had to fetch the twins home. Becky hadn't gone to the parade—she claimed she wasn't feeling well, that gardening all day yesterday had made her feel a little sun-struck, whatever that meant.

He headed down Main to the town wharf, where the parade broke up. After sifting through the dispersing crowd, Brett found the twins talking to that old pervert Captain Mayhew, who took tourists on "deep sea fishing trips" in Penobscot Bay, which was hardly the deep sea. Once in a while somebody caught a ten or fifteen-pound striper, and the captain posted a photograph on the wharf to lure other suckers aboard for a long day of heat and frustration.

Brett mentally kicked himself. He realized he was in an unaccountable mood and was silently taking it out on the captain. Old Mayhew had an eye for the ladies, but he wasn't really a pervert, didn't overcharge the tourists any more than anybody else did, and kept his boat clean and in good repair. To atone for his unfairness, Brett greeted Mayhew as warmly as he could. "Hey Captain, how's the fishing?"

"Come out with me some morning and we'll find out. Just for fun. Bluefish'll be running in a couple of weeks."

"Sure thing. What do you use for bait?"

"Bluefish'll take anything. I like to cut up a beef liver. Gets a little blood into the water. The bluefish go nuts." The captain smiled like a sand shark.

Tired and getting whiney, the twins wanted to get home and out of their costumes. Brett was happy to oblige. He was remembering his great-aunt and her terrible struggle with cancer. Liver cancer, now that he thought of it.

Captain Mayhew had innocently triggered that ugly memory. Brett hadn't much liked his great-aunt, who never had a kind word for anyone, least of all her great-nephew. But her pain had touched him, and for her last few weeks he and Becky had visited daily to help out in her sickroom. She had begged for morphine, but the nurse, with stoic self-righteousness, had warned that she'd become addicted if she didn't look out. When the nurse took a break, which usually lasted several hours, Brett had dosed his great-aunt with so much morphine that it was a wonder it didn't kill her. Maybe in the end it had. The nurse had to know where the morphine supply was going, but she was probably just as happy that Brett rather than she was doling it out so generously, keeping the old lady quiet.

Brett hadn't expected to be mentioned in his great-aunt's will. She hadn't much money, and Brett hadn't especially wanted this house. "A white elephant," he told Becky when they inherited the place. "We'll sell it."

But they hadn't sold it. They had kept it, and had now spent four and a half summers there, renting it out for the winter cheaply, unheated. Brett pitied the people who lived there through the cold months—usually academics looking for a quiet place to spend a sabbatical. It was quiet, for sure, but the huge un-insulated house gobbled heating oil at an astonishing rate. One renter, a Boston University professor, had complained that he'd spent three thousand dollars and still had shivered all winter.

The twins surged through the front door and up the broad oak stairway to their rooms to change their clothes. In a few minutes, they'd rush out and play in the yard, or beg Brett to take them down to the water to scout for tiny sea-creatures to torment. Behind the house a meadow swept down to the bay. Brett owned and paid taxes on a couple of hundred feet of rocky shoreline, good for nothing except starfish and tiny crabs.

"Hey Becky," Brett called. No response. He stumped upstairs and opened the door to their dim, curtained bedroom. Becky lay on her back with a wet washcloth on her face. He remembered his great-aunt lying on her back on her deathbed. She had looked healthier than Becky did at that moment. "Hey Honey, still feeling bad? Can I get you something?"

"Just keep the twins quiet, would you? I can't move," Becky sighed.

A stutter of fireworks erupted next door, behind the brick Federalist house. The neighbors loved fireworks and all summer played with firecrackers, rockets, roman candles, and cherry bombs. The twins, now headed downstairs, cheered. Brett shut the bedroom door and followed them into the back yard, where his gas grill stood unused and unloved. He had wanted to barbecue something today, maybe a pair of chickens neatly halved, but Becky had seemed too glum. This house, Brett thought, hates Becky, tolerates me, and sort of likes the kids. Yet Becky was the one who insisted on keeping it.

The wind streamed across the bay, ripping blue corrugations into the surface. A great day for sailing, but without Becky to look after the kids he couldn't even consider it. The twins ran through the mass of field flowers beyond the narrow strip of mown lawn. Tansy, meadow rue, Indian paintbrush, the first pink steeplebush. Brett followed. So we're going down to the cove to play in the tide pools. The sharp blue of the bay hurt his eyes, He needed a drink, wanted to dose himself with whiskey iced to kill. He liked that phrase: *iced to kill*. The children parted the tall grass and flowers like sharks cruising for small fry.

The New England summer at its midpoint looked too bright and confident to ever succumb to foul weather, but Brett knew how quickly it could change, the storms billowing up the coast in a rage of wind and rain. He had been caught out on the bay often enough by gusts so sudden they had put him on beam-ends before he could react. Luckily his buoyant little boat righted itself as readily as a kayak, and he'd never felt in real trouble. But he wondered what it would be like to go down in a whirlpool of storm-green water the way those Gloucester fishermen had, his tiny craft sucked into the depths and his fragile body crushed by the sheer weight of the water before he could inhale enough of it to drown.

The thought cheered him, and he ran to catch up with the twins. They turned and laughed at their hurrying father, and Brett thought he might salvage a little of this day after all. Tonight maybe Becky would feel well enough to listen to Nadia Boulanger on the hi fi, or maybe even Joan Baez. They had both loved Baez when they were first married. Or maybe they'd just listen to the wind off the water, smell the salt and feel better about each other. Brett would build a fire in the deep old fireplace and they'd watch the birch logs crumble. The whiskey would burn inside of him like the embers of their lives. Maybe someday they'd retire here. Already, as Brett panted down the slope, the twins were splashing in their favorite shallow pool. They screamed in unison as the boy picked up a tiny crab and waved it at his sister. Beyond, toward Nautilus Island, a wood-hulled ketch tacked against the sturdy wind.

Road Games By Arthur Carey

A bartender waved a remote and tweaked the satellite dish for the day's early football games as Larry walked into the Watering Hole in San Jose, California.

"Michigan-Wisconsin?" he asked.

The bartender pointed. "Over there."

Larry hunkered down at a table with good sight lines to a 50-inch, wall-mounted TV and picked up a menu. It was too early to drink, so he scanned the breakfast offerings and decided on the Field Goal Special—three scrambled eggs, Cajun links, home fries and Texas toast.

By the time his order arrived, the place was perking like the coffee. Customers—mostly male—trickled through the front door wearing shirts and caps emblazoned with images of college mascots: an alligator… a tiger… a bulldog… a badger. They reminded him of those little drawings by cages at the zoo.

Larry wore a 1997 Rose Bowl shirt purchased on eBay. He had an extensive collection of college sports apparel, which he added to frequently. This shirt featured a snarling Wolverine with a bad overbite. He had cut off the long sleeves at the shoulder, revealing muscular arms. One was decorated with the tattoo of an eagle, globe and anchor over the letters *USMC.*

"Okay if we join you?

He looked up from his eggs to see two men standing by the table. One, serious looking with sandy hair and out-of-style aviator-type glasses, wore a gray T-shirt stamped Michigan Athletic Department; the other sported a pronounced gut like Larry's, barely restrained by a wide black belt. He had a white cap with *Wolverines* in bold blue script.

Larry nodded a welcome. "Grab a seat. I'm Larry, '88."

"Ralph," replied one, eyeing the tattoo. "This is Bernie. We're both '01."

"Should be a real barn-burner today," said Larry. "Both teams have only lost one game." Last night, he had checked out the TV schedule for early games back east and in the Midwest.

Michigan and Wisconsin were on tap as Saturday's top Big Ten match up. So he had fired up his iPad and started reading about the game in the Ann Arbor and Madison newspapers. Then he quickly scanned the schools' websites for more information.

So much for dredging up chit-chat for the early game. Then he had turned to the local sports pages for information about San Francisco Bay Area teams, to see if they were playing in the afternoon. He had found lots of ink about Stanford (on the road at Oregon), but little on California, which was enjoying a bye that week. The San Francisco Chronicle's online coverage of the Stanford game had been comprehensive, but he had checked the Stanford and Oregon websites, for more background anyway.

After taking a sip of lukewarm coffee, Larry turned his attention to the morning's game and ventured an opinion on the Michigan running attack. "Looks like Caroll's good to go. Wheels are working again. Maize and Blue should roll!"

"Let's hope," grunted Ralph. "What do you do, Larry?"

"Internet sales," Larry said. He didn't offer any more information about his job. "You?"

Ralph yawned and looked around for a waitress. "Accounting—Intel. I'm Biz Ad and Bernie is Engineering. He designs light bulbs for G.E. that burn out early."

Bernie snorted and rolled his eyes. He'd heard that one before.

"I was general studies," said Larry, "refuge of the indecisive." That drew smiles and no questions as usual.

Ralph ordered scrambled eggs, hash browns and toast. Bernie opted for pancakes. Both had coffee and Larry joined them for a refill.

On the screen, sportscasters sitting behind a circular desk rattled on about other games in the Big Ten that day. The three men ignored them.

They killed time until the game started the way strangers usually do: hunting for common ground for conversation. "Nice weather for November," said Ralph. "Probably better than we'd have if we were in Ann Arbor. I can remember freezing my butt off at the Ohio State game at the end of the season more than once."

Larry nodded. "Midwestern weather is flaky in the fall."

"Nice thing about wearing a heavy jacket though," Bernie said, "you can hide a flask of brandy pretty easy."

"At least we never had to put up with anything like that Snow Bowl game," said Ralph. "When was it...back in the '40s?"

"A little later," Larry said. "I believe it was in 1950, the same year the Korean War started." That was one of the tidbits of information he had picked up on the Michigan website.

"Good memory," grunted Bernie. "I never win at trivia." He leaned back so the waitress could clear away his plate.

"Where did you do your drinking on campus?" asked Ralph. "I killed a few pitchers of beer at the P-Bell when I turned 21."

"Oh, here and there," Larry responded. "No favorites."

He turned their attention to another TV screen. "Hey, it looks like Miami scored. Pretty good team this year."

Kick-off time came for Michigan and Wisconsin after another commercial and final sportscaster chatter. The game began. Conversation between the three men turned to action on the field. Other Wolverine and Badger fans that had drifted in kept their eyes glued to the screen, too, and the air was punctuated with cries of "yeah!" and "no!" Halftime rolled around. Wisconsin led 20-7.

"Gotta hit the head," mumbled Bernie. "Too much coffee too early."

After he left, Ralph started to reminisce about the good old days at the 'U' in Ann Arbor, dredging up anecdotes about frat life and the bar scene.

Larry stood up. "Be right back... spotted a guy I was looking for."

Larry hadn't seen anyone he knew. In fact, he had never been in San Jose before last night. Nor had he gone to college. Larry drove a moving van cross country and wound up in a different city every weekend. Right now his 24-foot Luxton box van was parked at a nearby motel that offered ample parking and Wi-Fi. Another trucker had tipped him off about the motel on CB radio. Today was Larry's day off; tomorrow, he'd be back on the road, headed north to Portland. But wherever he was, a sports bar was his home away from home, and sports his companion—football in fall, basketball and hockey in winter, baseball and golf in spring and summer.

He killed some time at the end of the bar, pretending interest as the Miami Hurricanes blew away Texas A&M. When the Michigan-Wisconsin game resumed, he returned to his seat.

Michigan put up a good fight in the second half, but Wisconsin's reserves, inserted like replacement bulbs in a string of Christmas lights, ground down the Wolverine defense. Final score: Wisconsin 37, Michigan 21.

"Nice meeting you guys," Larry said as Bernie and Ralph got up to leave. "Tough loss."

"The Illini are due in next week," said Bernie. "Should be a "W" for the Wolves."

"Go Blue!" Ralph added. They left.

At the other end of the room, under the flickering screens, a scattering of red and green coalesced as fans arrived for the Stanford-Oregon game. Larry picked up his sports bag and headed for the rest room. Once inside a toilet stall, he stripped off his Michigan shirt and rooted in the bag until he found a Stanford sweatshirt with a large, monogrammed S. He slipped it on and returned to the bar room.

Spying an empty seat at a table with two crimson-attired men and a bored-looking blonde woman, he walked over. "Room for another Cardinal fan?" he asked. Assured there was, Larry sat down and ordered his first cold brew of the day. His eyes roved the blinking screens. As game time approached, he smiled, nodding whenever one of his new acquaintances grew nostalgic about college days on "the farm."

Larry was a player, just as much as the athletes on the field. But his game was assuming different roles, blending in like a chameleon in a constantly changing environment. He earned a living driving a truck; but his favorite pastime was watching sports with other fans, even if it had to be sitting in a noisy bar before a bank of television screens.

He could have enjoyed the same color, action and excitement alone in his motel room. But he would have missed the warm feeling of inclusion and acceptance that he experienced mingling with other sports enthusiasts, even if it required pretending to be something he wasn't. But he never thought of himself as a fraud. The strangers he met he considered new friends. And he always tried to fit in. Sports fans were Larry's family, and it was always nice to come home—even if home was always in a different place with a different family, rooting for a different team.

Smokin' Marlboros down Metedeconk
by Jim Meirose

Marlboro came back from the porta-potty and told his wife he was going in the river.

Come in the water with me?

Raising a hand, she said No, not yet. You go. I'll sit in the sun a bit. It feels good.

In the machine shop, magically make long steel bars into tubes. How? Well with big strong honking machines, is how—at the big factory. Five days a week, eight hours a day. This is a shitty job but someone has to do it. Lord God please, the weekend.

Metedeconk!

Marlboro turned and went to the water. Once in knee deep, he leaned and touched the surface of the water with a forefinger. The horde of tiny silvery fish suspended and unseen in the water about him darted away toward safety. Once out waist deep in the water, he splashed and wet down his arms. Then, further, not shivering in the cold water, he went in up to his neck. Then, he ducked his head under for an instant, just enough that he actually didn't hold his breath. Risen once more, he washed the water down his face, smacked his lips, and smiled out toward the factory silhouettes sprawled along the far shore of the Metedeconk River.

Manually file the tube perfectly round. Perfectly! But how many laborious hours and hours it takes; another mind-numbing job. But the weekend will come. And then—

Metedeconk!

Looking at the factories, Marlboro thoughtlessly peed in the water like everybody does. The pebbled bottom pushed up at him as though saying naughty, naughty, and naughty, as his bladder gently emptied for the second time since their arrival. The water around his crotch and thighs warmed pleasantly as the flow continued.

Place the two barrels side by side apply silver solder, and apply flux. Place the barrels in a small furnace at 90 degrees Celsius.

The barrels are now joined. But here come two more to do the same with; and two more and two more and—

Metedeconk!

A dead fish drifted further out, catching his eye. Marlboro figured it to be a carp, otherwise known as a giant goldfish. It rode high in the water filled with the gases of death. In it Marlboro saw once more the large catfish he found on the bank of the brook back home when he was a boy. The catfish was bit right in half. He looked out over the water. Something's in this water that's big enough to bite a catfish clean in half. Marlboro all at once found himself walking back to the beach. He had been in the water full of piss and snot and dead more than long enough.

Place long rib atop barrels, solder it in with a hand torch; boring, laborious, the air is too damn close too. Friday is coming; Friday!

Metedeconk!

Reaching the beach, he came to where his pretty wife sat with a towel for him. Rising at his approach, she draped it around Marlboro. Once fully wrapped, he sat by her.

Hey, I bet I never told you, he said idly toward the sun—did you know I once caught a fly in my hand and squashed it while I stood over the toilet peeing?

What?

What I said. And I bet there aren't that many people who can do that. But never mind. You should go in the water with me you know. The water is a bit cold, but fine.

Oh—

Yes, he said, rising—we came here to swim, after all. How about we go in now?

But you just came out—you—

Rising and tossing down the towel, he said No, let's go in. Now.

All right, she said, pulling her hidden feet from the sand, rising. They walked together down to the water and sloshed loudly in toward where it was waist deep, holding hands.

Use the abrasive lapping rod now, slide back and forth and back and forth to smooth the bore. Back and forth back and forth, one rod after another sliding in, back and forth, comes out, then another—another another another—

Please, Metedeconk!

The same little silvery fishes filled the water around their thighs, all hovering stock-still, all facing the same direction, shining from the sunlight cutting down through the water.

Smells funny out here, she said.

Yes.

Polish the barrel's exterior to a shiny finish. Finish this one, then there's a next one, and a next, and a next, all day every day.

Metedeconk!

The fishing hole back home where Marlboro came from had smelled like this place. Though it stank like a swamp, and was probably gone now, he had been there and had fished there, and sometime he caught a bass, or sometimes he caught a pickerel, or sometimes he caught a pike, or sometimes he caught a fat sunny, but now here were her eyes wide open at him, right now, staring at him, out here in the chest deep Metedeconk river.

Get the roughed out action body. Hold it in your hand. Hold it tight. Don't drop it just hold it. Never mind why. You just need to.

Metedeconk!

They squeezed their hands together, loving the water. They squeezed their hands together the same way as when he had led his future wife down a gully they discovered on some big old farm. They stayed at the farm's B&B for a night, halfway on their way to someplace else, but after breakfast it struck them to explore. They got into the pasture and went to the edge, and found the gully widening down through the tree line into a rocky ravine. At the very bottom they came across a dead calf's skeleton lying completely intact on the rocks. The calf wandered from its Mother long ago and fell into the gully, and went lower, and lower, and finally gave up, and died slowly, injured, lost, hungry, and afraid. Mother stood at the head of the ravine, lowing. Mother stood at the head of the ravine for three days, three nights, and then the days piled up on the days months years and the Mother was dead long ago now, too; the days piled up to now with Marlboro realizing the water was getting a bit cold; a bit uncomfortable. He turned to his wife.

I'm ready to go in now. It's a little nippy out here. How about you?

Sure. It is chilly, plus I feel a bit hungry. Sure, let's go in.

They turned and walked toward the beach. Animals turn and walk back to places too. Sometimes they wander off, get lost, and die. As they walked the water lowered from neck deep to chest deep to waist deep and lower, and they came up across the sand, a light wind chilling them. They rushed to the blanket for the towels. They rushed as he had rushed wandering back and forth down the road in his first Ford, and the cop pulled him over, and smelled liquor on his breath; mother, mother, cussed Marlboro; mother! But, the cop had just saved him from himself, he knew deep down. Mother had found her baby safe. Marlboro had burst into tears at the police station. His wife right now knew nothing about it. The memory felt embarrassing to Marlboro so he snatched up a towel from their bag and wrapped it around himself tight, and warm, and the memory went.

Place the action body in a bath of molten paraffin. Don't touch the paraffin—don't touch, wait, remove, pass on, get another action body, place in the molten paraffin—

Metedeconk!

Wrapped in their towels again, they sat. She was tossing back her head and brushing her hair down very rough and hard.

That water really woke you up, she said, brushing. Pretty cold.

That's right. So—where are the sandwiches?

In the big blue bag right there.

Okay—

He half stood, mind filled tight with the inside of the bag pushing his hand around seeking to find a sandwich, and his mind did not see the ants coming on the blanket, then going up his wife's back one at a time, the ants for some reason wanting to smell the smell of her hair. It's the new hair of one who's not been here before. It's hair that we want, now. It's new and we want new, now!

As the ants proceeded, Marlboro's mind pushed around with his hands looking for the sandwiches; as the moments passed he began to be certain they had not brought any, but his wife had said they had and she was usually not wrong. Looking, peering, feeling in a soft dark unknown place; like looking feeling for their future little daughter's face mask which years from now will lie lost at the bottom of the Metedeconk, that a boy all ugly inside and out will grab off her and hurl it deep out over the waves. He will speak to the boy's parents, and then, searching, he will go in the water and go under and look and feel and want to find it; the sandwich, the mask, his future little girl's Minnie Mouse mask, the sandwich not the sandwich no, the swim mask they will get special on their first trip to Walt Disney world. Here, what—up he came— not the mask, but a sandwich. No, no, no; why did she pack this way, why did she pack; but he found it, and knew, that somewhere out in the river, the mask would for sure be there in time, so in a way it's safe, so that made it okay and it was in the first sandwich bite he took, he saw, as his wife was still trying to unwrap hers, he saw; chewing, he started, he saw them, he saw; ants on her, up her—ants! He saw!

Get up! he cried—your back is full of ants!

What—

They both dropped their sandwiches in the sand. He valiantly began brushing ants off her back. They showered to the sand.

Ants are on me? she exclaimed. Get them—why are they on me?

Because; things like this happen. When you're in a wild place, full of wild things, for which there are no rules, things like this will always happen.

A spark erosion treatment gouges out the slots and makes the holes and recesses. Then, again, a spark erosion treatment gouges out the slots and makes the holes and recesses. Then, again, a spark erosion treatment gouges out the slots and—again and again—

Metedeconk!

She squirmed around, as he brushed briskly down her back, fluffing out her hair. Ants fell from the hair. Brownish green scraps of dead seaweed mixed with writhing fallen ants, fallen sandwiches, and grayish coarse sand. There, he said. I think I got them all. Yes.

Here, let me look—let me see—

She bent and his hand gently ran from under her hair all the way down her spine, to the end. There, he said. They're all gone.

God I was really scared, she said. Tiny ants like that are so creepy.

Oh God, he said, slapping his thigh—you, Mrs. Marlboro, are too easy to scare.

Maybe, she said. But look. We only brought two sandwiches. Now they're ruined. Shit!

Quickly, she bent and pulled the blanket from under the cooler and began rolling it up.

What will we eat?

I guess we won't, she said, the blanket rolled under her arm. Get the cooler, and let's put this stuff someplace, she said. Looking around like she was her profile cut down the beach spread off behind her to where a line of washed up dead seaweed marked the farthest the waves ever reached up the shore. Years ago becomes now again when you think of it now, again, looking around and around like this. Some things resist time, others just go off with it. She spoke sharply.

How about we just set our stuff on those pilings over there, and go and swim some more? We can't eat now, or sit on the sand, so we might as well do something while we're here.

Okay, said Marlboro. They started over and masses of tiny broken sharp shells stabbed their feet on the way to the pilings, but they made it, set the things down, and went for the water.

Get the intricate components and, one by one, carefully try them in the action body. One by one, delicate, no, don't

43

drop, don't. Now the next and the next and the next and, then get the intricate components and, one by one, carefully try them in the action body, and then—

Metedeconk!

Toward the water, yes; everything goes toward the water. The shore came at them like a flash flood coming into the gully, or ravine, or arroyo, they chose to bed down in only to get flushed out like a spider down a water spout. Reaching the water, they ran in, holding hands once more. Mrs. Marlboro kept up with her husband out until the water reached her breasts, then she froze in place, stopping him as though an anchor had been thrown out behind.

What's the matter, said Marlboro. Why'd you stop like that? Why that look?

I—I'm afraid I just went in the water, she said softly.

Of course you went in the water. What do you mean? I just saw you come in the water.

I don't mean went, like came into the water. I meant, I peed—in the water.

Shhh! Someone will hear you! he said, raising a finger to his lips, thinking why'd she say this? What's the big deal? Everybody pees in the water, and then it just swirls around and dilutes away to nothing. Everybody knows that. Nobody says I'm afraid I just peed in the water!

Blacken each component, put in place. Tap, rub, file, and repeat like the dentist does until the components all perfectly fit. Sit in the dental chair, be a component. Tap, rub, file, repeat tap rub file repeat tap—repeat repeat repeat—

Metedeconk!

I don't like that there's pee in the water around me, she softly told him.

Well, dear, he said even more softly, as he waved toward the faraway factories on the other side of the river—to tell you the truth there's guts and blood and shit in the water too, and bugs and bacteria and water striders and all kinds of dead things in all stages of rot and decomposition.

Again and again blacken tap rub, file, repeat; repeat, repeat, repeat again, until everything is perfect; practice makes perfect.

Metedeconk!

I want to get out of this water, she said.

What.

I want to go get dry. I want to go home. This is an awful place. Nothing is right here.

Seeing the words come in the air between them, he clasped her hand, nodded slightly, and turned and led her back to the shore. As the water level fell lower and lower with each step that they slowly and silently took, she hugged his arm harder to her. They came from the water; all life began in the water; once there was no life at all but then water came to wake the world up. Water's not to be feared, water's to be loved—

I love you sweetheart, he said, as they stepped out of the water. I really do.

Oh God—yes, I love you too.

Guess what?

What?

My foot is asleep.

Check the lugs that will hold the barrel to the action. Do it fast, because here comes another and another and another and more—all week long—

Metedeconk!

Well, shake it out then—that will wake it up.

All right.

They went in the sun's heat up the sand across the broken shell and ants and got their things from the fat damp pilings. They decided to go up on the boardwalk to the Briar Penny Wreath and Duffer grill and bar; the only place around. In the back of that place, unknown to them, swarthy men hit small birds on the head with frying pans, killing them for dinner. Not knowing this, they ordered the fried breaded birds.

The waiter came to their table with the birds, and told them that these were living things, with eyes, ears, and mouths, about a half hour ago. Now they are meat on your plate. Bon

45

appetite; but, they heard none of this. To them, he had only said, with a large toothless black gap of a smile, here you are. Enjoy!

Thank you.

As they dug in, Mrs. Marlboro paid complete attention to her meal, and only Mr. Marlboro looked out to see that down on the beach where they had been, an old man pulled a severed horse head from the waves with a stout rope.

The rope, the old man told Marlboro somehow silently intensely—pull the rope, and hurry up—it's your own world while you live, so keep on living—come on, and hurry up!

Fat eels squirmed out the empty horse eyes mouth and nostrils.

Make sure they fit face to face flush perfect. Each and every one of the hundreds that roll by for checking all day after day after day, must all fit face to face flush perfect—

Metedeconk!

The old man said the world will not turn all different when you die—you'll just be gone. Marlboro blinked and in the blink the old man receded away into the water leaving just the rotted horse's head on the grey sand. Marlboro went with the old man, without ever actually leaving the table, back into the school of fish, which did not move and all pointed in the same direction he would go. All at once an old Daily News front page picture lay before him so long ago. The picture showed a wide car trunk packed tight with white packages.

The horse's head lay on the sand.

Heroin Seized! yelled the big headline. Marlboro even so young had heard of heroines. Heroines were grown up women who did great wonderful brave death-defying things.

Mrs. Marlboro continued quietly eating. Mr. Marlboro looked deeply into the picture. No heroine there. No female hero there at all. Often he remembered that picture and the feeling it brought of being completely in the dark. But here he was now, anyway, with his fresh new wife all these years later, at

Metedeconk bathing beach, up in the Briar Penny Wreath and Duffer grill and bar which was the only place there was.

The eels had all escaped the horse's head and squirmed back into the river.

Lock, stock and barrel. Stand, stretch, yawn, repeat. Lock, stock, and barrel. Bit rub repeat stand stretch yawn repeat—

Metedeconk!

Marlboro yawned gazing into the old car trunk feeling that was he felt right them until his wife spoke; her voice made her face rise up out of the pile of heroin so he looked back at her.

Yes dear?

A penny for your thoughts. You're out cold daydreaming sitting there.

A penny for my thoughts? Oh, I don't know. None really.

How about you give me a penny for my thoughts.

I'm not sure I have a penny.

Then I'll give them to you free, then; I really love you, Marlboro.

Before he answered back to her, he looked out the beach.

The rotted horse head was gone.

I love you too, he said.

She nodded.

Test the action locks, test, redo, test, redo, until perfect. Test hundreds and thousands and millions one after the other and each exactly the same—

Metedeconk!

Hey listen, he said fast. Finish up that bird there. We need to be taking off soon.

Get the template onto a big slab of Turkish walnut. And after that another and another—

Metedeconk!

But you haven't eaten anything, she said.

I'm not hungry. I don't know why I ordered it. I'll have them wrap it for us to take.

Yes you can warm it at home.

I know. Are you done eating now dear?

Just about.

Fit the action to the stock—this may take a good forty hours. Forty after forty. Hours, Years, Centuries—five days a week eight hours a day fifty two weeks a year—

Metedeconk!

Okay, that's it, she said. Where's the waiter?

The stock will now go to the finishing specialist, who will finally use linseed oil and hardener. In the stink all day every day for weeks and weeks on end—

Metedeconk!

Marlboro rose at her question and scanned the place for their waiter. Long ago, when faced with this, tough strong men fought it out with shields rifles and clubs. Where is the waiter? Cluster round the rats, and the cheese is with you. Where can he be, now? Cluster around the bulls, and the silage is with you. Where is he where—you must not fail her! Cluster around the corncrib and the rats are with you. Suddenly, their waiter appeared, sliding down a slick firehouse pole toward a sudden Norway appearing below.

The engraving artist will now use a graver made of high speed steel to gouge out all the fancy decorations. Black ink and varnish finished this off. It does look good but there's no time to savor. Must let it go and do the next and be cheated of the savor and again and again—

Metedeconk!

From the Norway the waiter shuffled up.

Is everything to your liking? he said coldly and flat as things said all day over and over end up being said.

Here. Wrap mine for takeout. I'll eat it at home.

As you say, sir—

And also—the check please.

Yes—just as you say sir.

He turned and faded away to nothing gone somewhere only waiters do, to do things only waiters understand.

Heat treating process now. Hot, hot. Burned thick fingers. Put in, turn on, wait, take out, send to side, put the next in, turn on, wait—

Take out!

Metedeconk!

Oh Marlboro, she said, wiping the corner of the mouth with a napkin. Look out there; they've lit up the beach all blue. I want to go wading before we head out. You want to go wading? Look— there's people wading.

Marlboro tilted his head to reason with her. There were dead horse heads, eels, and swarm upon swarm of tiny fishes in the water. The water sluices through their gills to keep them alive, but he had no gills; try breathing water like you've got gills, and you drown; that's what will happen for sure, if you go back in the water. And then, also, there is the old man—

I'm afraid I'm too pooped for wading, honey, said Marlboro. I really would just like to get and pay the check and head home—the home they lived in where their cat ran endlessly after Marlboro's tiny radio controlled car. The car made the cat crazy; she said it's my cat, not yours; so she made him put it away. Ever since then it has been up on a closet shelf. After enough years go by the time will come move it to the attic or maybe even put it in the trash because the cat will be dead as the unused car battery will be then, now, too.

Cut out grooves for gold barrel inlays and barrel number. Cut, push in gold, smooth with abrasive stone. Cut out grooves for gold barrel inlays and barrel number. Cut, push in gold, smooth with abrasive stone. Cut out grooves for gold barrel inlays and barrel number. Cut, push in gold, smooth with abrasive stone—

Metedeconk!

The silently gliding waiter brought the check. This is a lot of money, he said, ducking under the water in his head immediately. Look at it. Add it up. I can't do that in my head but you can.

She took the check, and he let it go, hoping she would speak before he would drown right there in front of her, right inside his head; and she would not even know why it was he keeled over; but instead she lifted the check and pointed to it.

Send shotgun off for firing tests. It will be returned marked with certifying proof marks.

What's this say here, the waiters name- is his name Frustrum?

Mr. Marlboro looked at the check and the word. Frustrum? That's not a name.

I bet it's some foreign name. See, you learn something every day-

He gazed at Frustrum on the check. How horrible, horrible, damning even, to live life with a name no one ever heard of. Everytime you say it, the one you say it to will say What, I didn't quite catch that. It must be noisy in here. Loud band or something. Couldn't have heard that right. Say again please?

The waiter drifted over and picked up the check she had laid money on.

Change for this? asked the waiter lightly, in a liquid voice.

Yes.

They always ask if you need change when they can clearly see that if they didn't bring back change, they'd be getting a fifty percent tip. How full of snot are they.

Don't count on it.

They paid, leaving a fat tip regardless, and went out down a path to the parking lot. In the cool light air, she looked up pointing.

The moon, she said. It is beautiful.

And it was, but he was in a hurry. As they got in the car, she still eyed the moon.

It's a crescent moon, she said. And it is beautiful—but just then she was fully in the car with the door slammed and the moon invisible. The doors shut, sealing this visit to Metedeconk down, lost, and over, and just tucked away in memory now. As he started the car off toward the highway words came across the windshield, and he read them, as Mrs. Marlboro's chatter flowed across also; We went there, you will go there—I really had fun today, didn't you—your children and their children will go there too—but the ants the damned ants damn, nearly ruined the day— and then, then, you will simply go off someplace to die—but it was fun, really fun, just like us.

He glanced at her.

50

Fun? Like us?

Yes. Us. Just like us.

Each customer may have to order their gun years in advance, before it's finally shipped to them in a very expensive must-have-for-vanity's sake high end locking double strapped brown leather case, which they may carry out, put down, open up, brag about, and laugh over, before they hit the woods seeking their first attempt to kill some innocent woodland thing stone dead.

That Patch of Land by the Tree by Fariel Shafee

She had chopped up that mossy charcoal protrusion a myriad of times with a silver ax.

The story has many beginnings -- some silly and others bizarrely contorted, several involving a medley of softly colored emotions almost forked out from an insipid sentimental film. It wore on like a discolored hand-band you are too averse to look at but are incapable of throwing out. Emotional glues don't wash out in the thin teary rain. They spread out to the past through a bridge of cut out memories that stands recklessly upon life's stream.

Then some other tales are wrapping on swiftly, almost unnoticed at first, and soon pushing in, slowly, and then vigorously, like an anaconda you had not taken note of in that swamp that always existed.

These sagas start and then spread around in the realm possibilities. The stage bears the players almost like the story books that ask the reader to choose. Do you wish to go left? An emotionless voice inquires. The cake, yes, do you eat it or, walk past? If you eat that cake, then turn to page eighty.

The stories she endures, though, move on, sleekly from page seven, to eight and then to nine, or directly to page ninety nine where the sky is dark and purple in an eerie land. At times, she would think she chooses those turns. But she knows she really does not. You gravitate towards the nooks and then get thrust up to the clouds. It is an unknown force. You live through it.. It plays with you. It makes you believe you are a player. But that move goes through your skin and through your mind. You twitch and feel and then float. Then you fall freely once again.

The narrow road forks repeatedly. One, once again, expects to live and die, to love and loath, to discover conflicting aphorisms. Entropy is supposed to increase. More choices and states should open up. But that expectation gets severed. The saga twists around and then moves about, promising to lead to unknown terrains. It doesn't though. The ending always curls back to that tree-- tall and ancient, with a slightly moistened bark and a host of large round leaves throwing out offbeat patches of deep blue within the lush.

Dina closed her eyes. She did not wish to see that tree. It looked ugly under the midday sun. The bark was torn at places, and the leaves were parchment dry. The vines had crept out like a hand with lusting fingers. That tree looked naked under the leafy head, beneath the bark that promised to fall off. It looked bare, rotten, evil -- with rope-like hair and a toothless smile in the crescent tear where the larger branches pushed out.

It was the roots, she know -- the magic strings of being that would not let go. Black magic is more the right word, Dina had mumbled to herself.

Once there was this storm, and the tree swayed about like an unstable ship atop tumultuous waves. The blackbirds that had nested in the boughs were unsure if they should fly up to the sky lest their home crumbles onto their necks. The ones that had randomly chosen to embrace the ice cold drops had lived in the end. The bark had twisted into mangled wood and the leaves had withered in a week when the sun was up.

The dead creatures had rot with the dead tree's flesh. The animals decayed with a louder protest and reeked of hatred when they left. Then the land was smooth and grassy. Children huddled in to the flattened soil from the nearby huts and giggled as they ran and chased each other, kicked around their balls or jumped the ropes.

They had thought of building a school on that land. Behind that cast off patch was the jungle -- wild and unpredictable, vines and snakes embracing in the heat of uncaring proliferation. "There are bears," mother had warned. But the ancient tree bore sentiments. It had witnessed generations of droughts and showers, the births of sons and daughters. So that tree had stayed, spreading out to heaven with its daring hooky nails, and the parents had bickered over the price of land elsewhere, further due North.

The storm had brought ashore a new house in the end. The summer hut was small and raw, made of half seasoned wood atop a greenish stony floor. Dina had played upon that bare soil before the piles of wood were stacked, and later, when the roof was thatched, she chanted after the slender girl who taught math, the tables of multiplication.

Those summer days were long and speckled with routine drills, exercises and failures, pulling together and redoing. The shingles were thick above-head but the windows were large. The numbers melted at times in the airless heat, and then the children put them back together, sequenced them slowly to reach a thousand and more.

"We have a chance to move on, to live, not like this left out stale bread on this table you see, but like the picked out apples, the ones they take to stores," mother had uttered the words with clarity. Her eyes had brightened, and her fingers had danced on vigorously through the kitchen air. "Look Dina, we really never thought. The big school's almost three miles away.. And that's another village. I would have thought twice to let you go. The boys out there are wolves."

The tightly held lid that the storm had torn apart from the jar of daily banality had made that blue sky fresh and bigger, and the days longer. Mother now thought about the little tears in the skirts, and about the exact sweetness of the dried out plum. She wore lipstick at times, the only one she had in the shade of chocolate. She shouted at the children as she shouted in the bygone days. But the tone was light and cheerful now, the anger more a dressy layer on elation.

Dina trimmed her hair short and tied gaudy red ribbons, and then she walked up to the gray blue mound where the road forked to the school.

Mother waved at her from the roadside, and the cycle van picked her up with the girls. The road was narrow and wavy and went up and down with the hills. The girls were tired when they reached the yard, but they were jubilant nonetheless. That terrain brought in freedom. They were out under the sun when the bell rang loudly for lunch. Then they giggled and they ran. The lessons at time were hard and the slender teacher screeched, made them stand out in the heat if they failed. But they knew that the pain was short lived, and soon the bell would ring again so that the hot sun above-head would melt into golden joy.

Dina went every day to that school, even when it rained, even when her cousins came from the city.

She was there that day as well, seated on a rickety stool, staring out if the window at a thin blue layer of sky when the floor crackled.

"Look, look," little Suzie had screamed.

"She kicked me," the new stout boy had yelled.

The teacher was busy with a notebook. All at once she had appeared annoyed, her rubicund cheeks looking even deeper, the color of an apple.

"Suz.." the under certified instructor had started, her pointer raised, the indication of a coming short lecture with a punishment.

She did not end that line. That day, the all knowing teacher, Miss Debbie, looked confused like a hushed out kitten in rain. She knew she should have stayed away, closer to her desk, calmly and with dignity, but she walked up, joined the gaping children, and gasped.

"What on earth?" she had exclaimed.

That day, the children did not go out to the yard for lunch. So the patch of land sat quietly, as its terrain shifted and performed the dance of rejuvenation and destruction hand in hand. The children that did not freeze in the moment until they perished inside that large opening and into a simmering pot of discontent went back home in agony. Some had cuts and bruises. Others did not speak for days.

Mother looked doleful, hurt. Then she paced about the kitchen angrily, tightening her fist to protest against the unfair ruling of one who called Himself the omnipotent. Then she sat down on the worn out chair that had been wiped carefully just in the morning to accompany her into the sunshine land. That night she did not cook. Father said nothing like always. The new life did not knock on his heart in the beginning. Its departure made no bang. He looked at mother and then took out leftover bread-loafs, dipped them in the gravy from the morning, and then went to bed.

Dina did not return to that makeshift school the next day. Her mother had forbidden.

"It is the wretched roots," she had grumbled as she had simmered water for soup in the morning.

"They never quite ever go. You would think the monster is gone."

Mother gasped, and little Dina stared at her from the floor where she was engrossed with a painted cardboard star.

Father had said nothing once again. He had sat silently with his potatoes, pretending that gravity was more profusely scattered in the greater world, while mother had waded in her murky pool. Then he walked out through the blue gray door of time with his rake and a sack.

"I will bring potatoes," he had said finally.

When father did not return that night, Dina sat quietly in the yard.

The stars were bright and blue, mocking the darkness.

Inside the house, mother cried loudly. Her feuding sisters had dropped by. Whether the act was that of commiseration or of enjoyment of misery was unclear. The two had been bickering over the house left by the parents. They had demanded the whole three rooms.

"Alice, dear," the bigger girl had been arrogant. "You don't need a room. Look, your husband has one. We have three kids each and a dog. Mother would have been hurt."

Mother needed the room. Potatoes were dear, and butter was a rare luxury. She wanted to get a frock. Dina needed a uniform, new ribbons to go with that. The sisters' sons were young and strong. They could work well if they wished to. It was not sickness that made them drink.

"Alice dear," the superficial sweetness would have been annoying, patronizing. But mother was just not listening. She was drowning in her sorrow, and the slime and sludge about her had little room for what those women held in their hearts.

"Oh my God," mother had simply held her hand and cried.

Dina had walked out of that room then. Those words had made her nauseous.

That night with the stars was long. It was frigid, she had heard later from the neighbors who had come with bread and soup. Dina did not feel that coldness. Her tears had brought out warmth with all the anger that her body spewed out.

She was angry that she would be alone when she would need a lesson in words after class. She was angry that there would be no candies in the weekends, and she was angry that no one would be seated in the living room ignoring mother's tantrums. She would have a dirty frock and a pair of old blue sandals because the man who was to replace those in the coming weekend was gone.

What did it feel like? She had thought for a moment when she had stared up at the sky that night. What would it feel to die? She had shivered a little and then she had thought more about the present and about the coming days. The one who was gone would feel no more. But she would feel the pain, the needles of needs pricking relentlessly.

Dina had remained in the village for three more months. She did not go to that school. The books stayed tucked neatly under the bed. From time to time, she would turn the pages, and an apple or a giraffe would gawk at her from the whitest sheets of fear.

The patch of land near the wilderness, where the deserted walls still stood with broken ribs and legs, lay downhill towards the marketplace. It was a forty minutes walk, and the market was ten more minutes from there. With father gone, Dina now brought home the veggies and the cooking oil, the stale bread from the baker's rack on discount. The children met at the teacher's house, twice a week, in the backyard, the women whispered next to the oranges. Dina was not invited. Mother had crossed it out. She also had no money. A woman had come in with papers within a week of father's demise. Those were bonds, she said. Obligations. That's what he had left them besides the emptiness and the scars, and a lingering tale of a woman who claimed to be their kin. "Rubbish," mother had screamed before she had packed up all his shirts in a discolored suitcase that bore a hole, and lurched it out into the empty barn with the decaying hay.

On her way to the marketplace, Dina looked at that room that was once so dear to her. Grass had grown in the yard. Those were tall and rowdy leaves that grew precariously. A herd of cows moved lazily -- brown creatures and then those black ones. Those were wild cows. No man would take his animals where the eagles now had nested.

The tree was perhaps as high as her shoulder the first time Dina caught sight of it from the winding road. The next time, maybe two weeks later, the plant was the height of two large men added. It had grown out through the roof, throwing out the shingles with its vigor of life. The leaves this time were bluer, but it was a deeper shade of blue -- one that almost glowed, challenging the blunt hue of the weathered stones.

"It was the roots," Dina remembered. Those had spread out like a net beneath the bark and those had fed on rain and decaying cells. The roots had grown stronger under that school, and one day, those roots had shrugged off the bricks that had held them down in their dark prison. The plant that grew sprouted out from lumps of soil with its velvet layers of damnation. It was a monstrous plant, and those netted veins were the magic roots. Black magic, that is.

In her nightmares, years later, when she chopped that tree up again and again, Dina thought about those large blue leaves, the little sharp strands of hair sticking out of the blades, and the pungent smell. It was suffocating. The sun was relentless, and that tree breathed. The tree exhaled its fury upon her neck as it violated her in that nook upon the stiff wild grass.

It was a different meandering road that led to that tree each time. One road went through the jungle where she had seen blue birds flock like drizzled gems. The other was paved with red hard rocks and it carried her through a town huddled with yellow brick homes and men with tall black hats. She had taken those roads with the magician -- the man who had picked her up from the woods.

He was a shadow at first, a stranger then. Later, he was just human.

Dina was cold and pale, and her legs hurt. In the fog too he had seen her lips bleed. She was helpless and she was alone. She sat there in the grass like a fearful rabbit. Some magicians and wizards hunted rabbits in the wilderness. They played games of cats and mice in the shadowed stage as the trees stood still and as the birds flew off. But this man gave her water. He then offered her a deal.

He cut her many times with his shiny swords, and then he glued the pieces up, put her all together. The people who stood by clapped, threw in pennies and whistles. She bowed to them in her dazzling golden swimsuit. Groups of younger men ogled alongside some older ones as well. The mature eyes were the dirty pools. She pretended not to see.

At night, when he embraced her, she thought of that haunting tree. It was large and strong. The vines had pushed into her flesh. His breath was not so hot. Yet at times she thought of the fuming hatred exhaled by the pores that had sat tightly next to her skin until she had given in to the sun and to the sprinkled dust.

Two large men had carried her home that night. She did not know who they were.

"They had found her in the grove, lying in the mud," a roundish woman had explained to a slimmer paler one who had walked in with the flattened shapes of light that spread about the floor.

"It was a savage day," she had gone on. "That tree is dead. She had scratched the fallen trunk. Look, there was blood right on that bark. Now her finger nails are stained."

Dina remembered them speak. She did not remember her nails. Those were tucked inside another world from which a large brown hairy bear had also shifted to her bedside. It was a happy bear, and it smiled.

It was that bear, she knows, that had pointed to the wilderness.

Mother was seated in the kitchen on the dirty chair when Dina had run out to the yard. Mother did not look up to check. In the stove, something burned with the bitter smell of spoiled sweetness.

Those days, mother did not speak much. It seemed as though father's ghost had found refuge in his earthly wife who now mimicked his act of apathy.

This silence had angered Dina when she had found herself lying in the bed. Her legs were numb but her belly ached as though monsters had danced upon the flat ground. Mother had brought her a glass of water before resigning to the kitchen. She was hurt and sorry. But it was mostly about herself, and what had gone wrong in her life. Dina had wanted to scream, to point to herself and demand love. But she said nothing much. "Shhhh," the bear had signed. It sat right next to the bed and swung its leg like a small boy by the pond.

On her way out, Dina had quickly glanced at the kitchen while melting into the shadow of the front door. Perhaps she expected her mother to waive warmly at that shadow, ask the door to stay, and plead how lonely she was. Mother did not such thing but stared blankly at the stove. Something burned. She did not care. She sat still, almost like a tree, as though roots had dragged her down right to the floor where she was affixed hopelessly.

Epilogue

Dina looked at the grove. It was no larger than a basketball court. It lay covered with grass and a sort of purplish wild flower in the shape of a distended circle that had also been crumpled at places about the circumference. The trees were no more than a dozen, and those were scattered about the veneer of green and mud, though there were more of them where the soil was slightly reddish.

"It is just a tree!" Dr. Honey had asserted. She was a middle aged woman with a long and thin face wrapped with dry wisdom. Her glasses were too large, but within them, her small gray eyes pretended to look eager, concerned.

"Just a tree, Dina," she had repeated with stress. "It does not walk, chase you, strangle you or hop into your body like an alien parasite."

Dina had sat there stupefied that day, almost the way mother did in that kitchen when she left the village. In the doctor's clean and climate controlled room, her eyes looked still, and her lips were dry like paper. She felt it still in her feet, in the arms, under the skin. It shifted and it protested. It demanded to be let out. It was the tree, she knew. Years back, when she had lain helpless in that patch of land, the vines had cut through her flesh. The tree had let its spores out free into her blood. Those had grown now, and those marched about her body. The roots lashed out from within to spread into the bigger world, and then to affix her to that swamp behind her house.

"Just a tree, Dina. Why don't you take some time off? Go back to that village and then take a look at that tree. I'd say take a picture. It is there, in that village. Not inside your body."

Dina did not inform her neighbors where she was headed. "Vacation in the Pacific," was the rumor. People nodded and dispersed. There was only a momentary spark of interest in the vacation details of a waning diva. That city was where the stars rushed in and glowed. There were many of them in the sky that now dazzled brilliantly.

So these days, the passers by still paused in front of the many photos of the retired woman in her flaunting gowns of youth, showered with flowers and singing birds, all hanging from the papered walls of her foyer. "It is you? You looked fabulous!" they would exclaim. What lay beneath that faded glory was disconnected from the happenings, from what mattered.

So they would all leave then, let her be, together with the tucked in photo of a dead magician with a single invisible stab and the memory of a ruthless tree with its magic roots.

They did not care. She had provided for them and she had pleased. She had built her own castle of fame in which she had shrunk, slowly. The ones that dwelt alongside, acknowledged Dina's existence, and the opulent walls, and then they walked back into their lives, and into the bustling streets of the present.

Far away from the man made lights, the tree looked ancient, frail. It was the largest in that grove. The bark was mossy and black that bore many scratches of time. The leaves were round and pale with a tint of gray. It looked just like three more trees that lay about. That larger tree had no shimmery blue necrosis and no animal vine. As ancient as it might be, it was indeed just a tree, like the others solidly planted in that grove.

Dina looked at her own hand and at her finger nails. She was unsure if those were stained still. That image was inside her own mind.

The wind blew. It was a gentle summer breeze. The dispersed leaves swayed a little, and then went back where they were, pulled in by the receptacles. Her legs felt soothed. It was the trees that were fixed solidly to that land. She could walk away if she wished to.

Many times had she chopped that tree up with a silver ax. Then the tree had grown again, deep inside her heart.

But at last she was free. That tree had become banality, an earthly decaying shadow of a bygone fear.

Dina turned around. The train to the city would leave at nine. Five more hours to go.

She would walk back to her old house, and then she would look for the graves of mother and father in the village cemetery. She would take flowers with her, white lilies and yellow chrysanthemums.

Later, she would walk back to her old room. Dina did not know what exactly had happened to her books or to that gaudy red ribbon. She would look beneath her bed, and then she would walk up to the kitchen where the colorful heavy clay pots were stacked neatly. She had written to her cousin. He surely had the keys, somewhere in that old chest of drawers now buried in the attic.

"Sister," he had exclaimed. "Oh my long lost sis!"

Dina had felt annoyed then, when that letter had made it to her house, although she herself had connected. The most vicious village bully groveled to the fallen star from the city. The cowards now craved to touch that opulence, the easy way, by becoming the greatest friends. That path was wild for Dina -- and contorted. At times she looked at her chest. The cuts from the swords were there still, dried out yet embossed, almost like a seal stamped in by her master.

She loathed her cousin when he had been nice to her in the end.

Now she felt nostalgic.

It was five more hours, and then she would pack her past in a suitcase and go back home --- to that city of sun dried bricks. She would return a jolly free bird.

The breeze had brought in an aroma. It was fresh and wild at once. It came from far away, from an ancient life, a life that could have been, but had spewed her out to the wilderness.

Dina closed her eyes. She let her skin soak in all that rawness.

The air danced about and hopped, and then stood still.

Then something breathed. It breathed almost like that tree.

Her legs felt heavy, numb, like a tree trunk.

Dina turned her head with intense pain. Her eyes did not wish to see, but they HAD to.

That woman was still afar. She stood right beneath that ancient tree. Her house was there, in that great trunk, and she had flown out on a stick like a nefarious witch.

It was her eyes, she knew, the gray blue eyes, that had gotten stuck into her own skull. Those had crept into her blood.

Dina screamed. She wanted to scratch those eyes out of her own head and then run free. She did nothing though but stared helplessly.

The witch, however, laughed out aloud, hysterically.

The Shipping Report
by Victoria-Elizabeth Whittaker

"...southwesterly 7 to severe gale 9, occasionally storm 10; rough or very rough, becoming high; rain or squally showers; moderate or good, occasionally poor. Dogger, Fisher, German Bight, Humber: southeast 7 to severe gale 9, veering northwest 5 or 6; moderate or rough; rain then fair; moderate or poor, becoming good. Portland, Plymouth: southwest 6 to gale 8, veering northwest 4 or 5, becoming variable 3 or 4 later; rough; rain then fair; moderate or poor, becoming good. Fitz-Roy: in south, variable 4, in north, southwesterly veering northwesterly 5 to 7, becoming variable 4, then cyclonic 5 to 7, perhaps gale 8 later; in south, slight or moderate, in north, rough or very rough; in south, occasional rain, in north, rain; in south, moderate or good, in north, moderate or poor, occasionally good..."

The hearth's embers sputtered in the downdraft sweeping through the low ceilinged aerie. Lead paned windows overlooking the choppy waters of the port rattled with each blustering gust, propelling the tabby cat ever deeper into the homespun woolen blanket. The cultured velvety voice of BBC Radio 4 droned softly, reciting the shipping bulletin.

"...Lundy: west, backing south later, 5 to 7, occasionally gale 8 at first, decreasing 4 for a time; rough or very rough; rain then fair; mainly good. Rockall, Malin, Hebrides: west 7 to severe gale 9, Hebrides occasionally storm 10; very rough or high; squally showers; moderate or good, occasionally poor, Hebrides, moderate or poor, occasionally good. Bailey, Fair Isle, Faeroes: mainly westerly 7 to severe gale..."

This nightly ritual, deeply embedded into the fabric of British life, soothed and calmed those on land or near sea. Firmly woven, the broadcast was as reliable as Big Ben, ticking smoothly and elegantly in a mystical, metronomic rhythm. Switching off the jabbering telly; locking up the snug house; putting aside the tired book and tuning in to the midnight mantra, delivered in a mesmerizing cadence that only the BBC could muster.

An orchestral overture swells with a tidal ebb and flow, swooping across the landscape; serene as a warm summer breeze; fluttering violins and trilling flutes, leading into a phlegmatic well-worn adagio.

> *"...Mull of Kintyre to Cape Wrath, including Stornaway: southwest backing south 7, occasionally gale 8 later; rough or very rough; occasional rain or drizzle; moderate or good, occasionally poor later. From Cape Wrath to Rattray Head: southerly 7 to gale 8..."*

The cat, snuggled into his duvet nest, can rest assured, complacent in the knowledge that—though tempests, *severe gale 9, occasionally storm 10,* may rage over churning Irish seas, English channels, German bights, Scottish firths and bays of Biscay—he is sensibly tucked up safe on dry land, with a slate roof over his head.

Slumber pervades the house; its snoring creaks and muffled groans supported by its stone edifice, a stronghold against storming gales...

The wind howls off Ramehead, propelling crashing waves and the spew of spindrift. It is near reaching gale force and I feel a deep-seeded empathy for the plight of any vessel dueling with the channel in such conditions. Though, given the choice, I would take my chances, more than pleased to trade the shelter of my prison-house and this soiled scrap of parchment for the freedom of a poop deck and a ship's log.

While it was bearable I worked outside, finding an easy rhythm, carving a ship's fo'c'sle out of a chunk of English ash, while above, sentinels on the watchtower, overlooking the American wing, huddled in complacent silence. How the taste of summer's freedom has been replaced by winter's full-force of discontent. My men are disgruntled—torn from the valiant roar of our leonine ship—incarcerated in this most notorious of enemy prisons. By candlelight I will take pen to parchment again to plead our case with those in place to negotiate a prisoner exchange.

I, John Patrick Green, engrave this statement on parchment, 22 December, in the year of our Lord, 1781 from Mill Prison, Plymouth, England.

In Philadelphia I held the office of Shipmaster for a prosperous company trading in goods with England. When the colonies declared Independence, I commanded privateering vessels. As the Revolutionary War unfolded I was awarded with the captaincy of the *Lion* in the Continental Navy. In the late summer of 1781, the *Lion* was under chase by a British frigate, *Le Prudente*. My crew managed to evade the frigate for sixteen hours, before succumbing to capture off the coast of Brittany. My men and I were detained for thirty days on that stench of a man-o-war, before arriving at Plymouth.

Mill Prison has three wings, housing prisoners of war. We are separated by nationality and language. American detainees are, I've been given to understand, treated less harshly than their Spanish and French counterparts. We are viewed as kinsmen, even in war. This means that we are given license to move about and a higher level of food and hygiene. The exercise yard is wide, though enclosed by imposing walls. The southerly winds off the channel freshen imprisoned minds and blow the stink out of our stagger. Though we are not tortured, my crew and I implore that our case be given greater urgency; that we do not molder here throughout the long cold winter.

The glass-hued sea is tossing angry waves under a ceiling of dark clouds, stealing the meager daylight of Winter Solstice. The gale is blowing harder, spraying mist mixed with sleet that digs into the back of my neck at a piercing angle of pin-pricks. Pulling my shawl around my head, I amble along the hill above the port. A few old salts skitter on the cobbles, seeking shelter in the Fisherman's Arms where Maggie is sure to have a sturdy stew on the hob and burly brew in the keg. I pause to scan the horizon, peering across the channel to envision my home—St. Malo, Bretagne. But the surging gale defies me and I must avail myself of such hopes.

Monsieur, I am contentedly ensconced in the snug attic apartment of this strong stone edifice atop Lambhay Hill. Here I am soothed and calmed by the familiarity of the language of the sea. The winter gales are upon us now but as you know, I, Sophie Mirielle, have faced many a storm in my young life and am ever-ready to brace the onslaught. I am, of course, much obliged to your succour in my time of need, else I might not have survived. I know you decline to accept my indebtedness; determined by your sense of obligation, but you must understand that I will never view our arrangement as thus. Alas you have implored me not to speak of it and so I must not further.

Today, as I turned the sharp curve descending Lambhay Street, I felt the brunt of the westerly gale and was confronted by the imposing walls of the Citadel below. Despite the distressing conditions, the exercise yard of Mill Prison was not vacant. Men straggled around the perimeter, cowered along the western walls, shivering and troubled, some wearing tattered berets of France and Basque Spain.

One man, an imposing figure—well over six feet tall—shaped like a bear with a barrel chest over long, tapered legs, had a thatch of flaming red hair, the texture of flax. He stood in the middle of the graveled yard, fiercely facing into the wind, without mantle or hat.

Protecting my package with ever more resolve, I clutched it snug against my cloak like a swaddled babe. Seeing that man only added to my determination, fueling the courage to face the wet, cold sleet.

Gales have ushered in the new year and I continue to lobby for the release of my men and myself. To date I have written countless letters on their behalf, urging for attention in the matter. The increasing disparagement of their morale is my heavy burden and I have endeavored to look after the welfare of the crew, encouraging them to take exercise in the yard of the Citadel to keep fit. Hobbies and past-times are hard to come by, yet I have taken to carving ship models out of scraps of wood generously provided by the warden, along with all the parchment I do require for writing. Of course, the Warden reads all my letters, hailing me for writing so well- being an Irishman full of ballyhoo.

Dearest *Grannaine*—I've hopes that this missive finds ye well, and all the family yonder in BallyMacRoss. I'm told that a post ferry leaves for dear old Eire weekly and as ye know there's no family left in Philadelphia now. Da' is sure to be haunting your barrow, a-looking for your bannock cakes; I can remember the smell of them right here in the midst of the gale; smothered in heather honey and creamery butter. Donna' be surprised if I land on your doorstep before all this is thru—I may decide to stay a spell. So much hangs in the balance...

I'm doing well and keeping my spirits up for my men; some of them feel it heavy and so they should. But we are treated better than most of the detainees and I write to lobby for our freedom relentlessly. Such is all one can do in times of war. Appeal with the pressure of a banshee and the blarney of an advocate. I may turn in my captaincy for the life of a barrister—though I'll be sure and stay close to the coast. Keep well, old dearie.

Though England is a foreign ground, the taste of the sea breeze is not. The *cractch* of the gulls is screeched in neither French nor English; and the storms' wrath show no discrimination or partisanship. That appears to apply to stray cats as well. One took up with me along the quayside, full of fish and seeking a warm, soft shelter. Satisfied with the interior amenities, the cat snuggles in my lap and we peer out the lead paned windows overlooking Hoe Park, the Citadel, the port, and, far off in the distance, but close in my memories—Bretagne. I have read that cats can see far greater into the distance than mere humans and asked if he could see St. Malo on a fine day, to which I received a neutral *miao* in reply.

I am determined to christen the cat *Malo* to which he has responded approvingly. Perhaps he too has sought refuge from across the sea. No one appeared to acknowledge his origins. Like myself, no one knew what had brought this *mignon* to the coastal port.

Scandal. Treason. A web of intrigue. Rumors flow like a deep under-current. Whispers that echo in the sussurance of wavelets swishing over the pebbled cove. All that is known is that I arrived on a sloop from St. Malo, owned by a member of the English nobility, above suspicion of any misconduct. Having defrayed the cost of my living expenses—establishing a lodging with a reputable landlady— he had insured that my mind remain untroubled and at ease. No matter the conditions that had exiled me to a foreign land, it was acknowledged that I had indisputable relations with one who could shield me from any further degradation in society.

Though my society here is that of tavern maidens and fishermen, a bookseller and the group of knitters forming the circle of my waking hours. I have been content to drift, knowing that my secrets are discreetly concealed by an honorable and steadfast benefactor. I owe him a debt that I could only ever hope to repay.

Oh, our secrets! Embroiled and entangled; linking us as fixedly as a bridge spanning the English Channel. His ability to provide for and protect me was in no way bribery—for who would believe a foreigner in time of war—were I to cast aspersions on a peer of the realm? Nor have I ever felt beholden to bestow my feminine favors, for he would never demand such remuneration. No—ours is a bond based on loyalty, compassion and humility.

Monsieur, you will be amused to hear of my insistence to the warden of the Citadel that I be permitted to deliver my hand-knitted goods personally. I assured him that a few words spoken in the language of their home soil would give the French prisoners more comfort than a muffler. The warden was skeptical; his bristling mustache twitched briskly. I feared he took me for a spy—what with my unknown origins. I offered that, at his word, I could procure a reference if necessary but he only smiled— implying that he indeed did know of my relations with you. Yet he was discreet, which I know we both appreciate.

But here is the joke, Monsieur—the warden referred to what he termed my *feminine beauty* which would serve as a *disturbing distraction.* I shook my head violently. I gestured to my sober garments; my pale complexion and severe chignon. How could I disturb when I presented a figure no more alluring than a gentle sister?

I was persistent and strong-willed. I convinced the warden that these were noble patriots, who had fought for the freedom of other men and deserved some kindness and humanity during their time of confinement. And do you guess? I won the battle! I now visit the Citadel each week with a package of knitted items and pass them out with words of encouragement for *les garçons,* most of whom are far too young to live like casualties of war.

Another day, another wintry squall, another letter to be writ. The quill slips from my gnarled fingers, cold with damp and calloused from carving. The ink has frozen into a sludge like my granny's *parritch.* The men huddle together to gather what warmth they can. Today I leave off my nagging as it's no' fit for exercise out in the yard.

> Henry Laurens, Esq., Fleyder Street, No23, Westminster
>
> Janr. 19th 1782
>
> Sir, I had the honor of addressing you early in the month of December. I am a'feared that letter never came to your hand. We don't hear any news of our country and are uneasy at our long captivity. It is rumored that Doctor Franklin has made proposals to the Court of Great Britain to exchange part of Lord Cornwallis' troops for American prisoners now in Briton. I hope this will be the means of liberating us; we are much crowded in this place, tho' healthy and in good spirits. Letters we have wrote to Doctor Franklin have not been fortuned with a response. You will oblige us much if you can give any encouragement of our being released—

A diversion has lifted the men from their morose solitude. I hear a bantering and hooting as if a host of angels had descended upon us. The warden is presiding, ushering a tall figure, wrapped in a voluminous black cloak. I canna see what all the commotion is about, but the men are behaving with euphoria coupled with gratitude. Perhaps a special meal has been allocated.

I decide to bring the letter to an abrupt conclusion so as to hand it off to the warden while he is conveniently at hand. Whatever the event, I am obliged to hear my men singing with such lively voices again. For they are sailors of the sea and whatever the storm—how ever strong the gale—their spirits always hold sway, not to be defeated or captive to any but the sirens of the deep.

Monsieur, quietly our needles have become a force and the knitting circle have reckoned to match each other, stitch for stitch, enabling us to amass such a quantity that I can disperse hats, mufflers and socks to all the prisoners: French, Spanish, and American.

Wool has arrived from unseen crofts in Devon, Cornwall and the wide moors that stretch to Exeter; obtained by word of mouth and a sense of goodwill. I have taught the English ladies to knit the Basque-style beret familiar to the Spanish and French.

The bookseller has helped me to recite a few phrases in Spanish and you will be surprised to learn that my English vocabulary has grown much, as I have fraternized with the towns-folk. No one has tried to pry into my past or cross the boundaries of my soul. These good, sea-hardened people have taken me in and allowed me to be a part of their community.

I have ceased to surprise the warden; I feel that he appreciates that I am a woman of resolve. When I arrived in the midst of a squall he just shook his head at my snow-covered cloak and offered me a tankard of hot cidre. As is usual, I relinquished the package for his inspection. As he unwrapped the bundle, I requested in perfect English to be escorted into the American wing. He examined the indigo dyed woolen berets, embellished with eggshell-hued stars— the design of a proud Plymouth knitter, I exclaimed.

Well, didn't he chuckle! With fond accolades for our collective, he declared that if the war were in the hands of the Plymouth knitters, the Americans would easily be defeated- for no colonial could knit as well as a Devonshire woman!

I admit, it was pleasant to laugh on such a day and I was a bit delirious as the cidre was quite hard.

I had yet to venture into the American wing. Instantly I noted its superior qualities, of natural light and cleaner accommodations. The men seemed less gaunt, more fit, though in their eyes, less brown, more blue, I saw the same despair and dejection as the Europeans. You cannot imagine how their pleasure brought tears to my eyes, for they showed such gratitude and joy at the starry emblems on the simple berets.

I was met by the more stoic and serious visage of a man who waved to the warden with a parchment. He was addressed as Captain Green and I could see the grey-green hue of the sea in his eyes, from which cast a reserve and a resolution to survive through the most demeaning and puncturing of circumstances with fortitude and finesse. A life at sea crackled his skin with deep, salt-encrusted furrows. I saw myself in those eyes of glasz—the Celtic Sea that foamed on the shores of our nascent countries—for every freckle punctuating his red-haired beard proclaimed him an Irishman. In his craggy face I saw the lichen and moss-strewn rocks that bordered the pastures and built the fishing shanties. In his voice I heard the dialect of a fiddle moaning as fog shrouds the horizon, the briny taste of mussels, the whiskied scent of loam and peat.

Words could not penetrate more than the language we exchanged in our gaze. Forgetting my practiced Anglais, I tendered the *monsieur* with *un chapeau*, demonstrating that the flat, pancake of wool be worn on the head. He accepted the beret with much *politesse,* befitting a gentleman. Gracefully he endeavored to perch the beret on his flaming thatch of unruly hair. To no avail, and to the amusement of all, he failed to achieve the desired *panache* of a Bretagne fisherman. Suppressing my smile, I soberly promised to return with a more fitting *embrasure.* He thanked me with those quiet, briny eyes and I took the measure of the man and locked it in my memory for safe-keeping...

The marmalade tabby uncurled from its woolen nest, stretched its limbs, pried open its gray-green eyes and began to lick its flaming thatch of fur. The draperies cast aside from the lead-paned windows revealed a heightened sense of diffused light peering over the eastern horizon, beneath scudding and tortured clouds. The whistle of the tea kettle announced a steaming English Breakfast; the aromas of kippered herring and Cornish potato cakes. As the gale unfurled itself against the slate tiles of the roof, the cat licked his whiskers before settling on the divan, his attention absorbed with the contents of the knitting basket and mesmerized by the cultured voice emitting from Radio4.

"...And now, the shipping forecast...There are warnings of gales in all areas except Biscay, Trafalgar and Fitz-Roy. The general synopsis at 0 5 double 0: Low Fair Isle 989 losing its identity over Sweden by 1 8 double 0 Friday. Atlantic low 600 miles north of the Azores, expected southern England 1013 by same time. The area forecasts for the next twenty-four hours—Viking, North Utsire, South Utsire: westerly gale 8 to storm 10, occasionally violent storm 11, veering northwesterly 6 to gale 8; very rough or high, becoming rough or very rough; showers; moderate. Forties, Cromarty, Forth, Tyne, Dogger: west 7 to severe gale 9, veering northwest..."

Between Morrisons and Merkland
by Kate Hodges

George fights the tide of students rushing out the door, a massive wave of bodies jostling, screaming, joking, laughing, running. He dodges past one and then another and tries to protect the flowers he's holding in his arms. The students barely notice the raindrops spitting down around them.

"This must be how the salmon feel," he mutters to himself. His wife took her class on a field trip to the Falls of Feugh to watch the salmon jumping. (He was a last minute chaperone.) His father was an angler. Sometimes, his dad would let him help on the boat. He liked fishing with his dad. They would sit in silence for hours since talking would scare away the fish. George liked the quiet. The boys at school would howl and shout at recess. They were always pushing or kicking something. Home was full of shouting too. George's father always said his mum had an "Irish temper." After a big row, his dad would say, "George, if you have to get married, make you sure you marry a nice, Scottish girl instead. They're sweeter."

George finally makes his way through. He walks down the corridor. It smells like old juice, sour milk, sawdust, and chalk. The lino is sea green and grey.

Outside Room 109, student projects sell valuable planet real estate. Icy Jupiter's brochure features an endorsement by Superman. (Supes' vacation fortress of solitude is there.) Another pamphlet promises a romantic honeymoon on Venus' desert.

Across the hall, outside of Room 110, a poster with smiling crayons and tap dancing pencils reminds students that 'Today is a Great Day to Learn Something New!'

He turns left and ducks into the main office. He goes to the counter to sign the visitor log. The secretary is on the phone, "Then the Principal told me to speak to the children in gentle tones, like a pastel because he didn't want them to be afraid to come here. But the only ones sent down here are the troublemakers like that

Patterson boy, Callum. If you ask me that bairn doesnae need a reassuring pastel pat, a "there, there." He needs someone to speak in primaries."

George coughs to get her attention. He mimes signing in. She sighs and turns around to grab the binder. She sighs again as she opens to the right page. "That family has always been trouble. His father-"

George coughs again. She glances up. "Hold on a sec. Someone's signing in."

"Do you have the time? I can't put the time in. It's the first box."

She points to the clock. "Anyway, they say that Callum's father ran-"

"Excuse me." The secretary puts her hand over the bottom of the receiver.

"Can I help you with something else?"

"I don't have my glasses. I can't see the clock."

"It's 3:38." She shakes her head and begins speaking into the phone again. "Now, Mary, like I was telling ye, Callum is just a bad seed. It runs in the family. The apple doesnae fall far from the tree and-"

George coughs louder this time. The secretary glares at him. "Hold on a sec, Mary. He's still here. The visitor. One of the teacher's husband." She drums her red nails against the desk. "Yes?"

George uses his free hand to pat his pockets. "I'm sorry. It's just I can't seem to find a pen. And I know you wouldn't want me to overhear anything confidential."

She talks into the phone again. "I have to go, Mary." She thrusts a pen at him. "Here."

George heads up the stairs and makes a right. Here, book reports about *Lord of the Flies* line the wall. He skims a few and is surprised to find himself agreeing with the scratchy handwriting (complete with hearts dotting the i's).

He stops at room 213. His wife is stapling letters to the bulletin board. He hides the bouquet behind his back and calls out, "Close your eyes, Mrs Cameron, I have a surprise for you."

She turns around and smiles.

"Come on, close them. No peeking."

He walks in as Patsy closes her eyes. He brings the daffodil and rose bouquet forward. "Any guesses?"

She reaches forward. "Well, it doesn't feel like an apple...." She opens her eyes. "George, they're beautiful, but you shouldn't, we can't afford... especially roses..."

"Relax, Mrs Cameron, our ship has come in!"

He picks her up and spins her around.

"I got a job today. Well, an offer. We're going to be okay." He brushes a kiss on her lips and carefully sets her down amid maps, and----

He is surrounded by Lego maps and pirate ships. "What's going on here?"

Patsy smells the flowers and smiles.

"*Treasure Island*. The students are using Lego men to make 'the book is better the than the movie' trailers to convince people to read the book."

"That sounds amazing. The kids must be having a blast."

She puts the roses down, and straightens the desks.

"It is. We're going to have a book club premiere. Mrs Dawson is going to bring in her old red curtains to make a red carpet. The kids are so excited."

She erases today's sentence diagrams from the chalkboard.

"When's the launch?" He takes the erasers and leans out the window to clap them. She begins to sweep the floor.

"In a month. We only have the computer lab for one hour a week. And they'll need time to edit."

"Oh. So, still a while then.....I wish.." George trails off.

"What do you wish for?"

George shakes his head. "I was just going to say that I wished I could walk the prettiest girl on the Isle home from school.

What do you say, Mrs Cameron, may I have this walk?" George offers a slight bow.

"I don't know. All of the other teachers will be jealous. And what will Ms Dee say?"

"Ms Dee?"

"The secretary."

"Plenty, I'm sure. You'll be the talk of the faculty room. Risk it?"

Patsy starts to gather up the papers on her desk and puts them in her overstuffed bag.

You're not taking work home?"

"I have to finish grading vocabulary quizzes tonight."

"I thought we could go out to dinner to celebrate."

"It won't take long. I promise."

"I'll hold you to that."

George helps her into her coat and places her scarf around her neck. He cups her face for a moment before loosely tying her scarf. The print is a mix of daisies and sunflowers.

"What was the challenge word this week?"

"Exodus."

Patsy grabs the yellow roses in her right hand and takes her husband's arm with her left.

They walk past the janitor mopping the floor. He sways as he sings,

"Cause I never seem to notice time
When you're with me
You can tell it to the birds.
You can tell it to the bees."

He dips the mop.

"Sorry Gus, we'll walk on the edges."

"Like I tell the kids, just stay in the right lane." He gestures to the mostly dry right side.

George steps forward. "Don't let them work you too hard."

"Aye. You know I want these floors to sparkle."

George points to the mop. "She's a lucky lady. Getting twirled around the floor."

"I only have eyes for Mrs Cameron, but you got there first."

Patsy laughs, "Flatterer. I heard you say the same thing to Miss Lane yesterday. Go back to your mop."

They start to head down the corridor.

"Hey, Mrs C?"

Patsy turns back around.

Gus drops to one knee.

"Please don't go rushing by
Stay and make my heart fly."

They exit the building and take a left onto Union Street. The rain is coming down a bit harder and has turned into a steady drizzle. The signs above the shops used to be pops of colour against the grey granite. Now, they're a faded backdrop. Pale yellow signs advertise 'Everything Must Go' sales.

"Thank you for the flowers. But we should be celebrating you. Tell me about the job. Is Horizon taking you back on?"

"No, Shell is. They've even offered us a moving bonus. We'll be able to finally afford a new house."

"Wait. We already have a house."

"That we can't afford. They are going to help us sell that too."

"*Where* do they want us to go?"

"Indonesia." He reaches over and tugs her scarf. "You definitely won't need that there. The average temperature is 30."

She stops walking and pushes his hand away. "We can't go that far."

"Why not? Think of it. A tropical paradise."

They turn onto King Street. They walk past all of the take-a-way chippies that they always say they'll try later.

"We can swim in the Great Barrier Reef. Think of that."

"When? When do they want you to start?"

They pause by the Morrisons. But she doesn't mention dinner.

"Don't you mean us? When do they want us there?"

Patsy just shakes her head.

"In two weeks."

"I can't go. We have the premiere. There's the academic bowl and the Reading Olympics. I can't leave them. They need me."

"Indonesia has high poverty rates. Those kid will need you too."

"You don't get it. Those are MY desks. That's MY classroom. Those are MY kids."

She crosses her arms.

"I don't get the big deal. You'd have a new class next year anyway."

A woman walks out of the grocery store. Two kids, a boy and girl in a navy uniform blazer and wellies run out in front of her and straight up to Patsy.

The girl hops from one foot to the other. "Mrs C, did you grade the vocabulary quiz yet?" The boy chimes in, "What did Callum get?"

"State Secret. My lips are sealed." She makes a zipping motion with her fingers and then 'throws away the key.'

"Callum walked around the house all week spelling exodus. He was talking to himself repeating the definition. He even made his wrestlers use it in sentences. She shook her head. "It was..."

"...weird." Her brother finishes the sentence for her. "Callum is always weird."

The woman catches up to them. George takes a closer look at her face. She has dark circles under her eyes. Her coat is worn. She's carrying a reusable bag in each arm. She's prepared then. George always forgets to bring theirs. "Jimmy, Julia, stop pestering Mrs Cameron. She sees enough of you during the day."

"That's alright. I always have time for my favourite students."

Jimmy turns to his mother. "She says that about everyone in her class."

"That's because it's true. You're all my favourite in wonderfully different ways."

Jimmy rolls his eyes.

"I mean it. Like when I needed someone to turn on the Smartboard, you were my favourite as the tallest one in class. And when I needed someone to show the new kids around, Julia was my favourite because she talks to everyone."

"Jimmy, Julia take these bags and run on ahead. I want to talk to your teacher for a minute."

Julia makes a face. "Mum, can't you make Jim do it? Last time, I had to carry the bags all by myself."

"No way," Jim argues back. "Last time, you had a tiny bottle of milk in one bag, and a loaf of bread in the other. But the time before that, I had to carry all of the Iron Bru cans and all of the pasta sauce."

"That's it. No more arguing. If you want to eat actual food for dinner tonight, then you each have to carry a bag home." She hands one to each child. "Now go and be careful. And no running."

"But you just told us to run ahead," Jim argues.

"Well, I take it back, now go." They groan, but take a bag, and start to walk ahead.

"Mrs Cameron, I want to thank you for all you've done for Callum. His stutter used to be so much worse. And it's not as much of a struggle to get him to do his homework anymore."

"Callum is an absolute pleasure to have in class. I wish they were all like him. I'm sorry. I didn't introduce you to my husband. George, this is Mrs Patterson. I've taught her twins and now I have Callum."

George shakes her hand. "It's nice to meet you."

"You too. I don't want to keep you from your tea." She nods at Patsy. "I'll see you at the Parent Meeting next week."

"I look forward to it. Good night." She waves as Mrs Patterson starts to walk down the street.

Patsy turns to her husband. "Why would you think you could do this? And without discussing it with me?"

"We're discussing it now."

"Are we though? Do I get a say in this? Or did you already tell them yes?"

"I.....I...well, I had to tell them something."

She frowns. "That's what I thought."

George laughs. "We are drowning here, you know? I couldn't take the chance that they would call the next guy on the list. So, you don't have a choice. But, I don't have a choice either. We don't have any other appealing options." His laughter sounds bitter. "We don't have any options."

"But I had plans." She starts to walk fast. "Julia, Jim, and Callum have a younger brother Nicholas. I would have liked to have taught the whole family. And Callum is really trying. He's coming out of his shell. He wrote the entire script for his trailer already."

George takes another stab. "Someone else can finish teaching the unit. There are volcanoes and rain forests and...it's paradise," he finishes.

"Can't get to Heaven on a sinking ship."

Patsy trips on the street corner, "Stupid Merkland!"

The drizzle has turned into a downpour. They are being pelted with fat rain drops. George pulls Patsy into a covered bus stop. She is staring at the ground, dipping the pointed tip of her shoes into a puddle, creating tiny ripples. George points through the clear plastic sides of the shelter. "If you squint, you can see the North Sea." But she doesn't look up. "I want you to be happy about this. When we got married-"

"My mother wanted me to marry a doctor." Patsy remembers. "A doctor's work is never done. Doctors will always have a job. They are always in demand."

"When we got married, I promised that I'd give you the world. I can't anymore. I can barely pay the electric bill. This could be an adventure."

"We have adventures here. We drank from the fairy pools in the Isle of Skye. We climbed the Cairngorms."

"You dropped your wedding ring, we had to dig for it for hours in the snow. There's no snow there. I can take you to Bali for vacation. They are no seagulls there. So we can picnic in peace."

Patsy mutters, "You always hated the seagulls."

"They're huge! They are more like pterodactyls than birds. A menace."

"Floyd isn't a menace."

"Just because you feed a stray bird doesn't make it a pet. Could you for once just be happy? The albatross is off our necks. You think I'm not upset-that I don't care. I'm losing this too. I remember racing you to the end of the golf course. We climbed to the top of the hill. With all of the hills in Scotland, you would think we would be better at climbing them. But we had to stop and catch our breath halfway through. We looked up. I was a little drunk on whiskey and the smell of summer on your skin. The night started off clear. We counted stars and lost track and counted again. I remember kissing you. You tasted of strawberry lipgloss and candy floss. I remember us watching the Ferris Wheel lights bouncing off the top of the water. You snuggled in closer. Clouds blew in and turned off the stars. In the darkness, you pushed my hand away and whispered, 'We can't go that far.'" George looks around. "The rain is starting to let up now."

Patsy offers a sad smile. "It's supposed to rain off and on all day."

"And me without my wellies. How embarrassing." He takes her hand. "What do you say Mrs Cameron, want to make a run for it? Reckon, we'll make it home?"

Who made thee? by David Perlmutter

To say we were shocked about it all was a bit of an understatement. I mean, nobody wants to go around, living their lives and what not, and discovering that they actually didn't do the things they thought they did, and said the things they did, and whatever else happened in their lives because, supposedly, someone else came up with all of that. And that we three were just supposed to shut up and go off gentle into that good night when they supposedly figured out how to do our job better than the way we did it. Even though we had done our job well, and effectively, for what we thought was quite a long time.

Or else, that's what we assumed was going on when we were told about us being replaced. And we were not happy about it, of course. So we did what we had to do, that's all. No words, just action. Because that's just what you do when you save the day for a living, isn't it?

What? Oh!

I guess we've been away longer than I thought, if you haven't heard of us at all. I have this tendency to plow into discussions verbally when I get approached directly for a conversation like this. I suppose that's why I got named Babbles in the first place, I guess.

I got a photo here if you don't believe me. Let me get it out....

There. You can see me in the middle. I'm the blonde. My role is kind of uncertain and fluctuating, although I'm a bit less of an innocent boob than I appear to be. Or, I should say, we all are. The redhead is Britomart- she's the brains of our outfit. The brunette is Barracuda- the muscle. They must be somewhere around here. If you had to separate us like this, you really must think that we....

Oh. You're just questioning us separately, not holding us. You'll let us go as soon as we finish up here?

But where will we go to? We have no home left! You destroyed it! Trying to destroy us, I might add! Wipe us from the face of the Earth as if we never existed in the first place!

Well, that's what I'll tell them at the hearing when this comes to trial. And it's the truth! The three of us don't trade in deception, and we don't like it much, either.

Huh? "Elaborate"? What does that....?

Tell the whole story, huh? Finally! Somebody's got to!

I thought everyone had heard of us, but I guess I was wrong.

Anyway, the three of us are-were-no, are the Jet Puffed Girls. The fastest, strongest and most otherwise empowered young ladies on the planet. The friends of all good people and the nemesis of all bad ones. When trouble struck, we were always prepared to fly into action and set things right. Sometimes it took our fists, sometimes our wits, sometimes some weird combination of those two things, and sometimes it was just dumb luck. But it always happened, somehow. We always saved the day and kept our home town from falling into the peril that seemed to be threatening it.

Until today, that is. When we found out about what a sham our whole existence was, and successfully avenged ourselves on those who had done us wrong. Even if it might be against the "laws" of whatever this world is where we are now, it wasn't against those we govern ourselves by. Superheroes aren't controlled or controllable by any "higher" forces, regardless of what you might believe, Mr. Policeman.

This is what happened:

We had been called in for what, for once, was a fairly routine proposition. One of those monstrous creatures that emerges from the seashore every once in a while and wreaks havoc because it doesn't know any better and feels threatened by the human race. That sort of thing. We had hoped this would be one of those kind that was able to talk, or communicate with us some other way, so we could get their version quick, resolve things, and then get on with our lives.

No such luck.

This was the other kind. The one that struck quick, drew blood and looks on you as nothing more than a chance for a bite-sized meal. And not just us. Everybody and everything in town, if it felt so inclined.

We knew this wasn't a time to fool around. And we didn't. So we went in, with fists and legs flying and attack cries in our throats. As we predicted, it was too stupid to counter-attack when we three went at it at once, so it was beaten and dead right quick. As it should have been.

But what should not have been happened when Barracuda kicked the lifeless corpse and it sailed off into the air, back to the Island of Monsters where it came from, presumably.

Instead of traveling in a straight line high in the air, as we had all become accustomed to seeing, it travelled only a short distance before it ripped a hole in the space-time continuum as if it were simply a sheet of fabric (at least, that's what Britomart said happened; I couldn't figure it out for myself until much later on) and a giant burst of wind howled out of it, sucking anything and everything in its path towards it without any resistance. Even- and especially- us.

We were right in the path of the wind, and even with our super-speed, we weren't able to move anywhere out of its way before it hit us and pulled us in.

We were helpless and powerless to stop it. Can you believe that?

Really, we were. All we could do was drift helplessly along, in the breeze, as if we were just simple leaves. Until....

We ended up here.

Well, not here, of course. Not this building. We only got to this building just now when you captured and arrested us. I mean the other one. The one the three of us completely trashed just now. For justifiable reasons.

The wind spit us down into something resembling a drainpipe attached to a large building, and we tumbled down it, landing somewhere on one of the building's floors in a heap. We quickly got to our feet and tried to figure out what had happened.

Or, rather, Britomart did. She's always been faster on the draw in that respect than me and Barracuda. That's why she's our boss.

"If I'm not mistaken," she said, "this is not where we belong. Whatever that wind was, or, more likely, whoever was responsible for it, wanted to get us out of the way for some reason."

"That's obvious," said Barracuda, with not a little bit of sarcasm. "But what are we gonna do about it? To start with, how are we supposed to get back to where we came from and deal with it?"

"Not really sure about that yet," responded Britomart. "First thing to do is figure out where we are, and then figure out where we came from. That's the only way to handle...."

She paused suddenly at that moment. Because we all managed to hear, with our advanced hearing, some laughter than sounded very familiar to our ears.

Because it was ours.

But we weren't laughing. Far from it. So who was doing it? And why were they sounding the way we did?"Who is that?" uttered Barracuda.

"And why do they sound the way we sound?" I asked.

"No time to be wasted asking those kinds of questions," concluded Britomart. "There's only one thing we can do. Follow the sounds and see where they lead us. That's the only possible way we can get out of this trap, whatever it is."

So we flew down the hallway, burning rubber. We only stopped at the end of the hallway, where some very big wooden doors stood guarding the entrance to some sort of video recording facility. We guessed that by the fact that it said "STUDIO B" in white letters over the middle of the two doors, along with the smaller legend "Do not enter the room while the red light is on, because recording is in progress." The red light was over to the side, and it was on.

But was that going to stop us? When we'd been abducted by the wind without notice, and had no possible way of getting back where we came from, and this was the only way we could find out how to get back?

Not likely!

We smashed the doors like they were made out of paper, and flew in.....

.....and we faced the world where we had come from!

It was our home town, meticulously recreated from stem to stern. It looked good enough to fool anybody who'd never been there to assume that they actually were in that place. But not us. We knew it wasn't where we really came from. However, somebody was obviously familiar enough with us and our activities to want to recreate them in some way, in flattery or otherwise.

But that wasn't the biggest shock.

There were people milling around, obviously in the midst of producing a film or television project involving our hometown that we had, somehow, interrupted. They looked at the three of us in the same level of shock we had expressed on seeing the constructed town for the first time. It was understandable.

None the more so than the three young ladies who were in the center of the whole thing, who bore a very similar appearance to the three of us!

A fellow who had been sitting in a canvas-backed chair- the director of the program, obviously- got up towards us, and demanded to know what was going on here.

"That's what we want to know!" retorted Britomart, hotly. "And we aren't going to be leaving until somebody manages to explain what's going on here!"

"And why should we?" said the director.

"Because we are the Jet Puffed Girls," came Britomart's answer. "The real ones."

Well, that wasn't apparently a good enough answer for him. The director said that there couldn't possibly have been any "real" Jet Puffed Girls because that was "just" a television program that had been made a long time ago. One that they were in the process of remaking at that moment, as a matter of fact. So, as there had never been any "real" Jet Puffed Girls, how could we possibly put forth the idea that we were the "real" ones if it was a made-up proposition?

"What the hell do you mean by THAT, buddy?" snarled Barracuda. "You want to see how real we are, just try us!"

"You could just be some animatronic or robotic recreations," said the director. "Pretty good, but not good enough to...."

"Not GOOD ENOUGH?" Britomart flared. "How can you possibly get away with saying that? After all we did to make sure that the world was safe for....?"

At that, the director burst our bubble further by explaining that the whole universe we had come from was a fabrication. It was something that had been planned all along. Everything that we had supposedly done, or said, or whatever, had been preordained. It was a completely dystopian outfit of control from afar and pre-programmed ideas, designed simply to provide the avaricious people who ran all the affairs at the top with more wealth they didn't need, from filming our "exploits" for television broadcast without our knowledge or consent, to putting our images on the cheapest and most expedient merchandise they could find for a further level of profit!

We had had no say in how things happened, no say in what we said, no say in how we acted. Nobody else in the environment we came from had any say, either. Even the ones that we loved and trusted hadn't. We were all just puppets meant to be played with by higher powers, and nothing else.

And now they were going to do it all again, with those three little....clones....of us. And we wouldn't be able to have any say about how this all happened, any more than we had before.

Or so they thought.

We just exploded then. Even I, who am not known for having a temper, blew up at what we had discovered. We just completely went to town then, and no one was spared. We wrecked the whole building, but we let most of the people live.

You can probably guess who didn't.

So that's why we did what we did. If it was wrong, so be it. After all, they ruined our lives by exploiting us in that cheap fashion to begin with! We always were the ones who responded to threats.

We didn't cause problems. We fixed them. Tit for tat. This was just another one of those cases.

In any event, there are only three Jet Puffed Girls in the world now, and there always will be.

Even if we don't have a real home anymore, we can still find ways to make things all right in this new one.

If you can forgive us for what we did back there. I know it's not much, but it's all we can ask of you now.

Can't you?

Dedicated to Craig McCracken, from an admirer. Thank you very kindly, sir.

The Descent by Matthew Harrison

As he neared the mountaintop, Peter smiled scornfully. Marjorie had been so anxious when she saw him off, her brow quite furrowed with concern. Yet barely two hours later, here he was, almost at the summit. The path up had been winding, not overly steep; he had not even taken off his anorak. He felt good – he could walk miles more like this. It was almost a pity that he would have to return. Still... He sent his wife a text, and put her out of his mind.

Rounding a knoll, Peter strode the last yards through the rough grass and reached the top. The panorama of the Shek Kong plain opened below. Through the brown haze he could make out the small fields, workshops and the tiny bright-coloured boxes of the container depots that chequered the flat land, the whole surrounded by a rim of hills. He could see over the haze to the great peak of Tai Mo Shan and the waters of Deep Bay, pale in the late afternoon sun. Behind him, beyond Hong Kong's border, were the mountains of Shenzhen, cut by quarries and topped by telecoms towers. Yet the summit of his mountain was pristine scrub.

Peter stood for some minutes enjoying the view. But clouds were gathering from the horizon, and the wind had become cold. He turned to go back. Yet the housing estate where Marjorie was visiting friends lay ahead; was there a more direct route? Yes, the mountain was obliging – the path continued over the summit, pointing towards his destination. A happy chance!

Peter descended a little way, and stopped. Ahead, the path continued through bushes, its future course hidden by the convexity of the slope. Should he take it? He thought to call Marjorie, got out his phone– then paused. Why call her? He would decide himself. Just then, a gust of wind blew the anorak hood over his head. He snatched it back, and made up his mind. In the bushes he would be out of the wind: he would take the short cut home.

Deciding gave him new energy, and he descended the path in great strides. Going down would be easier than ascending, the hour or so before dark gave him plenty of time. He would surprise Marjorie. When he thought of his wife, her cloying presence seemed to settle on the bushes around him. She was too protective. And then he thought of *her*. Peter's lips curled with satisfaction, and he strode down through the bushes, sweeping at them with his arms.

But the bushes were not easily swept aside. They became thicker, growing in clusters that hid the path, forming an impenetrable barrier. Peter edged round, but the path shrank to indistinct marks in the grass, marks that divided and re-formed where earlier walkers had tried different routes, then disappeared altogether. Should he go back? But retracing would be wearisome, and time was getting on. The direction was clear enough, he just had to keep going.

To Peter's relief, the scrub grew taller, became woodland. It was dim under the canopy of leaves, but the bushes had thinned and he was no longer pushing through. Now he had to stoop under the lower boughs, and watch for the occasional bramble, but he could move at a good pace. Every step down took him nearer to his goal. In the silent gloom the crashing of his boots through the dead leaves was magnified. He was a giant striding down.

Ahead, the dimness brightened, and as he passed under the last boughs Peter found himself in a clearing. He paused and looked up. Through the gap in the trees the sky was clear, a steady grey. Far above, a tiny group of kites circled slowly, dipping and then soaring, impossibly remote. Peter dropped his gaze – and the dark mass of the wood loomed impenetrable before him. A chill gripped his heart.

Yet it was surely just the contrast with the sky. He shut his eyes, reopened them; yes, he could make out branches in the gloom. The twisted boughs formed strange shapes in the half light, goblins to frighten a child. *He* was not afraid. He balled his fists in his anorak sleeves and forged on.

Motion restored courage. But now came a new threat. The brambles that higher up the mountain had caught his bootlaces here grew more thickly. They formed a continuous matted layer that covered the ground and everything on it like a sinister sea, throwing up tangled waves that almost reached the lowest tree branches. Peter stopped, hearing his own breathing in the silence. How could he get through this?

He probed the matted stuff with his toe. The individual shoots were so entwined that they pulled one another down beneath his boot, the whole mass compressing to a springy mattress. Tramping on this mattress, he found that he could create space for himself beneath the boughs. Heartened, he took another tramping step, and then another. He could progress – and he would soon break through to easier ground.

The incline was steep. He tried to help himself by holding the branches overhead, sometimes swinging bodily over the more intractable brambles. Then, misjudging, he caught his leg and fell forward into a prickly embrace.

Peter landed face down, cushioned by the green mass, seemingly unhurt. Then his hands and face began to sting. He thrashed around before he could get a knee forward and brace himself. Panting, he struggled up, one leg thrust into the green shoots, the other braced against the slope. He dabbed his face with a trembling hand – a smear of blood. But mercifully, he had not hurt his eyes. Wiping his hand on his anorak, he stumbled forward.

Things had gone wrong, badly wrong. He should have returned the way he came. The mountain had tricked him. He would call Marjorie. But his phone was not there! Where was it? Panicking, he clutched at his clothing, his anorak, trousers. Nothing. Had he just dropped it? He parted the brambles with trembling fingers, heedless of the thorns, and peered into the gloomy undergrowth. But it was hopeless. He gave a shuddering moan and buried his face in his hands.

Moments passed; his legs buttressed him against the mountain's slope. He became conscious of the firmness of his legs. He was strong. It was darker, but he could see. He could still get down. He thought again of Marjorie, waiting with their friends in the housing estate below, making conversation, and then falling silent with that pensive look of hers. He must get on.

He stumbled forward. And, gradually, the brambles began to thin out, just as he had known they would. The smothering mass of shoots gave way to isolated shrubs and creepers. Holding the creepers, he stumbled and half-slid down crevices masked by dead leaves. Sometimes he slipped and landed joltingly, but he got up again and lurched on down.

The slope became steeper. At first Peter welcomed this. He half-ran down a gully of dead leaves, releasing himself from one dusty trunk and gathering speed until he caught the next. Each rush carried him nearer to his goal. The slope steepened further, and the gully became a torrent of leaves tumbling over outcrops of rock. Yet beneath the leaves were tree roots that offered footholds, handholds; he could still get down.

Now the slope became precipitous, each rock face plunging sheer to the next level which was itself little more than a ledge before the next drop. With sudden horror, he saw how the mountain had lured him. Here were the jaws of the trap, the bare rocks like closing teeth. He could not go on.

Yet he could not stop on that great slope. Instinctively he resumed his stumbling downward gait. And again, motion saved him: in motion, twilight made the threat unreal. He glided downward over boulders and tree roots, grabbing a branch, jumping, skipping downwards like a squirrel. The gloom was a supportive medium, water through which he could swim without falling, an enchantment.

Landing finally in a trough of dead leaves, he had to climb a little rocky rise. The momentary ascent broke his rhythm, and he paused, panting. Ahead in the failing light a curtain of foliage hung still and silent; below, the rock dropped sheer for twenty feet. A squirrel could leap through space to the boughs ahead. But the man hesitated, hearing the thump of his own heart. The enchantment was broken.

He shivered, and turned like a trapped animal. To one side, a ridge protruded from the cliff face. He stumbled up it. Beyond, a shale slope dropped out of sight, and with sureness born of desperation he slid and scraped his way down, rattling over the lip of the last drop to land with a thud on the mercifully level ground. He sat where he had landed. Was he down?

No. The shoulders of the ridge ran into the gloom on either side. Ahead, the ground pitched into darkness. Above, the dim sky was barely visible between the foliage. Soon there would be no light.

Despair rose in his gullet; his eyes pricked with tears. If he should get out of this, he would make it up to Marjorie: he would give up the girl. Sitting there on the dead leaves, he made a silent pact with the grave trunks. "One more chance!" he croaked. But the trees absorbed the sound without echo.

The darkness crept closer, and with it, the chill. Weakened after his rest, he got up and tottered over the rise ahead, stumbling down the other side. He crept slowly, bent double, not releasing one hold until he had gripped another. Nonetheless, he slipped on the moss of an exposed rock and fell, banging his hip. The mountain was toying with him. He began to want peace, to want the end.

Yet, automaton now, he got up and staggered on. The slope lessened, but he did not register this; the darkness of the wood had enfolded him and he could see only the next branch. He edged forward, pushing through black curtains of leaves. In one direction the darkness paled, and instinctively he turned that way.

The paleness hovered behind black trunks. He staggered towards it, pushing at the last spray of twigs. They yielded, then resisted his hand. Mechanically, he turned to one side, but a drift of dead branches blocked the way. He pushed forward again towards the paleness, through twigs that scratched his face, but again the leaves resisted. He pushed harder, and his fingers poked through wire mesh.

The lights in the living room reflected back from the windows and nothing could be seen of the darkness outside. Approaching the glass, the woman pressed her face to it anxiously, but the dark bulk of the mountain revealed nothing. The television played, no one spoke. Then came a knock on the door. The woman sprang up, and rushed to open it. Her joy at seeing the visitor was quickly stilled when she saw the torn anorak, the jeans and, worst, his face, scratched beneath the matted hair. She took his hand, recoiled at the torn flesh. Then, recovering, she gently held his arm and guided him to a chair.

A cloth and a basin were brought, and delicately Marjorie began to dab at the clotted mess. She saw that silent tears were running from the corners of his eyes, clearing a little path through the blood-caked dirt. She busied herself with the cloth and wiped the dirt away. What had this great child been up to that he had hurt himself so?

Later that week, when the girl who ministered to him had absorbed the full onslaught of his passion, she found him weeping in her arms, and the question that came idly to her mind was almost the same.

The Duel by Ken Leland

January 3, 1800

The line of men over by the river are wrapped in fur.
They stand in new snow near the footbridge.
Why do they stare at me?
Who are they?

". . . then you will both turn and fire." A pause. "Mr. White. Are you listening, Sir?"

"What?" I ask.

"I will count as you take seven paces. Then you will turn and fire. Do you understand?"

At grey dawn, we tremble on the plain beside the Don River. My adversary and friend, a tall, burly man preposterously named Joseph Small, glares down at me. Over his chest and arms, the wind ripples his long-sleeved, white shirt.

"I will ask one last time. Is there a chance for reconciliation... Mr. White?"

I glance at the grim, bloody-minded Small and wonder, did she confess? If not, how much does he know? How could I possibly ask what he knows?

I shake my head in despair.

The conductor of this dreadful business holds out a shallow, open box. "Both were carefully loaded," he says. "Take your choice, Mr. Small."

Small grasps one of the identical, walnut-handled pistols and holds it upright to cock the hammer. His face flames in driving snow.

"Have you used a pistol before, Mr. White?"

The steel barrel shines in my hands. The weapon is heavy. I pull the spring hammer back.

"If you fire before the count of seven, it's murder."

How ridiculous, I think, as we turn back to back. I imagine myself in my usual powdered wig, standing before the Court of

Quarter Sessions to ask one of those witnesses along the creek, "Did I, John White, Attorney General of Upper Canada, wait upon the count of seven before firing on Joseph Small, Clerk of the Executive Council?"

ONE

****

"Mr. Russell!" Pompy yells into the echoing hallways, "White and Small. They're fixin' to kill each other."

Limping, the Honourable Peter Russell, recently retired Administrator of Upper Canada, descends the mansion stairs. His gout is excruciating. Pompy, the black man Russell employs as his farm manager, waits inside the oak panelled foyer in a puddle of melting snow.

"Saints defend us, Pompy. What's all the commotion?"

"You got to come quick, Mr. Russell. I brought the wagon."

TWO

****

Russell's long, woollen scarf hangs down past the bouncing wagon bench as he struggles to button his fur coat. Once stout, the aging Russell has shrunk, withered like a late autumn pumpkin forgotten in a field. Pompy reaches out to steady him as the wagon lurches through the ice-rimmed slush pits that are Front Street.

"You! Woman!" Russell raises his fist and shouts at a figure on the plank sidewalk. "Confound you. What have you done this time?"

Mrs. Emily Small is a petite, enticing coquette with strands of long brown curls that peep from beneath her bonnet. Raising gloved hands to hide her tear-streaked face, she hurries down the street.

"On her way, no doubt, to wail to my sister," Russell growls. "Much good it will do her."

"I left White's boys still asleep," Pompy says, as they rumble through the frozen slough that is the intersection with Yonge Street.

THREE

****

"Miss Russell? Are you home?"

Miss Elizabeth Russell, greying spinster and sister to the now retired Provincial Administrator, Peter Russell, hurries into the foyer when she hears Mrs. Emily Small. At Miss Russell's close approach, Mrs. Small throws off her bonnet, clutches Miss Russell's hands and wilts to her knees in lamentations. Miss Russell, still in her dressing gown, wonders how Emily has managed to dress impeccably and yet achieve a state of emotional collapse, both before breakfast.

"Oh, Miss Russell. They've gone to fight each other."

"There, there, my dear," Miss Russell replies, amazed by the trace of thrilled anticipation in Emily's voice. "Whatever can you mean?"

Mrs. Small's face is upturned; flawless skin, sweet peaked nose and lustrous hair carefully trained into curls that fall to her shoulders. In Society, men babble insipidly in Emily's presence – though today, her tortured eyes spoil the effect.

"My husband didn't come home last night. Then just before dawn, he did," Emily says.

"Oh. I see," Miss Russell says.

"He spent the night at an inn."

"Yes, yes. I'm sure he did," Miss Russell says, slowing lifting Emily to her feet.

"And he was quite sharp with me. At first I couldn't imagine why."

"No, no. Of course, you couldn't, my dear."

"When he left at dawn, my husband said he was going to kill John White, in a duel across the river."

The aging spinster is aghast that two gentlemen she and her brother have received in their home for years could come to such a pass.

"Do you have any idea why?"

"John White pretends, he pretends that he and I have had . . . relations."

FOUR

****

Susanna Page hears the hard scrape of a wagon axle plunging into a frozen pothole. At the sound of an oath, she glances outside to see Peter Russell clinging to the driver's bench as Pompy's wagon careens towards the Don River.

John must have gone straight home, Susanna thinks. Pompy's already out and about.

Pompy was to stay overnight with John White's two growing sons while John slept in Susanna's arms. Early in the morning, long before light, John woke her sweetly with great longing. Gasping, finally, he clutched her tight. A little later he whispered how much he loved her and then rose to dress in darkness before going to the next room to kiss their two young daughters goodbye.

Susanna sighs as she thinks of John. My house here in York is just four mean rooms – and so dear at that. In Niagara, John and I had a brave cottage with flowers by the sidewalk and a garden. Fran and Lucy were born there and we were happy. But then, a year ago, Mrs. White sailed from Wales, bringing John's two fine sons and her fiery temper. Their reunion failed, thank the Lord. When Mrs. White returned to Cardiff in the fall, she left the boys behind in a ruinously expensive, second house.

Now John says he and I can share one home, just as soon as we can explain Fran and Lucy to his sons.

FIVE

****

Miss Russell and Mrs. Emily Small sit behind the fire screen next to the rose wood fireplace.

"Why would John say such an outlandish thing? Do you think my husband blames me?" Emily asks.

"Blames you for what, my dear?"

"At the subscription ball, Mrs. White was most horrid to me. Everyone heard her. Joseph was mortified."

"Oh, yes. It was scandalous," Miss Russell says.

"Why, of course the three of us lived together at first. It was so crowded in Niagara when all the government officials arrived together. And not even shacks to rent," Emily says.

Miss Russell nods. She remembers those early days in Upper Canada.

"But the things Mrs. White said! As if John White and my Joseph shared more than the house."

"No one credits that, Emily."

"Mrs. White thinks I'm a loose woman. Is that why she returned to Wales?"

"No, no. It's a blessing she's gone," Miss Russell says, knowing full well no woman would trust her man, no man could trust himself, under the same roof with the irresistible Mrs Emily Small.

SIX

****

Miss Russell stares quietly at the ash-strewn, parlour floor. The servants are hopelessly inept. After a moment she glances up at Emily.

"My dear. What exactly did John say to your husband?"

"They didn't speak. There was a letter."

"From John?"

"No, unsigned. Something about proof overheard at the Nag's Head."

"Tavern gossip, proof! And your husband believed it? Imbecile!"

Miss Russell shouts for her boots and winter coat.

"Lord in Heaven. Where's Peter?" Miss Russell asks in confusion as a servant hurries to bring her galoshes and wrap.

"Your brother and Pompy are headed for the Don," Emily says. "I saw them in the street."

"Emily, run tell Doctor Baldwin to harness his sleigh," Miss Russell says. "I'll be there directly."

SEVEN

****

I turn at the count of seven. The snow filled world spins past watching faces to settle upon a tall, white shirted man, standing alone. My arm is heavily weighted. In extension it waves past my solitary adversary, to the earth, then skyward.

A soundless effusion of smoke leaps towards me. My ribs are struck a hammer blow. I rock backwards, as my legs buckle. The pistol in my hand drags down my arm. I am startled by its explosion as I fall face down into the snow. A searing iron has plunged into my side and I begin to scream.

****

"I killed him!" Joseph Small shouts as he runs forward. A ring of witnesses already surrounds the moaning, writhing John White.

Small pushes through the crowd until he sees the tickle of blood oozing from underneath White's body. "Dear God! I've killed him."

Someone rolls White onto his back. His linen shirt is crusted with red, powdered snow, congealing upon the pierced cloth. White's wide eyes stare upward. As he clutches at his side, he spreads blood across his belly.

Pompy clears a path, the tottering Peter Russell calls to all and sundry, "Let us through."

In a gout-driven agony of his own, Russell kneels to take White's hand.

"John, are you with us still?"

White nods and grinds his lower lip to keep from wailing.

"Good, man. Hold on."

The sleigh carrying Doctor Baldwin, Miss Russell and Mrs. Emily Small arrives just as White is carried over the footbridge to Pompy's wagon. Emily cries out as she runs to her husband. Her hands smooth over his windblown shirt, then, satisfied that he is whole, she turns to the wounded man.

"Oh, John," Emily says as she leans into the wagon to touch his shoulder. His eyes focus when he turns to her voice.

"Never." White moans, loud enough for everyone to hear. "Never."

"Bastard!" Small snarls. "Still lying. Still denying your guilt."

The diminutive Emily wheels, and with the crack of a horse whip, she slaps her husband's face. "He's not lying, you precious fool! He never touched me."

Doctor Baldwin clambers into the wagon box to rip open White's shirt. The bullet has entered between the second and third lower ribs. There is no exit wound. The ball is lodged somewhere inside his belly.

"Take him to Susanna Page's house," Doctor Baldwin tells Pompy. "He's fading."

The witnesses part as Pompy lashes the team back towards town.

****

"Keep that door closed!" the doctor shouts to the neighbours clustered in Susanna Page's tiny kitchen.

White lies in Susanna's bed – their daughters, Fran and Lucy, stand at the doorway, eyes wide with fear for their blood-covered father. Draped in a shawl, Susanna sits on the bed in horrified silence, her eyes locked with John's as he struggles in hushed wretchedness. The doctor completes his examination.

"Miss Russell," Doctor Baldwin says gently to the aging lady, "please ask if anyone has extra clean towels." Miss Russell marches to the kitchen and begins to organize those she finds there. In the bedroom, her brother Peter leans back against the curtained wall to ease his aching foot.

"Pompy, we'll need warm water to wash him. At least two pails."

"I'll borrow some buckets," Pompy says as he heads out the door.

"Mr. Small."

"Yes? Anything."

"It's cold." The doctor glances at Susanna Page, who wrings her hands then reaches out to touch John's face.

"Mrs. Page is short of firewood."

"I'll buy some," Small says and squeezes his wife's hand before hurrying out into the snow filled street. Emily smiles distractedly as her husband departs, then turns to stare at the plainly dressed woman caressing John's cheek.

"Mrs. Page," Doctor Baldwin whispers, "come away, please. Just for a moment."

Susanna Page and the doctor enter the children's bedroom. The doctor closes the door. "Susanna. It's very bad. The bullet passed through the liver. I think it's lodged somewhere near the spine."

Alone and unnoticed beside the curtains, Russell watches as Emily approaches the bed. She drops quickly to one knee, leans close. John's voice is slow but clear.

"Never... tell. I go... to the grave."

A short time after Emily leaves, Doctor Baldwin and Susanna Page return to the bedroom.

"Laudanum," the doctor says as he places two thin, brown bottles on the dressing table. "Give him one now. He will sleep. When he wakes, give him the second."

"There's nothing else?" Susanna sobs. The girls clasp tight to her skirts.

"No, nothing. I'll return to clean his wound while he's asleep."

As snow swirls beyond the window, Susanna cradles John's head in her lap. Their daughters sit motionless at the foot of the bed. Russell limps over to collapse onto the chair by the door.

"This will ease the pain," Susanna says holding the laudanum close.

John gently pushes the vial away.

"A moment," he murmurs. "Susanna, my love, my only love. Had I found you first, I swear things would have been different."

"I know. I've always known. It can't be helped."

"I've nothing left, just debts. You must be strong, for our girls."

Russell frowns as he rises to limp out the door.

****

In summer's crushing heat, Pompy and Russell file into the back row of the smoky courtroom. With a handkerchief, Russell wipes sweat from his neck and then picks up a paper fan. A town warden approaches the high bench to address the triune judges.

"Your Honours, it has come to my attention that a Mrs. Page, a former servant . . ."

The warden coughs.

". . . of the deceased Attorney General and her two daughters are destitute, homeless. They pray relief."

The judges confer, powdered wigs bent close. "The Court is of the opinion that the Acts of this Province do not authorize such wastrel use of public funds. Next item."

Peter Russell leans on Pompy's arm. It is a relief to stand on the Court House steps, bathed in cool breezes from Lake Ontario.

"What will she do?" Pompy asks Russell.

"I don't know."

"You paid passage for his boys back to Wales," Pompy says.

"Yes. Yes, I did that."

"Miss Russell wants a better housekeeper. You got plenty of room."

"I can't accommodate all the strays in Upper Canada," Russell says.

"No. No you can't," Pompy smiles gently as he helps the old man down the steps. "Just John's wife and girls."

Charity by Gillian Rioja

The school doors open and the pupils tumble out. They look to Jenny like a flock of birds released from a cage, and in seconds they have fanned out to fill the playground. Mums, a few dads, grandparents and child-minders wait round the edges, their charges' meriendas – usually a foil-wrapped sandwich – clutched in their hands. Most children make for the adults. They dump rucksacks at the grownups' feet, grab their snacks and race off again. Some of the younger ones are swept up in loving arms and smothered in kisses. A few children cling to their carers. Chronically shy or just had a bad day? Jenny hopes it's the latter.

Jenny turns to Nuria, who is complaining that on Monday the kids have both a maths and a geography exam, and that she will have to spend a good chunk of the weekend helping Javier prepare for them. Jenny is glad Nicholas has a good enough memory to learn by himself the lists of facts that have to be regurgitated on a regular basis.

"¿Cómo es el sistema educativo en Inglaterra?" asks Nuria. Jenny thinks that children receive a better education in Britain but that it isn't tactful to be critical Spain. Also, she's not sure to what extent her admiration is a case of absence makes the heart grow fonder, so she just replies that eight year old kids certainly don't have so many exams.

Nicholas and Javier are among the last out of school. They run up, pulling off their coats as it's warm now, in the bright, winter sun. They are accompanied by Hugo, but he stops a couple of feet from the mothers and starts kicking a pebble round in circles.

Hugo, the traveler boy in Primary Three, used to go straight home after school with the rest of his family. They would leave holding hands, Hugo on one side, his elder sister on the other and two younger siblings in the middle. They reminded Jenny of a clothes line: the older children the poles, the little ones sometimes being swung up, like fluttering washing.

But Hugo is now friends with Nicholas and Javier, united by a passion for Pokemon. They know the names of all the characters, hundreds of them it seems to Jenny, and can recite all their transformations. If Pokemon was on the curriculum, the three boys would be straight A students, Nuria once said.

"Have a good day, darling?" Jenny asks.

"Bien," replies Nicholas in Spanish. This is the usual pattern of their communication except for when they have been alone together for a while, and then Nicholas slips into English. Jenny doesn't force anything; she is just glad he doesn't object to her speaking to him in English in front of his friends.

"Are you ready for your sandwich?" she asks.

"¿Qué hay?" Nicholas sounds suspicious.

"Peanut butter on granary bread."

"Ha-ha."

"Ham and cheese on a baguette roll, just like your friends' sandwiches."

Nuria is wetting a tissue from a bottle of water and smears it across Javier's dirty face.

"Pareces un gitano," she says.

Out of the corner of her eye Jenny sees Hugo, now flipping the stone from foot to foot. Did he hear Nuria telling her son he looked like a gypsy? Do these thoughtless remarks register with him? Hugo is a tall, skinny boy with thick, black hair and beautiful eyes. He is wearing a rather grubby, too-big Adidas tracksuit.

When Nuria has finished, the three boys bound away across the playground making strange, martial arts gestures; Pokemon fighting tactics. But five minutes later they are back. Nicholas looks in a mock-begging way between Jenny and Nuria:

"¿Puede venir Javier a jugar en casa? Por favor, por favor."

Then: "Can Javier come and play at our house for a bit?" Perhaps he thinks asking in English will help persuade Jenny.

"Fine by me. ¿Qué te parece, Nuria?"

Nuria agrees, as long as Javier does his homework as soon as he gets back.

Nicholas then turns to Hugo: "¿Quieres venir?"

Hugo shrugs.

"Can Hugo come too, Mum?" Nicholas asks.

"Of course." Jenny tries not to sound surprised. Her husband, Pedro told her that travelers generally are as suspicious of payos as many payos still are of them, but Jenny likes to think that is changing. Hey, aren't these three boys all good friends? Although Hugo never goes to birthday parties and isn't in the football club. She asks Hugo if he should check with his parents.

"No," he says.

Most of the pupils live in flats nearby but Jenny's house is on the outskirts of Logroño. She enjoyed the convenience of living in the city centre until she got pregnant when she suddenly longed for her child to have a garden, to help her water flowers and make mud pies. Now she finds it a bit of a drag having to chauffeur him everywhere.

In the car the boys chatter excitedly, butting in, raising their voices to be heard, the conversation changing direction in a way that is as impenetrable to Jenny as a watching a shoal of fish moving in unison. She has to pay attention to distinguish one voluble voice from another.

She parks outside the house. Javier is the first out of the car and rushes up the path. Nicholas follows but Hugo stands on the pavement looking round.

"Por aquí," Jenny says and holds the gate open for him.

Jenny was going to suggest the boys leave their coats in the cloakroom but they are already running upstairs to Nicholas's bedroom. She hears the door being flung open and the scrapping of chairs on the parquet floor. A crash, followed by a laugh as someone apparently bangs the chair from the spare bedroom into the door frame, makes her wince. Nicholas should tell his friends to be more careful, but at least he has friends and is comfortable sharing his home with them.

There is an hour before Jenny has to run them back and she decides to sort out the washing she left to dry. After rubbing the thicker seams of sweatshirts and jeans to make sure they are not still damp she puts the clothes into a wicker basket and goes upstairs.

First she had better check up on the boys and she half opens her son's bedroom door. Nicholas and Javier are playing the Harry Potter computer game; Hugo is looking out of the window.

"¿Estáis bien?"

"Sí, sí sí," reply Nicholas and Javier without turning round.

"What about your other friend?" Jenny asks Nicholas. Hugo turns around and looks surprised, as if he's never heard her speak in English before. In fact, as if he doesn't know who she is.

"He doesn't want a go," Nicholas replies. Jenny reminds herself to tell him later that he should have chosen a game they could all play together.

"¿Qué tal, Javier, Hugo?"

"Bien," says Javier. Hugo nods as he continues to stare at the garden.

In her bedroom Jenny places the dried clothes into piles: clothes for ironing and the non-ironing: her stuff, Pedro's, Nicholas's... The stripy tee-shirt is too small for Nicholas now. It's rather faded to pass onto Jenny's nephew so she'll give it to the second-hand shop. The threadbare end of one of Pedro's socks has finally worn into a hole; something else for the charity bag. She hopes no-one in Logroño is poor enough to want holey socks, but she's heard that the material from unwearable clothes is recycled.

Suddenly there's the sound of someone running downstairs and the front door being slammed shut. Jenny rushes after and finds Hugo about to open the gate. He tells her he's got to go home, now. No, he doesn't need a lift, he knows the way, but Jenny is sure he doesn't.

"Espera un minuto y te llevo," she tells him and runs to the house for the car keys.

Where did she leave her damned bag? Surely Hugo hasn't...? No, there it is, on the sofa. Jenny thinks about asking Javier to come as well but by the time he's collected his things Hugo might have run off. The boys are looking down over the banister.

"Dónde se ha ido Hugo?" asks Nicholas.

"I'm taking him home, now. I'll be back in about fifteen minutes. Play sensibly until I return. Ahora vuelvo, Javier." Jenny picks up her bag and leaves the house, worried about the other two boys being left alone.

Hugo is quiet in the car. He answers with one-word Jenny's bright questions about Pokemon and she desists. Who is she to force conversation on him? He asks to be dropped off in the Glorieta, at the end of a pedestrian street that marks the beginning of the rundown part of the old quarter. He jumps out of the car and, dodging passersby, runs off until he is out of sight.

When Jenny returns the boys are playing quietly with football cards. She takes Javier home, stopping outside the door of his building until he is buzzed in and Nuria waves from a second floor window to let her know he's arrived safely.

That evening Nicholas is subdued. Jenny believes him when he tells her they tried to include Hugo in the game but that Hugo just became quiet and then suddenly said he must go home.

When Nicholas is bathed and ready for bed Jenny goes into his room.

"You can read for ten minutes then lights out." She gets a chair to look on the top shelf of the fitted wardrobe.

"What are you doing?" asks Nicholas.

"I think the charity shop bag is up here. I'm going put your stripy tee-shirt in it."

"No, don't. Just throw it away."

"That would be wasteful."

"I don't care. I don't want my old clothes being given to someone else."

Nicholas is clenching his fists and looks as if he might cry. Jenny sits on the bed and puts her arm round him.

"Sweetheart, what's the matter?"

"Something happened at school a few weeks ago that I didn't tell you about."

"Well, tell me now, darling."

"Remember my Harry Potter sweatshirt you gave to the charity shop? Well, Hugo came in wearing it."

"Oh dear."

"And someone said 'Oh, Hugo's got the same top as Nicholas'. But I knew it had to be mine because Gran sent it over and no one is Spain can have the same one."

"You didn't say anything?"

"Of course not!"

"I knew you wouldn't. You're a good, sensitive boy." She kisses Nicholas on the side of his head. "And the other kids thought it was just a coincidence, right?"

"Yeah, but Hugo's never worn it again."

"So there's no harm done. But I promise I won't give any more of your clothes away."

Jenny strokes Nicholas's back until he's drowsy and then quietly leaves the room. She remembers the sweatshirt and the blackberry juice stain on the sleeve, the reason she didn't pass it on to her nephew. She sighs and goes back to the ironing.

Later she and Pedro have supper together.

"Poor Hugo," says Pedro. "He probably felt disoriented in a house so different, so luxurious, compared to his." Then he smiles in a slightly amused way. "Sorry your social experiment didn't work out."

"I just let him come round to play," says Jenny quietly and wonders at how differently she and Pedro sometimes see the world.

"We need more pepper," says Pedro as he turns the empty grinder.

"I'll put it on my list for the supermarket, tomorrow." Milk, bananas, pepper; a new tee-shirt for Nicholas. He's growing so fast.

Vinny Grasps The Nettle by Stephen McQuiggan

Vinny Cleaver sat in the green room of Studio 5 watching the game-show unfold on the monitor. His palms fizzed. He felt his legs spasm with the desire to move needlessly, endlessly, to assert their existence. He was on next. As his stomach began its relentless rise he wondered if he could go through with it, after all.

When he had applied to be a contestant on Grasp The Nettle he had done it as a joke; he had never actually believed he would be chosen. The show was halfway through its fifth run, with the recent Christmas celebrity special pulling in nearly twenty million viewers; that was a hell of a lot of people to see him fall flat on his ass, to turn the joke onto him.

On the wall, the clock banged out another minute, each cold, slow tick the fall of a guillotine blade.

Just remember what the producer said during rehearsal, he told himself, concentrate on the host and forget about the faceless folks at home, and above all have fun! But Vinny found the show's host just as intimidating as the thought of Joe Public scrutinising him over their microwave dinners.

Alex 'Brash' Bison had enough old school charm to stop the blue rinse brigade from flicking channels, whilst maintaining a certain ironic edge that appealed to the fickle 16 to 25 demographic. He was TV gold and the tabloids loved him for his unapologetic and undisguised excess. Vinny thought him the most insincere man he had ever laid eyes on. Maybe if he had met the mercurial Brash during the run through he wouldn't be feeling so damn nervous, but one of the backroom staff had taken the host's place, hamming it up magnificently. Brash only did the show once, when it was live and dangerous - 'It's the only way to stop yourself getting jaded,' he told Inside TV.

Josie, the pneumatic doll who led the contestants onto the set and, according to tabloid rumour, Brash's latest beau, popped her Domestos curls around the fake Chinese rubber tree that shaded the door.

"On in ten, Mr Beaver."

"It's Cleaver," said Vinny, but she was already gone, the artificial plant jiggling in her wake.

Ten minutes.

Six hundred seconds in which to compose himself. He took a few medicinal deep breaths and returned his gaze back to the monitor, watching the show, letting himself drift away on its mind numbing banality.

On screen, Josie was escorting a small, wrinkled man in an ill fitting suit onto the Terror Board. Vinny had spoken to some of the other contestants before the show, but not this one; the small man looked even more nervous than Vinny felt. Why do we put ourselves through this? The prizes were rubbish. Was it for the fleeting fame? God help us all.

Vinny surveyed the empty green room, he was the last contestant, the only victim left. At least now, he had the complimentary buffet to himself. He flicked open a dog eared sandwich to reveal a wizened slice of cucumber; great combination, he thought, bread and water; Victorian prison food aiming at sophistication.

On the monitor, Brash was doing his dance, the one imitated the length and breadth of the country. "Arthur Marsh!" he boomed, "I hope you're in fine fettle..." pausing, giving the crowd their money's worth, letting them pitch in and finish his equally imitated catchphrase, "...because now's the time to GRASP THE NETTLE!"

Grasp The Nettle was ostensibly a show about phobias, 'a breakthrough in psychological gaming' was how Brash liked to describe it on his many chat show appearances, though an exercise in maximum discomfort would have been closer to the truth. Like all successful shows nowadays, mused Vinny, it was really about making a fool out of the contestants and a hero of the host, of making the poor dupes degrade themselves, sell their souls in front of a baying nation, for prizes you would hand back at a funfair.

And yet here he was.

Was he truly any better than the idiots he routinely swore at every night before reaching for the remote? The thought added to his nerves, crippled his confidence even more; could he really go through with this, or could he just slink way now, damn the contract, and hide under his bed?

But the show was live. There would be no time to find a replacement, he would be sued by the network, hauled through every court in the land until even church mice offered to lend him money. That was the kind of fame he could live without. No, he had no option but to carry on, to go through with it, to face his biggest fear within the allotted timeframe before the inevitable humiliation. He turned back and gazed unblinkingly at the monitor.

"Don't be nervous, Arthur," said Brash, but Arthur looked to be scanning all available exits, his eyes moving independently of each other. "Tell all the lovely folks out there in Tellyland exactly where you are from."

"I'm from Milton Keynes, Brash."

"Milton Keynes! How about that! I once went out with a girl from Milton Keynes...she was a right cow!" Cymbal smash; a flurry of activity as the floor hands scuttled about holding up cards that read LAUGHTER to the audience. Arthur smiled directly into camera one as if he had never been happier.

"So Arthur Marsh from Milton Keynes, what do you do for a living?"

"I'm a freelance sculptor, Brash, specialising in-"

"Unemployed! Excellent! You could probably really use the fantastic prizes we have on offer tonight. Round of applause everybody for Arthur, who could really do with a holiday by the look of him!"

Vinny clenched his teeth. It was real edge of the sleeping bag stuff. He listened as Arthur said his hobby was collecting armour before proceeding to drop his qualifications the way adolescents dropped their testicles. And all the while, Brash smiled his false smile, the one that never reached his too blue eyes. Vinny knew that if he went out there and pulled up one of Brash's immaculately pressed trouser legs he would find, just above the mirror buffed Brogue, a comedy sock - Sex On Legs or something - because Brash was that kind of crazy guy.

The host with the most looked deep into the camera until the crowd grew silent. In his ear he got his cue.

"So, Arthur, tell us all what you are most afraid of."

"I'm...I'm...I'm afraid of swearing at authority figures, Brash," said Arthur, unaware that viewers were switching over in their droves; according to a survey carried out by the tabloids, viewers tended to prefer the contestants to be put in life threatening positions or at least covered in snakes. It was obvious that Arthur had only made it on in a misguided attempt at variety, or perhaps to add a comic element.

"Well, Arthur," said Brash, looking slightly bored (he would have snakes on every show if he could), "do you know what time it is now?"

A large curtain at the back of the soundstage rose up slowly to reveal a policeman, an army sergeant, and a vicar all standing on a podium.

"Now the talking's done...It's time to overcome!"

The audience, prompted by more dummy cards joined in on this too. Arthur Marsh looked like a man who had just given birth in the back of his trousers and was keen to put the child up for adoption.

In the Green room, munching a hospitality banana, Vinny was laughing. He knew he could go through with this now; the show's idiocy ceased to rile him now and in a way he found it oddly comforting. For the first time since his interview, he was actually looking forward to it.

Arthur was frogmarched over to the podium by the pneumatic Josie and placed in front of the three men, who stared back at him stony eyed as if daring him to speak. On the monitor, in close up, the sergeant's moustache twitched like an eager ferret, ready to bite. A clock appeared on screen for those who had a problem comprehending the concept of thirty seconds. When the crowd yelled, "GRASP THE NETTLE!", it began its inexorable countdown. Never had half a minute of television seemed so long.

"Come on, Arthur!" urged Brash, who loathed being off camera for more than a nanosecond, "Do something! Swear at them!"

"You dirty sods," mumbled Arthur, his eyes on the floor.

"Come on, you can do better than that! Get torn into them!"

"Buggers."

"They said your mother's ugly, Arthur, they did, they told me backstage!"

"Turds."

"Come on, Arthur, only a few seconds left!"

"Bum."

"They hate you, Arthur, they bloody hate you! It rhymes with truck, you can do it, Arthur, don't let them beat you!"

"FUCK!"

The hideous theme tune blared out to let everyone know that Arthur Marsh had reached round two and would soon be whisked off by the delectable Josie and dressed in an inflatable panda suit.

Alex 'Brash' Bison walked somberly over to camera four and stuck his rugged, intelligent face directly into his viewer's living rooms.

"Arthur grasped the nettle folks. He thought he would get stung, but still he's overcome. Don't you wish you'd done that?"

For some reason that was the one thing about the show that irritated Vinny the most.

"So tell me, Arthur, how do you feel about big, creepy, crawly spiders?" Brash rubbed his hand over Arthur's bald dome, drumming his fingers on the gleaming pate. "How do you feel about s-s-s-s snakes?"

"I'm terrified of them, Brash."

"Really?" Brash had a disdainful, disbelieving tone, as if he doubted every word foolish enough to venture out of Arthur's mouth; contestants had been known to lie before. "Well, we'll see after the break, stay where you are folks, back in three!"

Vinny slumped back in his chair as the ads came on, closing his eyes as cute cartoon blackcurrants urged him to drink their blood. He had a bad taste in his mouth like he had just licked rancid butter off a knife.

"Ready?" Josie popped her head around the rubber plant, again. Vinny stood up and smoothed the creases out of his trousers, fixing his hair the best he could through the grinning portrait of Brash adhered to the mirror.

Josie grabbed his arm like a favourite handbag. "Enjoy your big moment," she said, her voice as terse as a text message. Her hands were equipped with talon like fingernails that would not withstand foreplay, her weary eyes promised joyless, robotic sex; up close everything was flawed, mused Vinny, yet people were still ordered to enjoy it.

"I'll try," he said as she led him out into the blaring lights and the screaming crowd. He felt like a Christian at the Coliseum, about to play Blind Date with a lion. Here I come, he thought, sweaty or not.

"....Vinny Cleaver!" hollered Bison as Vinny was escorted down the glittering steps, trying his level best not to ogle Josie's jiggling breasts; his mum and dad were recording this.

"Well now, Vincent, don't be nervous. Everyone here wants you to win, and win big."

Up close, Brash was a mummified dog turd with shredded wheat hair that had been ironed into position. It was all smoke and mirrors, all one big lie from the start, that was the nettle that Vinny grasped tonight.

"Tell all the folks in Telly land something about yourself, Vincent."

"My father was a Yeti."

Brash looked puzzled, he had been expecting an anecdote about being chased by swans on a school trip; he carried on though like the professional he was.

"So Yeti boy, tell all the folks what you are most afraid of."

"Well Brash, my deepest fear is becoming just another pathetic wannabe, famous for being famous. I want to earn my fame."

Brash was genuinely fazed now, it said spiders on his card.

Vinny produced a pistol from the waistband of his jeans; it had been digging into him all evening long.

The report of the gun drowned out the shrieks of alarm from the audience. Afterwards, there was silence, there were no dummy cards for this. Vinny Cleaver sauntered up to Camera Four and, wiping the blood and skull debris from its splattered lens, put his smiling face into millions of stunned households.

"Hey, all you folks in Tellyland, don't you wish you'd done that?"

Twilight by John Mueter

The old Datsun spluttered and bucked, but it made it up the hill and to the end of the road, to the beginning of the trailhead. Marlis got out and surveyed the scene for a minute. There was the granite rock face of the mountain and, just visible to the right, the ledge she remembered. It had been just a year earlier, when Maxine was still alive, that they had climbed the trail together and stopped on the ledge to admire the view. Maxine had said, "Ooooooh, that is so pretty!" Marlis remembered the remark because it was one of the few times in their friendship of over thirty years that Max had expressed a sentimental opinion. She just wasn't verbal in that way. Maxine may have had a gruff exterior, but behind the façade there was the kind and loyal friend that Marlis loved.

They were both widows of a sort. Marlis' husband Jack had died of a heart ailment some twenty years before. Max's husband was still alive, wherever he was, maybe still with the slutty waitress he had run off with, maybe not. Max never mentioned him. The two women were neighbors and liked mostly the same things, especially hiking in the wilds of eastern Oregon.

Marlis was an artist, specializing in landscapes of the local scenery. And there were plenty of subjects to excite her. The view from the ledge of the secluded gully was one she had wanted to paint since that moment with Maxine. Max was gone now, had crossed over to the Great Beyond, embarked on the ultimate hike into the cosmic wilderness. Marlis still missed her friend terribly and had shed copious tears over the loss. Why was life so unfair? Why did a total scumbag like Henry Kissinger still see the sun rise every morning when her dearest friend, her only real friend, had to die and leave her stranded? But life went on. That's the way it was. Her painting of the gully would be a tribute to her friend.

Marlis eased her paint box over her shoulder, carried an easel in one hand and a camp chair in the other. It would be a strenuous climb to get up to the ledge, a challenge for someone her age, but she could do it. On the way up she thought of Maxine and her illimitable energy. Max, in her brown hiking boots and thick white socks, was always in the lead. Marlis used to admonish her friend not to rush ahead. 'Wait up, Maxie,' she would call out, 'you're off to the races again!'

Reaching the ledge, she flung her equipment onto the ground and caught her breath. She ignored the pain in her knees. There were at least two hours before the light would begin to fail. She would get back to her car just before the onset of darkness. It was not the smartest thing to be out in the wilderness alone that late in the day, but she had done it before. She knew how to scare off any lurking bobcats. Bears would be another matter. Fortunately, she had never had to deal with the most dangerous critters. She tried not to think about it.

Having long since outgrown the desire to paint imposing dramatic vistas, she sought the out-of-the-way spots, such as this, the places that most hikers barely noticed. Marlis' eyes, as old and worn out as they were, recognized the allure of the unobtrusive. And now, in the late September afternoon, the colors were glowing.

There was no time to lose. She gulped some of the lukewarm water from her canteen, set up her stool and easel, and mixed her colors. She loved painting outside, under the open sky; there was nothing like the pulsating light that caressed the landscape.

She contemplated the composition of what she saw in front of her: the sparse scrub pine that tenaciously clung to the sides the hills, the long since dried grass, and the few hardy shrubs that managed to survive in the gully itself. The dark purple of the shade, the mellow browns and golds of the hills, the rich green of the vegetation excited her imagination. Getting the shadows right– that will be the challenge here, she considered. Every painting was an attempt to express the inexpressible, an exercise doomed to failure. Marlis set to work, immersing herself in the scene. After more than an hour of unbroken concentration she was weary. She stood up to stretch her legs a bit.

It was an almost imperceptible movement of her heel on a stone, a stone that slipped just enough, that caused her to lose her balance. She teetered for a moment, her arms flailing, her brush and palette flying out of her hands. Once set in motion the momentum was inescapable, and Marlis fell over backwards off the ledge, twisting as she hovered in midair for those few seconds. The grace of her fall might have been lovely to watch had her body been headed for a plunge into a cool mountain lake, but it was on unforgiving basalt, jagged, barren and indifferent, that Marlis landed.

When she came to and was able to assess the damage she found that she couldn't move. Every breath was painful. She was on her back, one leg folded under the other. The daylight was fading fast, leeching the color out of the hills. Soon it would be night, it would turn cold. The stars began to appear and Marlis, drifting in and out of consciousness, gazed up at the heavens with the sense of wonder she had always felt. It might have been an apparition, she couldn't be sure, but she thought she saw her friend, beckoning to her. As the serenity of the twilight enveloped her, Marlis nearly managed a smile.

It did get cold that night, colder than usual, but Marlis Kennedy never even felt it.

Beyond the Reef By Don Noel

It is hotter tonight, sticky even without a top sheet. He knits his fingers across his chest, suppressing a desperate urge to feel, to caress, to plunge between warm thighs, to seek tactile assurance that there will be nights of conjugal embrace long into a revived future.

Rolling on his side, he props himself on an elbow to regard this wife whom he dares not touch, who is beyond his reach. Carol fell asleep a few hours ago still protesting even a light sheet on her inflamed skin. She appears to sleep well; the doctor's shot must have had an opiate. His own forehead is beaded with sweat. The overhead fan would be cooling, but she insisted she could not stand even that feathery touch.

In the thin luminescence of the moonlit window, the stretch marks of two pregnancies are hidden. The welts from the sea urchins' assault seem diminished. She lies on her back, her naked body handsome, voluptuous, inviting. He wants her. He hates her.

Perhaps, he should have left her after all, last year. "You wouldn't divorce me?" she'd said, less question than protestation. But the chasm between them in their queen-size bed was of her making. With both the children in college, he'd told her, it was over. He would no longer pretend to forgive and forget her infidelities, no longer stifle his mortification. Lying here in the Jamaican night, the memory of that angry confrontation festers.

He had rehearsed in his mind the arguments against a break. Suburbanite parents would object to their daughters' being sent for discipline to the office of a divorced vice principal. Their friends would have to choose between them. There would be degrading arguments over who would keep what. The cost of lawyers. Where Millie and Carl would spend vacations.

Against all that was the humiliation of betrayal, wondering how many friends and acquaintances knew, wondering if she'd fucked some he hadn't guessed. He had poured out his bottled-up anger, finally overcoming his inclination to swallow hard instead of spit.

Carol had not defended herself. She groveled. She had hurt him. She was deeply sorry. She could not imagine why she let these things happen, invited them. She had never loved anyone but him, not really loved. He did not, would not say, at that moment, that she was good company, a good mother, that they had shared ideas, even shared good sex if he could stifle imagining who she might have compared him with.

She wanted to spend the rest of her life with him. She would be a better companion, a true companion. She made herself so vulnerable that he wanted to believe her. He would not let her seal her promise with sex that night, but agreed to wait, to sleep on it, and at last they did sleep.

She had given him no reason to doubt her conversion in the weeks that followed. Showed houses only to husbands and wives together, calling that merely sound real estate practice. Invented no clients who had to inspect houses at odd hours. Was home for him at the end of the school day. Waited patiently for him to initiate love-making again, and when he finally did was wonderfully responsive, as passionate as when they'd courted.

By Valentine's Day, he'd been confident enough to plan this getaway. He found a perfect card, lovebirds on a beach. "Come away with me to Jamaica," he wrote inside. He found this remote inn, far from the tourist bustle, the ideal setting for a second honeymoon.

He suppresses the urge now to ease a hand across the bed, whisper-light on her thigh, a gesture as old as their early years and as new as their reconciliation. If she is wakeful too, she will reach down to pat his hand in reassurance: Glad you're here, darling. Usually they just doze back off, comforted by each other's presence. Occasionally, she brings his hand to her belly, turning to him.

He rolls onto his back and invites sleep; he dares not touch her. Not after what happened on the reef. It frightened him too, the physical assault she endured, nearly drowning and then being dragged over hundreds of venomous sea urchin needles. She finds the lightest touch excruciating.

He wakens again. The inn has fallen silent. The moon, still nearly full, is well risen; a shaft of light through the screened window touches the bare, wooden floor and is mirrored on the ceiling. No labored breathing. The doctor's hypodermic has done its job, despite her protestation that the marijuana she'd been using – Bo-Jim's ganja -- was adequate relief.

Bo-Jim. She has been finding comfort and healing in strange places.

He rises on one elbow again. She is not beside him. He sits up, peering through the moonlight, expecting a crack of light under the bathroom door. There is no light. No sound. A faint depression in the mattress where she slept retains no warmth.

He stands, slips into sandals, starts toward the door. Turns back to put on his pajama top, takes the flashlight from the nightstand, hurries down the stairs. She is not in the sitting room, nor did he expect her there. At the end of the garden, behind a thick stand of oleander, is the bench where Bo-Jim plied her with marijuana. He switches on the flashlight. The accusatory beam finds an empty bench.

He runs down the beach, frantically scanning the flat, moonstruck strand. A hundred yards, two hundred, three hundred. Breathing heavily, he moves inland and starts back toward the inn, his flashlight probing the shadows of the thick sea grape trees at the back of the beach. He calls, his voice ragged: "Carol! Carol!"

There is no answer. The beach is deserted. Regaining the garden, he collapses in despair onto the bench.

They had arrived two nights ago in time for drinks at a beachside table, watching the sun sink into a halcyon sea. Uniform ranks of gentle, unhurried waves tumbled against the barrier reef thirty yards out, rippling into the sandy margin.

"A new start," he said. "I hope you're glad we came."

"I am. I might not have picked so remote a spot, but I'm sure we'll enjoy it."

"Sorry. Wanted to surprise you."

"You certainly did that. Even squirreled the money away without my knowing it." He had opened a new teacher's credit union account. "Thank you. A nice Valentine."

The money might have helped minimize college loans, but the kids would manage. This would be an interlude of healing, of recommitment. He held her chair at a table on the patio, and handed her the short, wine list; wine was a taste she had acquired without him.

"Their Pinot Grigio is from Chile," she said. "Might be good."

That would be Jeffrey, he thought, wishing such thoughts didn't intrude. Warren, the one before, favored red wines. He ordered the Pinot Grigio. When the waitress brought it, he pointed to Carol's glass. "Anything would suit me. Yours is the refined palate."

She tasted. "Not bad. Pleasantly dry."

The waitress filled her glass, then his; he invited a recitation of specials.

"Broiled snapper," she said. "Grouper. Sea puss."

"Sea puss?"

"You call it octopus."

He liked the innocent, double entendre. "I'll try the sea puss." Carol chose the snapper.

They enjoyed the meal. Carol took a taste of his, as she often had years ago, and declared she might try sea puss the next night. She turned down dessert. "We've been up since three-thirty, Henry, to get through security and catch your crack-of-dawn plane."

A full moon – he had planned this vacation with great care – was up, turning the wet beach beyond the inn into an undulating, incandescent shimmer. "How about a stroll down the beach before bed?"

"I'm sorry. Tomorrow. Jet lag, wine, bed." They went to their room. She declared the king-sized bed comfortable, and was asleep in minutes. After a time, the sea's sibilance lulled him to sleep too.

Carol was cheerful at breakfast. "This mango is marvelous! And the pineapple is sweeter than what we get at home."

"Of course," he told her. "It's native to the Caribbean; what we get has travelled all the way from Hawaii."

"You're so smart. Where do you learn all these things?" He heard loving admiration in her voice. He caught the waitress' eye, invited another slice. "You're so patient, Henry. In so many ways."

A new day, and a fresh start.

After breakfast, they waded through the shallows, wearing reef shoes that seemed absurdly thick -- until they clambered onto the reef, a narrow, flat walkway of razor-sharp coral that made them glad for those heavy soles. It was low tide, no breeze yet astir, the sea, lake-calm. He explained to his city-bred wife how generations of coral polyps built the reef, contributing their skeletons to communal growth. A rainbow kaleidoscope of fish shimmered through slanting sunshine in the deeper water just off the reef. Hundreds of sea urchins clung to the edge, golfball-sized reddish orbs with toxic spines as long as darning needles. Despite the ominous-looking urchins, it seemed a friendly reef.

After lunch, the sea changed. The tide was in. An onshore breeze piled waves shoreward, burying the coral in rivulets of foam, entirely different from the morning's languid reef. They would try body-surfing. Two hundred yards from the inn, a break in the reef shaped a wide sandbar over which waves broke predictably. They waded out, the water only thigh-deep, caught a wave, rode it almost to the beach, waded back out. Carol rode the farthest every time. Then she, much the stronger swimmer, gave up surfing and swam out beyond where the waves broke, floating on her back, waving.

Suddenly everything changed: She was trying to swim back in. Making no headway. Losing, being swept out toward the jagged, outer rim of the reef.

The innkeeper – a nice man – had warned them: As waves break over a reef, the water must sluice back out. If you feel yourself sucked into such a surge, let it carry you out. The undertow will dissipate, and you can swim easily to a better landing spot. Don't fight it; don't wear yourself out. People drown, doing that.

"Carol, *relax!*" he shouted. He edged farther out, the water shoulder-deep now, making it harder to keep her in sight; he could feel the sandbar hollowing beneath him as he neared the sluice. *"Relax! Don't fight it!"* She persisted in trying to swim in, fright in her face.

He turned toward the deserted beach. *"Help!"* he cried as loud as he could. *"Help! Someone, help!"* A few steps brought him back to shallower water at the crest of the sandbar, from which he clambered on to the reef, balancing against the waves, the coral lancing his bare feet. He turned inland again; at the top of his lungs: *"Help! Help!"*

He turned back toward the sea, toward Carol, forcing himself to walk mincingly over coral whose sharpest edges and urchins were buried in foam, trying to avoid being knocked down. Painfully, he worked his way in the direction she was being swept. He wanted to jump in, try to hold her in his arms, calm her. He didn't dare: In her panic, she might seize him in a death-grip; he was no match for her in the water. But, if she neared the reef he might haul her up.

Then a miracle: Someone came running on toughened feet across the coral. A young man with muscled chest and arms, wearing cut-off denims, a coil of fisherman's rope in his hand. He thrust one end into Henry's hand -- "Hold dis tight, mon!" -- and jumped into the water with the other end in his teeth.

He reached her barely in time. She had gone under, swallowing seawater. Her arms flailed. Catching her with a cross-chest carry, he signaled Henry to pull them in. Henry hauled. The man turned as he neared the reef and clambered up, his calloused feet a shield against the urchins, holding Carol's hand to drag her limp body behind him through a forest of spines.

Bo-Jim – that was his name, they later learned – swept her up in his arms and ran back along the reef on feet impervious to the coral, choosing a shallow place to run in and lay her inert body down on the beach. By the time Henry caught up, he had her on her side, massaging her back to pump out seawater, rewarded by her gasping and coughing.

"Thank you!" Henry said. "Carol, are you all right?" Stupid question; he tried again. "You're going to be all right, dear." Breathing hard, she blinked up and nodded a faint yes.

"Got to get de spines!" the man muttered. "Dem pizen!" Henry could see them in Carol's flesh, like a pincushion of needles. The man produced a knife from a pocket of his wet cut-offs, rolled her on her back, bent over and with thumb against blade began prying spines from her arms and shoulders and then her thighs and chest, peeling back the top of her suit where a few spines had penetrated. Henry watched helplessly as this stranger ministered to his inert wife's wounded private flesh.

At last the man stopped. Bo-Jim. "Can't do no more wid dis knife! You down at de hotel?" Henry nodded, and reached to help Carol up. But Bo-Jim picked her up, cradling her in his arms, and loped effortlessly down the beach. Henry had run the 100-yard dash in college, but that was a long time ago; he barely kept up.

"Some ganja, mon!" Bo-Jim shouted to the man at the inn's desk as he gently laid Carol down on a lounge chair in the shade. He was a handsome fellow, with dreadlocks but not unkempt. A smooth face, shoulders and chest that could have been a body-builder's. There are women who come to the island to find men like that for a week of erotic pleasure, Henry had read, and there are men waiting to accommodate them. He brushed away the thought.

Carol was still dazed, pain etching her face. Henry took her hand. "I'll get you some help, dear. There must be a hospital near by."

Bo-Jim took charge. "You smoke, dahlin'?" She shook her head no. "Well, we gonna try. Your man gotta get you to bed to rest, but the pain gonna make you thrash around and make it worse. Nothin' take the pain away like ganja."

Henry had taken enough marijuana away from students to recognize the lumpy spliff that the desk man brought, already rolled. Bo-Jim held it up to the offered match, and turned back to Carol. "Now, dahlin', you jes' take a little puff. Don' breathe too deep at first, if you not a smoker a'ready. Jes' take an' hol' a little in your mouth, an' then let it go."

Carol looked up obediently. Bo-Jim held the joint to her lips. She put her hand on his, took a light puff, exhaled it, then drew in harder. She coughed, but drew again. "Dat's de way, dahlin', see if you can hol' it down in yu' chest a bit." She did. Henry felt useless while this young hero took charge. He tried to swallow the irrational resentment that rose in his gorge.

She visibly relaxed. Bo-Jim let her rest, then put it to her lips again. And again, almost until it burned his fingers. "All right, sah, dat's all Bo-Jim can do for now. She in shock, you know? But the ganja gonna help. Git her up to bed in a dark room an' she's gonna sleep. Kin you tote her up?"

Henry nodded yes. He didn't want this man in their bedroom. Didn't want his wife in those arms again. Bo-Jim lifted Carol from the lounge chair and laid her into Henry's arms. "Thank you!" Henry said as he started toward the staircase. "My God! How can we thank you?"

"Thas' all right," Bo-Jim said. "You get her to res' now. I goin' look in later." He was out of sight through the inn's garden and down the beach before Henry reached the landing of the stairs.

The innkeeper followed them up, tilting the window louvers to darken the room as Henry lowered her to the bed. He handed Henry a pair of scissors and a tweezers. "I'd cut that suit off if I were you." His clipped, British accent made the suggestion seem impersonal. "You mustn't pull it off. Her skin is too raw. And pull out any remaining spines."

"Can't we take her to an emergency room? Or at least to a doctor?"

"The hospital is fifty miles away, sir. Over rough roads that would make her pain unbearable. We have a physician who makes a circuit, comes to our town two days a week. I'll get word to him. But urchin stings are not uncommon. And not life-threatening. The usual remedy is bed rest."

As Henry turned to his wife with the scissors, the innkeeper stopped in the doorway, discreetly looking away. "You get her to sleep, then come down. I'll make you some weak lemonade for when she wakens. I'll find a straw. And some fish tea later on. Bo-Jim's right, she needs sleep. She mustn't dehydrate, but let her sleep for now."

He had to turn on a light. "Carol, can you roll onto your side so I can cut the suit away down the back?" She tried, but fell back moaning. Reluctantly, he cut the shoulder straps, then eased a scissors blade between her breasts and started down. Thank God for thin fabric, he thought. She cried out when he reached her belly; more spines. He started to tug the suit down her legs, but she sobbed so grievously that he finished cutting it open, aroused despite himself.

Her body was a dense patchwork of reddened welts. She moaned as he tweezed the last few spines out of the inflamed flesh on her chest, her belly, her groin. He started to pull a sheet over her nude body. She wouldn't let him; even that light touch of fabric made her groan. He sat in a rattan chair beside her, letting her hand rest on his. After a time, she slept.

She wakened enough to sip some lemonade when he brought it, and slept again. She cried out when he helped her to the bathroom. "No, no! Just let me lean on your shoulder! Don't touch me again. Please! Don't touch me!" Leaning heavily on him, she limped back to the bed, took a few sips of the innkeeper's cold, fish tea, and slept again.

At sunset, he went down to eat something with the other guests. It was a small inn; everyone had heard. "Come sit with us," one of the women said. "How is your wife? Has she seen a doctor?"

"The pain is pretty bad," Henry said. "The innkeeper hasn't located a doctor yet."

"Tell her we're praying for her," the woman said.

"Thank you," Henry said. He ate a little, but wasn't hungry. He excused himself to come back up to lie on the bed beside her naked body, careful not to touch her, and half-dozed.

Bo-Jim arrived. Henry heard him in the sitting room at the foot of the stairs, talking with the innkeeper. "How she doin', sah?"

The voice wakened her. "I've got to see him, Henry. He saved my life."

"Of course, dear. I'll tell him to come in the morning when you're feeling better."

"No, now. Please tell him I'm coming down."

Henry went down to send him away instead. "Oh, no, sah," Bo-Jim said. He winked. "I brought her somethin' for the pain." Henry was sure it was more marijuana. Before he could get rid of the man, his wife appeared on the stairs, wearing only the diaphanous nightgown he had given her for this vacation.

"Oh, Bo-Jim, I can't thank you enough!" She looked down. "I'm afraid I'm not very well-dressed. My skin seems so sensitive; even this peignoir hurts to wear."

The innkeeper turned away politely. Bo-Jim did not.

"Oh, miss, don' you worry none. We-uns don't care how you look; we jes want you to feel better. I brought you a little somethin' to he'p that. You think you can walk down to the garden there, behind them oleander bush?"

He turned to Henry. "You know dis ganja illegal, right, sah? One t'ing to ask dat man to provide us some before. Was a crisis, you know? But dis innkeep could get into a heap of trouble if folks thought he was providin' to his guests regular-like. You follow? You jes' wait here a few. I gonna bring her right back."

Carol was already out in the garden, moving more quickly than Henry would have thought possible. He wanted to follow, but the innkeeper put a hand on his arm. "She'll be all right, sir. We must wait here. Bo-Jim is right; it is better than neither I nor any of my guests see him providing marijuana here at my inn. Even you, sir. I'm sorry."

"How soon can we get her medical attention?"

"I'm afraid we're rather remote. I've sent word for the doctor. He covers a wide area."

Carol had disappeared into the dark at the back of the garden. Henry started to walk there. The innkeeper caught his arm to hold him back. A wisp of smoke rose above the dark oleander and grew, caught silvery in the garden lights. The sweet fragrance wafted back. It seemed to go on forever. Then she reappeared, alone, looking back toward the dark shrubbery. "Oh, thank you, Bo-Jim, thank you so much. I feel better already." Then turned to him: "Thank you too, dear Henry. Do you mind if I go back to sleep now?"

He led her up, letting her lean on him, but she turned him away at the bedroom door. "Not now, Henry, I'll be all right. I need to rest. Why don't you go enjoy yourself a little, and not worry?" The other guests had retired. He took a book downstairs to a rattan chair in the sitting room under a fan. He might as well have been reading Greek.

She had been hardly better this morning. The innkeeper whipped up a mango smoothie in the blender. She whimpered as she sat up to drink it, then lay back again.

But when Bo-Jim came in mid-morning she wakened, put on a bathrobe only slightly less revealing than the peignoir, and hurried down the stairs. Hurried. Off to the shelter of the oleander. Henry started to accompany her, but she turned. "Wait here." It was a tone of exasperation he'd heard often before their reconciliation. He hesitated, then turned back. He imagined the marijuana being held to her lips. He twice started to walk to the back of the garden, and forced himself to retreat.

After an interminable time, she walked back, giving a little wave to Bo-Jim as she started up the stairs and back to bed. She again urged Henry to let her sleep.

He walked down the beach to where the whole thing had begun. It was deserted. Inland, over a bit of dune, through a screen of sea-grape trees and palms, he could see the roofs of a few houses, some thatched, some with corrugated zinc. Bo-Jim must have come from one of those. The sea was calm, the reef as innocent as that first morning. With his thick-soled reef shoes he could easily have walked out to the spot where he'd watched her in trouble, where he should have dived in to help her instead of watching Bo-Jim rescue her.

He went up to the room at noon with another fruit smoothie. She was awake, lying motionless, still handsomely naked. He wondered if her pain would subside before they had to start home. "Oh, thank you, dear. Is it lunchtime already? Please don't worry about me. Why don't you join the other guests and have something to eat yourself?"

He left her reluctantly, but was in fact hungry, and welcomed the solicitous company of the other guests. So, he was in the dining room when he saw her, out of the corner of his eye, come down the stairs and disappear into the garden again. He got up from the table.

"Could we have a word, sir? Sir?" The innkeeper finally got his attention. Henry hesitated, then followed him into the little office.

"I'm glad to say, sir, that we can get your wife some medical attention today. I don't doubt the marijuana is helping, but there's a limit to folk medicine, isn't there? Perhaps Bo-Jim has done as much as . . . well, as much as you'd want him to. The doctor will be here in a few hours."

Henry got back to the table just in time to see her go back upstairs. He forced himself to finish a bowl of red-pea soup before going back to their room.

"Resting any better, dear?"

"Oh, yes, Henry. What Bo-Jim calls ganja seems to be helping."

Henry did not mention seeing her slip down. "The innkeeper has arranged for a doctor. Maybe you can sleep some more until he comes."

"Thank you. I'm not sure I need him, though." He waited until she dozed off, then went back downstairs to stare blankly at the book again. The doctor, thank God, arrived before Bo-Jim came again. A man wearing a faded suit, carrying the kind of black bag

English doctors once used. As he led the man upstairs, Henry saw the innkeeper hurry into the garden. Intercepting Bo-Jim? Good.

The doctor decorously slipped a sheet over Carol's hips, ignoring her wince. He put a thermometer in her mouth while he took her pulse. She winced again. "A bit of a temperature, but not serious. Heart rate just a bit fast." He produced a narrow, silver, flashlight tube and shone it first into her mouth and then into her eyes. He examined her welts.

"I think your wife is mending, sir. An urchin sting is not usually serious, but she has endured many of them. She may need another day or two of bed rest. You should let her decide that according to how she feels."

He turned to Carol. "The innkeeper tells me a local man has provided you some herbal relief. I would not continue that. I'm giving you an injection that should promote healing as well as ease the pain." Ignoring her protests, he swabbed her arm with alcohol, deftly jabbed with the needle and stanched the needle mark with a cotton ball.

"I'd bandage it, sir, but the adhesive would hurt terribly when taken off. I'll leave you some alcohol and a few swabs. Dab it carefully several times in the next half-hour. We don't want her to get an infection on top of this. If she still needs pain relief in the morning, have the innkeeper give me a call before I set out to the next village." He turned back to her. "Good luck, madam."

Henry followed to pay him. By the time he got back to their room she was sleeping soundly. He went down and ordered the sea puss again, but it was not like that first night. He nibbled, then came upstairs again, sweating, wishing he might use the fan.

The hotel fell silent. He rehearsed in his mind the events of these two days, wishing he had been braver, more forceful.

At last he slept. And woke to discover that Carol had disappeared.

Now, recovering from his fruitless race up the beach, he sits despondent on the very bench where she had sat with Bo-Jim. The night breeze is still warm. He tiptoes upstairs, hoping to find her in their room, her disappearance easily explained. But she is not there. Wretched, he exchanges the pajamas for slacks and a long-sleeved shirt, and goes back to the beach.

Walking now, he covers the full length, from coral headland to coral headland. He is no longer sure he wants to find her. Against the moon, the stars are faint, but Jupiter is bright overhead, and Venus sets in the west. He reaches the break in the reef where this all began.

The tide is up again. The sea is not as strong as the first afternoon, but in the moonlight he can see where the water sluices out. He kicks off the flip-flops, takes off his shirt and slacks and starts naked toward the water. Steps back to take off his wristwatch, tucking it into the thongs of the beach sandals.

He walks resolutely back into the surf, steps farther in, feeling the current at his thighs, coursing outward. He hesitates, half-turning to look once more at the dark beach, then dives forward into the sluice, feeling it carry him rapidly, silently, out beyond the reef.

Traveling Shoe Lament by Katarina Boudreaux

Evonne stretches her hands in front of her and grips the dashboard with both hands. Her mouth is dry and she knows her breath stinks, but she says, "Lord, Jims. They're going to pick us up for sure."

Jims does not look at her. Evonne decides it's better that way, and focuses on watching Jims weave them in and out of traffic like a mad criminal.

They veer close to an old lady in a flowered house dress, and Evonne yells, "You're a damn fool man, Jims. Why do you want to follow this ambulance? We aren't in any kind of a hurry, come on now. I could see the flowers blooming on that old lady."

Jims tsk tsks, and Evonne stifles a scream. She hates it when Jims tsks, and she hates it more when he tsks for no good reason.

Evonne shakes her head and replays the morning conversation, but can't find anything to cause mad driving in it. Simple enough, Evonne thinks: go down to Evette's and pick up a sweet potato pie.

She looks at Jims's profile; his head is regularly shaped, and Evonne can't see any signs of head trauma. Evonne knows that just because you can't see it, doesn't mean it isn't there.

Evonne wonders why she married him.

She can't think too long on it, because they are going fast. Evonne can hear the emergency sirens all around her and she wants to see her demise clearly when it happens.

The bank whizzes by, and it's like she is traveling in a time machine. Evonne does not like time anything, and she hangs on to the dashboard.

"Jims. There is no reason why you have to be driving like this. What's happened to your sense? Come on now, I don't want to be spending the night in jail, or in the grave, and Evette's pie is just not that good," Evonne says.

Jims doesn't take his foot off the gas, and they are still going like a chicken with no head. A car is parked a little too far from the curb, and Evonne lets out a squeak when Jims swerves into oncoming traffic to avoid it.

Evonne shifts her weight in the passenger seat. She tries to remember what she knows about preparing for collisions, but she can't think of anything but to double check her seat belt.

"At least this old truck is made of real steel, and not that cheap stuff they're making these things out of today," Evonne mutters, and pats the seat.

Jims bought Daisy when they were first married, and it has always been a good truck. Probably more reliable then the marriage, Evonne thinks.

"Not like I haven't tried, Jims," Evonne says, and remembers how she had tried to make a home baked cake for Jims on their first anniversary.

She had followed the recipe perfectly, and then the oven part came. She had watched her creation through the glass, so when the cake started overflowing and everything started smelling, she had not panicked.

She had cried.

Jims had laughed.

That was when it had all changed, Evonne thinks, and shuts her eyes as they go through a yellow light. The sirens are still pealing, and it looks like maybe Jims is going to keep driving like a lunatic until they pick him up and then shut him up in the padded room down on Main Street.

"I hope you like padded walls, Jims. That's where you're heading to, normal head and all. I can't see on the inside, but they can," Evonne warns and opens her eyes.

The dollar store is on the left, and Evonne wonders if the Christmas trees are already out. Evonne catches a glimpse of the pointy green tips when she peeks at Jims, and she grimaces.

Evonne hates Christmas trees almost as much as she hates fast cars.

"Just don't trust them," she says. Evonne never had any luck with them; they always looked one way in the store, all nice and pretty, but then in the house they lean and droop and just look like maybe they'd be happier in a field with some birds nesting in them instead of ornaments.

The truck lurches to the left, then to the right. The storefronts on Main Street are blurring together, and she tries to remember the order of them by heart.

She can't, and her stomach is starting to feel funny.

The sirens are right in front of her now, and Jims is still hot on the trail. "Not going to be much good when we get to Evette's and she does not even have that sweet potato pie out of the oven yet."

Her voice is small, and Evonne decides she needs to save her strength and just be quiet. She imagines Evette in her kitchen, all efficient. Evonne's always been envious that Evette can cook and put up jam.

Never have been alike, Evonne thinks, and remembers the matching dresses they wore when she and Evette were young. The big bows would slide on over to the side, and people could always tell which was Evonne.

Her bow was always untied.

Evonne shakes her head and tries logic on Jims. "You're making good off of someone else's misfortune now, Jims. You're sinking low to be doing that. We've crossed half the world in five minutes. Why not go regular over the rest?"

Jims grunts, and runs through another yellow light and Evonne tenses her muscles for an impact. Evonne would rather walk anywhere she needs to go. Sometimes, Evonne wonders if she was born maybe fifty years too late.

Then again, she doesn't like horses so much. Anything that big with that small of a brain does not need to be carrying her.

Jims is humming a ragtime tune, and Evonne shuts her eyes hard. She's always been more partial to songs with words. She tries to remember the name of a song she likes, then the words, but can't.

Evonne swallows hard and says, "Guess I don't need to worry about the rest of our supper, seeing as we aren't going to even make it to Evette's with all this speeding around."

Her stomach flips as Jims turns the corner on two wheels, and Evonne feels like she is losing her grip on the dashboard right along with her mind.

"Somebody is in that ambulance dying, Jims, and here you are following it like you want to be next" Evonne screams then opens and closes her eyes twice.

Something strange is happening inside her body, and Evonne thinks that maybe the double serving of coleslaw at lunch was not the best idea. Tasty, but not the best idea considering that Jims is trying to outrace everything that rolls.

The sirens are clanging in her head now, and Evonne thinks maybe there are really a million four year old children clamoring around in there looking for buried treasure or sticky treats.

"Jims, I'm turning bad in here. You're following all this noise and death like you aren't even worried about living. And for a pie that isn't that good," Evonne says.

Evonne's right hand is starting to twitch on the dashboard, so she places it gently over her stomach like it is a bowl of expensive cherries.

Coleslaw, she thinks, and wonders if she will be able to last until Evette's house. Things are churning around, and Evonne does not think she can take much more of the siren and the driving and the blurring of things.

"Jims," she says and lets her left hand drop to her stomach.

She remembers how Jims had held the child, and how he had let the child go when it was time to let the child go. Evonne never wanted to let Christian go, but she knew when she was talking to the wall, so when Jims said that Christian should go, she had held her tongue.

Now he comes on back from the big city once every year. Maybe twice.

Evonne shuts her eyes. I'm left all alone with a man that doesn't talk, doesn't love, doesn't drive like a decent citizen, Evonne thinks.

"Jims," Evonne whines and opens her eyes when the truck stops. The ambulance is in front of the hospital trying to turn in, and at least Jims is sane enough not to rear end it, Evonne thinks.

Evonne watches the ambulance turn in slow motion, and she wonders if Christian is still doing good, or if he had fallen in with bad elements, or if he was sick, or if he missed her.

"Jims," Evonne mutters, and when her stomach empties, she aims for his right shoe, thinking maybe now he'd slow down for the rest of the drive.

The Visitation by Gary Beck

I was definitely feeling pleased with myself. I made it to the private clinic without the usual escorts, for a check-up that would tell me how to deal with my upcoming departmental physical. It was a rare treat to be alone for a few minutes without any responsibility. There was a knock on the door. I called, "Come in," and a pretty, young girl entered.

"Good morning, sir. I'm Eva, from transport. These men are here to take you to x-ray."

Two identical looking men, wearing blue jumpsuits, pushing a stretcher, came in. The only problem was that I wasn't scheduled for x-ray. I lifted the sheet, grabbed my weapon, shot both of them, and they slumped to the floor. Eva froze, waiting for the lunatic to shoot her. Since she couldn't run or hide, she tried to make herself invisible. Smart girl.

"Eva," I said, gently.

"Yes, sir," she quavered.

I pointed and said, "Give me that tray, please."

She cautiously brought the tray. I put my weapon on it and told her to put it on the counter. She quickly rejected trying to use it on me, since she had absolutely no idea what it was, or how to use it. Smart girl.

"Give me your cell phone, please."

She did. I called headquarters, apprised them of the situation, then waited for the police. A minute later, a cop came in, weapon drawn, ready for anything. He quickly eyed the two bodies, the girl, then me. I read his nameplate.

"Sergeant Jefferson. Please search me, so you'll know I'm unarmed."

He approached, carefully, as I slowly pulled down the sheet. He was thorough, even checking under the pillow and bed.

"What happened here?" he demanded.

"You'll get a phone call in 30 seconds that will start a process. In the meantime, don't let anyone else in, and if you can't stop them, make sure they don't see my weapon."

He started to ask me something, but his phone rang.

"Yes, sir. Yes, sir. I understand, sir." He disconnected and looked at me. "Homicide is going to be pissed when they can't get in."

"Sergeant Jefferson."

"Yes, sir?"

"This is not an ordinary homicide."

We waited quietly. Two minutes later the door opened and Parker and Lindner, my executive assistants/bodyguards, rushed in. Parker took in the scene at a glance.

"We have 10 agents deployed, air cover and a team is searching the building. A support team will arrive in eight minutes... Did you really have to go off on your own, sir?"

I ignored her and said:

"This is Sergeant Jefferson and Eva. They have been exemplary. They will be offered opportunities."

"Yes, sir," she replied. "Can we move to a secure location, so the containment team can get to work?"

"Sergeant Jefferson."

"Yes, sir?"

"Is there anyone you have to contact until tomorrow?"

"Only my watch commander."

"He, your Lieutenant and precinct Captain have been notified that you are temporarily assigned to a federal agency. Eva, do you have to notify anyone?"

"I live with my sick father. I have to make dinner for him."

"What if we send some good, Spanish speaking people to take care of him tonight?"

"That would be wonderful."

"Then call him and say you're spending the night with a girl friend. Take care of it, Lindy."

Lindner made a few quick calls, then said, "Ready to go, sir."

As we headed for the door, Jefferson asked, "They aren't human, are they?"

I just looked at him and didn't reply, as our team guided us to waiting SUVs.

We raced, with helicopter cover, to a campus just outside Washington, D.C., and entered a special building through a series of well-protected tunnels. Parker arranged comfortable quarters for Sergeant Jefferson and Eva, told them to use the house phone if they needed anything, then informed them they would be interviewed at 7:30 a.m. Then Parker and Lindner joined me in my office.

"We have two questions to consider," I said. "How did they find me and why didn't they send a hit squad?"

Logical Lindy stated, "You didn't tell anyone you were going, so x number of people may have seen you leave the campus. I'll check anyone who might have seen you go. We may be under observation. You may have been noticed in transit, or entering the clinic." He looked at me and Parker. "Have I omitted any possibilities?"

I couldn't think of any, so I shook my head no, then nodded to Parker.

"The only thing that makes sense," she said, thoughtfully, "is that they didn't have time to muster a strike force and took a chance on a simple snatch."

I couldn't think of a better explanation, looked at Lindner, who nodded agreement with Parker.

"Alright," I mused. "We obviously have some work to do."

"May I make a request, sir?" Parker asked. I knew what was coming, but nodded 'yes'.

"Please don't go anywhere again without us," she urged. "We'll close our eyes no matter what you do, we'll look the other way, or oblige you any way we can. Let us do our job."

We all knew it was more than a job, so I agreed.

"Shall we debrief you now, sir?" Lindner asked.

"Let's do it after we debrief Eva and Jefferson."

"Who first?" Parker asked.

"Eva. She was the eyewitness. Jefferson arrived after it was over. Be aware, I'd like to recruit both of them."

"Eva's a kid," Parker protested.

"You'll change your mind once you hear her account of the incident. Now. How about some dinner. I'm starved."

When Eva entered the conference room the next morning, if she was intimidated by the people at the table, the video cameras and other recording devices, she didn't show it.

Parker said, crisply, "Are you ready?" Eva nodded. "Then please tell us everything that happened yesterday afternoon."

She took a deep breath. "My supervisor at transport told me to take the two transporters to room 502 and bring the patient to x-ray. The two men were wearing some kind of blue work suits, like plumbers or something. They looked a little weird..."

"In what way?" An Admiral asked.

"They looked alike, but odd."

"Go on," Parker said.

"I led them to the elevator, we went to the room, I knocked and a man said, 'Come in'. I said, 'I'm Eva, from transport and we're here to take you to x-ray'. The two men came in. The man on the bed looked at them, pulled out some kind of gun and shot them. I had no place to run or hide, so I made myself invisible and hoped the madman wouldn't shoot me. Then he told me, gently to bring him a tray and he put the gun on it and told me to put it on the counter. I knew he wasn't going to shoot me, so I relaxed. Then he asked for my cell phone, which I gave him. He made a call, then the cop came in."

"Good, Eva," Parker said. "We'll stop here for now, but we'll talk to you again in an hour." Parker signaled an agent. "Take Eva to breakfast, please."

When she left, the group discussed her statement and agreed she handled an extremely challenging situation with exceptional poise.

"What do you think, sir?" Parker asked me.

"We'll discuss that after you debrief me. Now let's have Sergeant Jefferson."

An aide brought Jefferson in and I saw him quickly scan the room, noting the high-ranking military officers and the cameras.

"Good morning, Sergeant Jefferson," Parker said. "Will you please tell us about your response yesterday."

"I was passing the clinic in my patrol car when I got a report of some kind of disturbance on the 5th floor. After a brief search, I found the room, drew my pistol and entered cautiously. There were two bodies on the floor, a girl was standing in the corner and a man in bed said, 'Come search me. Sergeant Jefferson, so you'll know I'm unarmed'. I approached, carefully, made sure there were no weapons, and he said, 'You'll get a phone call in 30 seconds that will tell you what to do.' I saw a strange weapon on the counter, but before I could look closer, he said, 'Don't let anyone else in the room. If they do come in, do not let them see the weapon'. Just then my phone rang, my Captain instructed me to cooperate with the agency taking charge and disconnected. I told the man, 'Homicide is going to be pissed'. He said, 'This is not an ordinary homicide, Sergeant Jefferson'. Then two agents came in and took charge."

"Thank you, Sergeant Jefferson," Parker said. "We'll talk to you again in an hour." She signaled an aide to lead him out and he turned to me.

"Question, sir?"

"Of course," I replied.

"Will I be allowed to leave?"

"Certainly. You're not a prisoner. If you wish, you can go after the next meeting. However. You might want to talk to me before you go."

"Thank you, sir," and the aide led him out.

Parker looked at me quizzically, and I said, "We want to hear their opinion and perception of what happened. Then we'll analyze the incident."

We listened to Sergeant Jefferson's and Eva's account of what they thought happened. They were thorough and clear on what they did and didn't know. I met with them, one at a time, Jefferson first, Parker and Lindner sitting in as I reviewed his record.

"You've been on the force for five years, two years of army service before that. You have several commendations, one for a shoot-out in a deli that saved civilian lives. You are respected by your superiors, especially your watch commander. You are going to night school for a law degree. I offer you the following choices. You can return to your precinct with commendations that will put you on a fast promotion track. You can join our agency and we will train you in counterterrorism and other skills, and fast track you for a law degree in the area of your specialty. You would be working for a clandestine government agency, with many responsibilities and benefits."

"Do I have to decide now, sir?"

"No. We'll give you a contact number if you opt to join us. However. There is one stipulation. You cannot discuss or tell anyone about the events of the last two days, or mention the agency, under any circumstances."

"What if my watch commander asks what I've been doing?"

"Your chain of command has been informed you helped federal agents subdue two men who attempted to kidnap a government witness. Parker will give you an outline of the incident that will satisfy any inquiries. Lindner will arrange to have you driven home, or to your precinct. Good luck, Sergeant Jefferson."

Thank you, sir. One more question?"

I nodded and he asked, "What kind of weapon was that?"

I just grinned and Lindner summoned an aide, who led Jefferson out.

"What do you think, sir?" Parker asked. "Will he be back?"

"We'll hear from him tomorrow. Let's see Eva."

147

An aide brought her in and seated her.

I nodded, then reviewed her background.

"Eva Rodriguez, age 19, graduated from Woodrow Wilson High School, 4.0 grade average, ran track, scholarship offers, including one for track. Father became ill and you had to go to work at two low paying jobs. We can help you get a better job and arrange a medical policy to take care of your father. Or you can go to work for our agency, take special training, then attend college part-time in preparation for a medical career. We would provide assistance to your father while you were in training."

Before I could continue, she said, "I would like to join your agency, sir."

"Why?" Parker snapped.

"I know enough to realize something very important is going on and I would like to make a meaningful contribution. I also want the educational opportunity."

"Lindy. Have someone drive Ms. Rodriguez home. Eva, you cannot discuss the events of the last two days with anyone, not even with your father. Unless you change your mind, a car will pick you up at 7:00 a.m. and take you to a training facility."

"Thank you, sir," and an aide led her out.

"She's awfully young, sir," Parker commented.

"She's smart, tough, has good sense and good judgment. In her way, not unlike Jefferson. We're facing a dangerous menace that we don't understand and we seem to be learning everything the hard way. We need people who can rise to the challenge. As you both know, they don't grow on trees. We have to find out what we're confronting and need all the help we can get."

Parker moved closer, recognizing a real opportunity to question me.

"Who do you think we're facing, sir?"

"Looking at this logically," I replied, which made Lindner grin, "there are two alternatives. Either a powerful cabal has made incredible scientific advances in producing some kind of android that can almost pass for human... Or there has been an alien incursion that for what purpose has not yet been determined."

"Which theory do you favor, sir?" Lindner asked.

"There isn't enough evidence to reach a conclusion, but I would prefer an earthly conspiracy, to an alien visitation... Do either of you have an alternative theory?"

They shook their heads and Lindner said, "Better a human conspiracy. At least we'll be able to figure out their motives."

Where Late the Sweet Birds Sang by Paul Lamb

His father had once mistakenly claimed the call of a mourning dove was that of an owl. David was so struck by this error that he doubted himself. How could Dad be wrong? It had to have been one of the very few times he ever was. Yet while he knew his father had considered himself an outdoorsman, he was never much of a naturalist.

His old cabin looks weary now. Not so much run down or neglected as lonely. On the drive down David tried to remember the last time when they had all been out to it together. More than a decade gone now. Such a shame. So many of the important moments of his life had been lived at this little Ozark cabin. It had been Curt's eleventh birthday party. Marred, he recalled, by biting horseflies that had kept them inside while the cool lake called in the August heat.

He's parked on the gravel pad, just as he has countless times, the sides of his car, familiar with paved streets, now surprised by splattered mud. His father had called the place his Cabin at the End of the Road, but it's really just at the end of a gravel track, two miles of washboard after leaving the county blacktop. Even less passable now that it gets so little use. Jimmy, their neighbor and unofficial caretaker, will see a strange car at the cabin and know it's time to come by.

A weedy footpath forks soon after the parking pad. The short, level way leads to the cabin; the more steep route goes down the old stone steps to the lake. As a boy, David would fly down those steps, bursting from the car the same way his dog, Jack, had when they finally arrived from Kansas City. Now he picks his way carefully down the irregular stone steps, mindful of a tumble and the remoteness of the cabin.

As he approaches the water, two crows rise from the old dock and settle in a nearby tree to scold him. The leaning dock looks unsafe now; even the local kids, Jimmy reports, no longer dive from it. Yet there on the rotting boards he sees a fresh pile of fish guts.

This is what the crows had been after. Someone had been fishing off the tumbledown dock that very morning.

This lake, where he had learned to swim as a boy, is now almost fully ringed by cattails. His dad had fought them in his time, wanting to keep the shore open for fishing and swimming. But nature always wins, and he had slowly surrendered whole stretches of shoreline as the work grew too much. Since David had last been out, the cattails have nearly completed their flanking conquest. He shakes his head, wondering what his dad would say if he could see it, then turns to climb the hill to the cabin.

David is older than the cabin and the lake, though only just, and to him they have always been there. His dad often spoke of the golden weekends he and his mother had devoted to building the cabin. David in a basket or toddling about among the hammers and saws and stacks of lumber. He doesn't remember any of this. A superhuman effort, building an entire cabin without power tools. His dad had hired a couple of local Amish boys to help since they had the old skills.

For many years David believed that his father had made the lake as well, digging out the entire two acres one shovelful at a time. No one had told him this; it was merely the sensible conclusion of an adoring son standing in the comforting glow of a father who could do anything. By Ozark standards, two acres is just a pond, but his dad had always insisted it was a lake and always corrected anyone who got it wrong. David is supposed to have asked where they hooked up the hose to fill it.

The lake is silting in now, decades after it was first carved out of the howling wilderness. His dad would likely cry if he could see it, assuming he knew anymore what he was seeing, though he still might. His memory might stir from its stew of fretfulness and confusion. It needs to be drained and dug out and tidied for the next owner, but David is not going to do that. He's already decided he'll dicker down the price if he must.

The cabin porch is a mess too. Dried mud and overturned chairs and cigarette butts and faded beer cans litter it. Even discarded clothing. Evidence of trespassing kids from Hoega with nothing to do in town and no one to stop them from partying there. But it's always been a good porch, deep and shady, with a nice view of the lake below; he can understand why a bunch of bored kids would steal away here for skinny-dipping and drinking away their summer days. Whatever their faults, they've shown the courtesy not to break into the cabin. Maybe having Jimmy nearby restrains them. He used to call David whenever he spotted a truck bumping through the trees toward the place. But what could David do, two hundred miles away? If he'd had them run off by the sheriff, it would only make them spiteful, and they surely return with hard feelings. He told Jimmy to let them be as long as no one destroyed anything. Jimmy stopped by once or twice to say howdy; he says he knows most of the kids. They know that he knows, and that probably keeps them under control.

David realizes now that he'll have to put a stop to it so he can keep the place in better order for potential buyers. That's still a bit down the road though. So much clearing out to do first. This place was his dad's hard-won retreat; many times he had told David how he and his mother had scrimped for the money to build the cabin. He would have moved here after he retired if his wife had let him. Cooking his meals on the propane stove, staying warm by the potbelly, reading by lantern light. His true identity is found here. Rusted axes and saws and all sorts of woodland tools he must have thought he needed at one time; many he probably only used one time. A mouse-eaten rug Jack had slept on that his dad had picked up on a trip to Taos before he was born; it still has Jack's hairs in it. Framed photos. Cast-off furniture. Pots and pans. Stuff and junk. The accumulation of decades that all has to go now. To charity, or to the burn pile.

David can begin by clearing away the cobwebs on the porch. There is a broom in the cabin, and the key he hasn't used in a long time, which he could never remove from his ring, still fits the lock. The door is snug; he has to put his shoulder to it. A familiar, musty smell greets his nose, but his dad must have known earlier smells. Of fresh-cut lumber, of sawdust, of wood oil. He must have known every cut and joint, every dovetail and toe nail, every nail driven home. Such memories he must have had of the place, now mostly gone. He remembers the cabin. The nurses say he still frets about it sometimes. But he doesn't remember his son. He's gone down a different road now.

David's heel crunches something as he steps in. A piece of glass. A lens from the binoculars there on the floor. His dad had kept them on a nail by the door, ready to snatch whenever he would dart out to look at something, some movement across the lake that had caught his eye. Their leather strap has been chewed away. He could never make the cabin mouse proof as his wife had wanted. When they visited they had lived out of battered popcorn tins where they stored everything they thought a mouse might get into. She hated that, but she never told him, and he may have never realized it. Or did he assume she was just as in love with the place as he was, overlooking his beloved cabin's flaws just as she must have overlooked his?

The cabin is disordered within, not from vandals but from time and use, disordered from the snapshots of David's own memory that are outdated and inadequate. His dad had continued to visit the cabin after David had moved away and his wife had died. Until he became too infirm to be trusted alone there. Before his mind began to slip. Yet he had held on longer than David would have guessed. Perhaps the cabin, filled with memory, baptized by his own blood and sweat, was the anchor that let his mind hang on even as age was pulling it away.

In the murk David sees the familiar as unfamiliar. Chairs in wrong places. The unmade bed. Books scattered on the table as though only just set down. The window curtains that were a concession to his wife, who couldn't sleep without them despite the cabin being long miles from anywhere. She'd sewn them herself. They're filled with dust now; it rises to David's nose as he pushes them open. Yet with more light he can see better. Familiar and unfamiliar. His dad's cabin. His sanctuary. His retreat. Later his Fortress of Solitude. "I built this for you, you know," he had told David one day as they sat on the porch in the fading light, the setting sun putting the lake into soft focus below. It was David's farewell visit after starting his new job far away. His father was in decline then, though David wouldn't let himself see it, let it interfere with his own long-delayed rise. "It's a legacy, and it will pay off in time." He puffed weakly on his cigar as they sat. "But only after I'm a memory. Curt will come here when he has a boy of his own someday."

Time was running out for the man then, and the cost of his care, which stretches his son thin month to month, will be eased by cashing in his legacy now. It took David a long time to accept that he had to do this. But his father will never be able to return to his cabin; he won't even know the place has been sold. Does that make his job easier or harder? David wonders. His long, slow, tedious job of sifting through the accumulation of a lifetime, of cleaning and clearing and burning and hauling and selling and parting. He knows he has to be merciless, just as he had to be when he moved his father out of his house.

The old tractor and brush hog were late additions to his dad's arsenal, kept in repair by Jimmy, who uses them to work his own meadows and occasionally clean up around the cabin. To David these belong least of all because they arrived after he was gone, after his own memories were fixed. They'll be the first to go, and Jimmy will arrive soon to discuss a fair price, which they both know won't be fair. Why would he pay much for things he already has free use of? That he has sweat equity in? They both know that he will win, though it isn't a contest, and David hopes he holds some regard for his dad, who he'd seen much more in later years than David had.

The dust from the opened curtains settles in the quiet cabin; his eyes adjust to the new light. The cut glass crystal that Curt had given his grandfather one year hangs in the window and casts tiny rainbows. He'd forgotten that detail. Below it on the sill sits the line of fossils David had collected as a boy. "We can only keep the good ones," his father had said because there were so many. Each with a story to tell.

It's not disarray he sees, after all, but use. Untouched for years yet seemingly left only days before. A spiral notebook opened on the table. A mechanical pencil at rest beside it. The chair pushed back as though risen from moments ago. A cigar butt in the ashtray. His wife had never let him smoke inside the cabin, but he evidently no longer heeded that after she was gone. His price, maybe, for the curtains?

His presence is here, from so much use and love. A new owner won't know it, won't feel it. Won't see him sitting in that hard wooden chair at that battered oak table.

Doing what, though? He was rarely a man of repose at the cabin. If the night or the cold didn't force him inside, he was outside, tending the campfire or sawing logs or clearing cedars. Swimming in the lake. Or just rambling in his Ozark hills.

So what, David wonders, is this scattering of books on the table and an open notebook before them?

He settles himself in the chair and leans toward the notebook. His father's handwriting runs down its page, marked at the top with a day four years past now. He flips to the front of the notebook and reads the inscription:

VISIT JOURNAL #3

Number three? Had his dad filled two prior notebooks with whatever this is? The man who couldn't be bothered to write a grocery list? What would his visit journal contain? What would be so important that his father could sit still and fill pages?

David flips through them. There are dated notes about the temperature, the weather. Chores undertaken or left undone. Animals seen. Had he robbed himself of his precious time outdoors to sit in the hard chair and write such things? It is his handwriting. It must be so.

liberated 27 Juniperus virginiana *today*

He always cleared cedars when they visited the cabin. "Liberating them from their earthly toil," he boasted. His fear was that with their oily needles they would transfer a harmless ground

155

fire into the treetops. Clearing cedars was another of his superhuman labors. A never-ending chore that would mock him now if he knew. Like the cattails, tiny cedars have reclaimed the forest around the cabin.

Yet in all the years his father had brought him here, David had never once heard him use a scientific term to describe anything, and certainly not the cedars he hated. They had bass and bluegill in the lake. Catfish of some kind. They had simply oaks and hickories and cedars. Just woodpeckers and cardinals and little gray birds. They had a kingfisher that visited the lake below the cabin, but never an *Alcedo alcyon*.

Alcedo alcyon *visited again today Entertaining*

Picoides pubescens *at the suet feeder*

A Peterson's guide sits on the table before David, its spine broken and its pages dog-eared and tattered. Highlighted and underlined. Checkmarks beside many of the birds. His dad's life list? Is that possible? The naughty-sounding *Picoides pubescens*, it turns out, is a downy woodpecker.

The many pages of his notebook have been filled with entries like these. Two other notebooks are somewhere in the cabin. Was he trying to nail down facts, David wonders, because he knew he was losing them?

KD and I visited today Chest doesn't hurt as much out here

Who is KD? He'd never spoken to David of bringing anyone to the cabin. Had his dad had a secret girlfriend? The pair of cigar bands taped to that page suggests a man, not a woman, but "KD" alone is surprising enough.

The weak November sun is warming the cabin. The metal roof pops as it expands. His roof never leaked; he knew how to do it right from a lifetime as a sheet metal worker. A job he hated but kept at heroically and one that he beat in the end with the victory, he said, of "still having all my fingers!"

forgot wallet again dammit!

Who cooks for you? Who cooks for you all?

David couldn't recall the first time he noticed his dad's mind slipping. Or rather, when he first let himself see it. His physical frailty had alarmed him enough. This invincible man was shown to be human like everyone else. That his mind would give way too was more difficult for David to accept.

bring more AA batteries next trip

But there never was a next trip. His Visit Journal ends there, the remaining pages blank. A bittersweet testament of hope *and* defeat, and David suddenly wants to see the other two journals he'd filled with his notes, to glimpse at his cabin life after David had left.

He rises from the chair and begins looking in the obvious places. The bookcase with stacks of David's old Superman comics, probably worth more as tinder for a campfire than anything else. The table beside the bed. He opens all of the popcorn tins. But when he finally finds them, in the metal cabinet that was a mouse-proof improvement over the old tins, they sit next to a box of cigars. His dad's beloved Upmanns. Odd that he would keep a box of pricey cigars under such conditions. No protection from heat and cold or from the drying winter. Why wouldn't he keep his supply at home and just bring a fresh one or two each visit? Surely he didn't still fear his wife's frowning disapproval after she was gone.

David slides his hand under the notebooks. He'll skim them as he waits for Jimmy. Then, on an impulse, he grabs one of the Upmanns. Never once had his dad offered him a cigar on their visits. Certainly not while his mother was around but not even after she was gone. He'd never invited his boy to enjoy them as he did, though David suspects he would have been welcomed to if he'd asked. Yet even as a boy, David had watched his father. How he first put on lip balm. How he cut the tip. How he let the match finish flaring before he brought it to the cigar, the flame never quite touching it. How he puffed his cheeks to get the cherry going. Whether it was ritual or just technique, it had fascinated the boy.

Perhaps fearing his mom's disapproval, David carries his own cigar to the porch; he will smoke outside the cabin. Yet it's breezy there – his dad had claimed that he'd lined up the cabin deliberately to have a breeze cross the porch for summer relief – and he has a hard time getting the cigar lit. Stepping inside for a moment he has better luck, but before going back out to where the journals wait, he sees one of his dad's old flannel shirts hanging from a nail near the bed. The November morning is cool, and his jacket is in the car, so he lifts the shirt from its nail and slips into it. It's blue and red plaid, one he recalls Curt picking out for his grandfather. There is a small yellow thread running through it, and Curt had said that it made the shirt "pop." It smells of woodsmoke.

David settles into one of the righted chairs, snuggling into his father's old shirt, and looks across the lake. He'd forgotten how much he enjoyed this view in November, after the leaves had fallen and he could see farther into the forest. He takes his first real draw on the cigar. The smoke trails up his nose and he coughs, but the smell of it brings his own memories. Him lying on the porch floor with Jack at the end of the day. Reading the same comic books over and over. His parents sitting in their chairs, relaxing after their chores or swimming or dinner. His dad's cigar smoke blending with the murmur of their voices. In David's memory these were perfect moments, and he thinks they truly were.

VISIT JOURNAL #1

The information here may be useful. I'll put it down and see what might be made of it.

temp 58 degrees at 10:30 a.m.

birdsong plentiful this morning

    The paper crinkles in his fingers, brittle from having gotten wet sometime. A cigar band is taped to the page.

    The old cigar in his hand is brittle as well. The wrapper is flaking. The glue on the band dried long ago; it hangs loose and he removes it, slipping it into the pocket of his dad's shirt. He spits flecks of tobacco from his lips.

splendid solitude!

cut some firewood must stack

.

sandwich for lunch cookie. iced tea (unsweetened, of course)

need more black sunflower seed for feeder

leaves starting to turn – hickories – shagbark?

what is gray bird with crest?

    A snapshot, a moment years ago. His father being reflective. Inquisitive. Passive. A side of him David rarely saw, especially at the cabin.

righted Jack's stone

David and his father had buried Jack up the hill behind the cabin. He'd found a spot that had some actual dirt, though they still needed the pickaxe to break up the rubble that comprises most Ozark hillsides. David told himself he was too big to cry then. Fifteen. But his dad knew better. He showed David how to swing the pickaxe then put it in his boy's hands to break the ground and make a final resting place for his dog. They took turns digging. Working silently. Later his dad found a slab of sandstone and scratched Jack's name in it deeply with a nail. On some later visit, when David was probably too busy with his friends to come along, his father had tugged that stone up the hill and set it over the grave. Sometimes it was toppled when they'd returned, and they'd set it up again. David thinks he should hike up there later.

For a long time, David thought his father could do anything; and then, he couldn't. Maybe his mom's death had robbed the man of some strength or some need to prove himself. He'd built a cabin with her. He'd built a life with her. With them. Then David moved away. And his mother died. They sold the house and put his dad in an apartment, but he refused to sell the cabin and lake. Not that David would let him. His dad claimed to love his solitary life, but his son was never sure. (After all, who is "KD"?) They spoke twice a week. His dad sounded delighted to hear from him, and maybe he was. David visited as often as he could. Dragged Curt along sometimes. Bought his father new clothes, new glasses when he needed them. Did little things around his apartment. Met with his doctor, though his dad never liked that. Made a few weekend trips to the cabin where he could see the gloom lift that had settled on him. Mostly they'd sit on the porch together and his dad would smoke a cigar. Later they would build a fire and sit around that, maybe drink a couple of beers, tell a few familiar stories, but his dad would get cold and they'd retire to the cabin for an early bedtime. Simple oatmeal for breakfast. His iced tea that he'd brought from home. A few chores just for show. Then they'd go back to his apartment in Kansas City. And then David would go back to his home.

funny pain in chest, right side again comes and goes.

hip hurts some but can still get around fine

This is in his first visit journal, the oldest one. He never willingly shared his ailments with anyone. David feels guilty peeking into his secrets like this. Into his private memories, even if his dad will never know. He's sure his dad meant to retrieve these notebooks, maybe burn them in some cleansing campfire. He'd surely never meant for

160

anyone to read them. But he'd lost that race, and now he sits unmasked.

gunfire over ridge, getting ready for deer season?

mostly blue sky, some cottony clouds

crows calling – bring peanuts for them next time

Aster anomalus *in bloom*

no more swimming this year

Had he still been swimming in his condition? David wonders. In the lake's condition? On the next page is a photo taped to the paper. His father holding a bass. The familiar lake in the background. Apparently he had still been fishing too. David had had no idea. Did "KD" take that photo?

Jimmy found old Ford tractor and b'hog that will work for mowing

As though summoned by his name on the page, Jimmy's old pickup comes rumbling down the hill. Here to strike the deal. Too soon, David realizes. His own splendid solitude is now at an end.

David closes his father's journal and taps the ash off his cigar. It's obviously dried out; it's burning much faster than he ever remembered his dad's doing. He doesn't know what one should taste like, but it probably isn't like this. He stubs out what's left of the cigar and rises to meet Jimmy.

Jimmy steps on the porch and surveys the mess David has yet to clean.

"Saw your car." A pause, and then, "Came over quick as I could."

As tight-lipped as David remembered him. "Hello, Jimmy. It's been a long time."

He evidently agrees or at least doesn't have anything to add because he says nothing. David offers his hand, which Jimmy crushes in his to establish their roles in the negotiations. Not that they will get to it right away. In this part of the country there are rituals of greeting to perform, seemingly unrelated small talk that must be passed through before the business at hand is reached.

"Nice morning," David says, rolling his head to look at the sky beyond the porch.

"How's your father?" Jimmy avoids eye contact, looking instead down the hill to the rotting dock and the lake.

"As well as can be expected. Forgetful, mostly. And frail."

"A good man, Mr. Clark."

The crows have returned to the dock and are sparring over the fish guts there. Jimmy eyes them.

"Looks like someone's been fishing this morning," David offers, considering for the first time whether it might have been Jimmy who had.

"Imagine there's some lunkers in that pond after all these years."

"Lake," David corrects, wondering if Jimmy's words are an admission.

"Yep. Your dad spoke of getting it dredged. Made nice once again"

David was never allowed to go in the lake by himself until he earned his water wings by swimming all the way across and back without resting. A middling swimmer as a child, he was mostly content to fool around in the shallows where he could touch the bottom, afraid of the fish below, always within a quick lurch of the shore. Or he'd hang from the side of the dock, his dad or mom watching him from a folding chair. Their willingness to sit idly in the sun and supervise, of course, rarely coinciding with the heat of the day when he wanted to splash around. Eventually this motivated him to master the impossible distance across the lake.

It was on their traditional Fourth of July trip to the cabin, in the heat of the Ozark summer, when David boasted that he was ready to pass his father's test. He was not allowed to dive from the dock, gaining unfair distance and momentum, but had to start from the shore, wading out until the water was deep enough to swim and then going on from there. His father stood on the dock where he could watch his son the whole way.

The lake was maybe three hundred feet across in those days, but to David it was an ocean. He had little difficulty reaching the far shore, but as he made the turn he felt fatigue catching him, turning his arms and legs to lead. He began to doubt he was going to make it. He looked across the water, and there was his dad. Standing on the end of the dock, his legs planted firmly apart, his fists on his hips. He had a bright red towel draped over his shoulder, and he'd taken off his glasses, ready to swoop down and rescue his son if he faltered. "Keep your head up," he had urged. That image of him, strong and watchful, stirred in David the strength he needed to finish his return lap, and that image has stayed burned into his memory ever since.

Jimmy has droned on about the tractor and brush hog. Not sure the old things are worth much anymore. Need constant maintenance. Hard to find parts. Wants to be fair.

David thinks now that his father had left his journals so he *would* find them. The mechanical pencil sits on the table inside the cabin. He wants to begin filling in the blank pages of Journal #3 with notes of his *own* visit that day. Tape his own cigar band to the page. Count the cedars he can liberate. Leave his own memories for his own son while he can.

The young cannot understand the old until it's too late. But at least they can come to some understanding, if they try.

The Witch by Columbkill Noonan

The witch hung, and the people cheered. A trial had been had; evidence had been presented; the jury had deliberated and found the woman guilty. No matter that the trial had been a farce; no matter that the evidence was spurious at best; no matter that the jury had been far from impartial. A show of justice had been made, no matter how half-hearted and unfair, and the woman had been sentenced to death. The people had done their duty, and the thing was done.

And so the witch hung. Her name was Susannah, and she had grown up with the people who now watched her die. There, in the front, was Becky. Susannah and Becky had played together as children, had tied ribbons in each others' hair, had giggled and whispered together as they skipped down the dirt street that served as the main thoroughfare of their town, hand in hand. Now, Becky cheered Susannah's death with all her might. In fact, she cheered so exuberantly, so loudly, that the apple of her fat, round cheeks turned red from the exertion. Beside Becky stood her husband, Adam, cheering no less enthusiastically than his round, red wife. Adam had always fancied Susannah; indeed, he had asked for her hand in marriage many years ago. Susannah had turned him down, leaving Adam to wed Becky, instead. Still, though, he had watched Susannah with an unhealthy lust, even after his marriage to Susannah's erstwhile friend. Now, there was a light of malice in his eyes, the kind of angry hatred that can only be felt by a small-minded man who feels that he has been unjustly denied something which he covets and finds that he cannot take. Becky, too, had seen the way her husband gazed at her old friend, and had grown to hate Susannah for it. Together, Adam and Becky had begun the rumors against her, the rumors that would grow and bloom into a sentence of death for Susannah.

And so the witch hung, and she watched the people whom she had known all of her life rejoice. There, the grocer, who had smilingly greeted her every week when she did her shopping, until the rumors began to fly. There, the lawyer who had made his ridiculous case against her, who had brought together those who hated her, those who feared her, those who were simply bored and seduced by the thrilling and terrifying thought of a witch in their midst. There, the judge who had allowed the absurd stories of the witnesses against her, who had given credence to their tales of curses and spells and midnight dances with the devil by listening with gravid interest to them and by silencing her denials of the hateful and impossible things of which she was purported to be guilty, things that fell from the witnesses tongues as blithely as if they spoke of the weather.

And so Susannah hung, and died, and it took far longer than she would have thought possible. In fact, time seemed to slow down (or did her mind simply speed up?), so that she could see every detail, hear every noise. There, the spittle flying from the lips of her very own nephew, an avaricious and lazy twit who, as her only surviving relative, stood to inherit the house that she herself had inherited from her father. There, a tear in the eye of her maid, who, afraid of arousing the suspicions of Susannah's accusers, blinked it away quickly to hide her distress at the execution of the mistress who had always been kind to her. Susannah could see every speck of dirt, every rotten tooth, every droplet of sweat, which decorated the faces of the people who had gathered there today to watch her die.

She had been unlucky; the rope had not broken her neck as she fell, and so she dangled for a time, slowly strangling. Her thoughts grew strange, even as she contemplated the crowd that cheered and jeered and rejoiced in the spectacle that was her death. It didn't hurt as much as she had thought it would. True, it was difficult to breathe, and the rope pinched at the skin of her neck most uncomfortably, but these things she found she could bear. There was a bit of a breeze, and so she swung a bit, her body twirling in a lazy inscription of an eight. She found that the outer arcs of her swing offered her some respite from the pinching, so that she looked forward to the apexes of her loops, while the bottom increased the pressure, so that she steeled herself as her body began the inevitable descent that followed each glorious turning.

Her feet kicked, vigorously at first, as though the movement of her legs might somehow, miraculously, release the pressure about her neck and allow her to breathe once more. Of course, that didn't happen, and her feet slowed until they moved lackadaisically in time with the cadence of her swing.

At last, the lack of breath overcame Susannah. Her mind slowed along with her feet, until at last her body gave up, and her life was ended. Still, her body swung, back and forth, forth and back, and the people watched it as though it were a mesmerizing pendulum. They stared for a few moments, until, satisfied that the witch was dead, they began to disperse one by one. Susannah's maid was the last to leave. She waited until she was sure that everyone was gone, and then she quickly, surreptitiously, darted up to the body to place a flower within Susannah's shoe. It was a small act of kindness and not of any practical use to Susannah at all, but still she watched her maid do this with no small amount of appreciation.

Yes, Susannah watched her maid do this, and watched the people as they left the square to go on about their lives. For Susannah found that though she was dead, still, she was there. She could see her body as it swung, could see the ugly way in which her tongue lolled out of her mouth, but she was no longer bound within it. She was dead, and free of her body, but it seemed she was not yet free of the earth.

The world appeared gray and misty, as though a great fog had covered the town. Susannah, confused, knew that she must move on, that her spirit must leave the earth, but she knew not where to go. She looked up, hopefully, but saw no light, no heaven waiting to admit her to eternity. She looked down, with some trepidation, but no black hole was there, no demons waiting to grasp her in their cruel talons and drag her off to the eternal fires of hell. There was nothing but the fog, and so Susannah waited.

After a time, she grew impatient, and wondered what she ought to do. She thought about all that she had heard about the fate of the soul after death. The ministers, of course, said that one went to either heaven, or hell, or purgatory. According to them, there were no other options, but it seemed apparent to Susannah that she was in none of these places, nor did she have the slightest idea of how to get to any of them.

So, she thought of stories that she and Becky used to whisper, tales meant to frighten each other in the dark of night, things that had been told them by the servants that served Susannah's family, or by the lone African slave who served as a maid in the minister's house next door. The maid's name was Mgbeke, (although, fearing the heathen sound of that name, the minister had bestowed upon her the good Christian name of Mary) and she told the girls tales of ghosts, of souls that could not find rest. Always, in these stories, the ghost had some unfinished business that needed to be attended to, some vengeance that must be wrought, before the trapped soul could move on to the afterlife. Susannah supposed that she did indeed have a great deal of unfinished business, and some revenge to seek. Hadn't she been falsely accused, because of jealousy, and greed, and pride? Hadn't the people of the town, people she had called friends, people she had known since birth, been all too willing to believe the stories about her, simply because she lived differently from them? In their judgment of her choices, in their refusal to understand how a woman, even one who had inherited enough money to live comfortably on her own, could refuse suitors, could choose to remain unmarried, they had been willing to believe that she had instead chosen to marry the devil. In their boredom with their own lives, they had gladly accepted the tales spun by the nephew who wanted what was hers, or the man who had hated her for rejecting him, or the wife who was jealous of her husband's desire for her. They had maligned her, and falsely convicted her, and wrongly taken her life.

Yes, Susannah most certainly had just cause to seek vengeance against those who had wronged her. Before the hanging, while she had languished in the jail, with naught to do but to think on the unfairness of her accusers, she had imagined what she would do to them if she truly were a witch, if she truly had the powers of darkness at her disposal. So many times had she imagined the ruination of Adam and Becky, and her nephew, and the judge who looked upon her with disgust, smug and stupid in his surety that she was evil. But, strangely, now that she was dead, she found that she simply didn't feel quite as angry.

Susannah thought more of Mgbeke. Since Christianity was proving somewhat useless to her at the moment, perhaps Mgbeke's religion, which she had brought with her from Africa, could help Susannah. Odinani, Mgbeke had called it, her religion of spirits and charms and simple magicks. As a good Christian, Susannah had of course pretended disbelief in Mgbeke's heathen nonsense, but secretly she was intrigued. The stories of uneasy spirits that haunted the living, the promise of herbs and potions and spells that would make any man fall in love with a girl; this was the stuff of excitement and fantasy that was sorely lacking in this strictly Puritan town.

Yes, she had, when younger, used Mgbeke's love potions (for, unmarried though she was, still a woman could yearn for the touch of a man, though the Church might deny it), although she had never used the potions on Adam, as Becky claimed that she had. Indeed, were it possible, Susannah might have used a potion to instead deliver herself from Adam's unwelcome lust for her, rather than to incite it further. Then, perhaps, Becky would have been spared her wild jealousy that had so quickly changed her friendship into animosity.

How absurd it was that an entire town could be brought to fear, and at last put to death, a simple, single woman, only because another woman was envious of her husband's attentions! Susannah laughed a bit at the thought, and then checked herself with surprise. She wondered how she could feel amusement at such a thing, when by rights she should be horrified, angry, ready to rain down unholy vengeance upon those who had wronged her. Yet, she was having a difficult time holding on to such thoughts. Those emotions seemed to her somehow heavy, while she herself felt lighter than air. She tried to clear her thoughts, to steady herself, to decide on a course of action. Truly, it seemed that Mgbeke was the only person who could help her. And so, resolved, she made her way to the minister's house.

She came upon the minister and his wife sitting in their parlor. He read quietly from the Bible; she sat opposite him, mending a shirt collar with her needle. It was a scene of idyllic domestic tranquility. Susannah wondered how one could sit there so calmly so soon after watching one's neighbor swing from a tree. How could the minister read from a book of love and compassion, mere minutes after yelling that his God had forsaken Susannah, and that He would smite her soul into hell? How could his wife's needle find its way so surely, with nary a quiver, when not even an hour had passed since Susannah had seen her amidst the crowd, jeering and cheering with the rest of them? Susannah looked at them curiously, marveling at their hypocritical composure. There they sat, smug and cozy in their false righteousness. The minister's wife even hummed a gay tune softly while she sewed, as though all was right in the world. Susannah supposed that, to her simple mind, it was. A witch had been destroyed, the devil defeated, God had prevailed, and her husband's shirt collar was nearly fixed. Susannah watched the two in their contentment, as they enjoyed a surety of mind that can only be achieved by the truly enlightened or the truly stupid, and, as she knew them both to be far from enlightened, could only feel sympathy for their dearth of intelligence. But Susannah's business was not with the minister and his wife, it was with Mgbeke, and so she left the two of them to seek out their African maid.

She found Mgbeke in the kitchen, consoling Susannah's own maid, Sarah. Mgbeke held the girl as she sobbed. Tears fell from Mgbeke's own eyes as she spoke words of comfort to Sarah.

"Oh, Mgbeke," cried Sarah (for it was only the white adults of the town who called the woman by the name of Mary that the minister had decreed was her God-given, Christian name; the servants and children all called her by her real name). "Minister Halethorpe said that Susannah's soul would go to hell, but she was so kind to me that I cannot endure the idea!" The girl wailed in a renewed fit of weeping, and Susannah's heart melted with love for the girl.

"Well," replied Mgbeke, "it's not for me to gainsay the minister, but sometimes people say things that they just be making up, and that don't mean much of nothing. Saying somebody's going to hell is not the same as them actually going to hell."

"So, you think the minister is wrong?" asked Sarah, eyes wide with hope.

"Sure and I do," said Mgbeke. "If anybody's going to hell, it's..." she broke off, but Susannah saw that her eyes had strayed to the parlor where the minister and his wife now sat. "Well, let's just say that I can't imagine a God that wouldn't welcome our dear Ms. Susannah to him."

At that, Mgbeke happened to glance over to the corner where Susannah watched, and her eyes widened. With some surprise and no small amount of relief, Susannah realized that Mgbeke could see her. The woman drew in a startled breath, and then, calmly, gave Sarah a last hug before ushering her quickly from the kitchen. "Come now, child," she said. "I've got work to do, and so do you. Best you dry your tears and we get on with it, then." Sarah nodded and allowed herself to be pushed from the kitchen, still sniffling. Then Mgbeke turned to Susannah.

"I figured I might see you," she said, no fear whatsoever in seeing her dead neighbor in the kitchen, apparent in her manner. "Anyone who dies like that, is near certain to come back like this."

"Like what, exactly?" asked Susannah. "What has become of me? What am I?"

"You are a mmuo," answered Mgbeke without hesitation. "A spirit that is lost. A spirit that needs to find its way."

"Am I evil?" Susannah asked with trepidation, fearing the answer. She knew what the minister would say, that she was a witch, an unholy spirit, and that she belonged to the devil. But she trusted Mgbeke's opinion far more than that of the self-righteous man who sat on the other side of the house.

"You are what you will be," said Mgbeke, cryptically. "Mgbeke can't be telling you such things. They are for you to decide on your own."

Susannah paused, far from satisfied with this answer. She tried a different tack. "Why can't I move on? Do you know why I am trapped here like this?" She thought for a moment. "And why can you see me, but the minister and his wife, and Sarah, could not?"

Mgbeke nodded, somberly. "Aye," she replied. "I do know these things. And the reason that I know is the same reason that I can see you, where others cannot. I am a dibia, one who speaks with the spirit world. The minister and his wife, and yes, even Sarah, have closed their eyes to that which they cannot understand, and therefore fear. It takes an open heart to see things as they are, to see the truth of things. Some have hearts more open than others."

"So, can you help me? Why am I still here?"

"Your death was unjust, and your soul is troubled by it. You need to set things right, to restore the balance within yourself. Then you will be able to move on."

"So," said Susannah. "I must seek revenge upon those who wronged me."

Mgbeke pursed her lips and mumbled noncommittally, then let out a heavy sigh. "You must seek balance, in whatever form that may come to you," she said.

Susannah took this as affirmation of her intent, and made ready to wreak her vengeance. "Thank you, Mgbeke, for your help, and for your friendship. I go now, to pay a visit to those responsible for my death. I pray that you are right, and that then I may find my peace."

She made to leave, but as she did Mgbeke called out a warning after her. "Only you can find your path, dear girl," she said. "Remember, you are what you will be. Do not be that which you do not wish to be!"

Confused by Mgbeke's words, Susannah put them out of her mind, and made ready to do what must be done. To find peace, she must right the wrongs done to her. She decided that she would begin with the least of her malefactors, the one whose deeds had stung the least. The prosecutor's actions, although instrumental in achieving her execution, had been less personal to her, and so hurt her less. The judge, who had presided in a manner so biased against her that it would have been laughable had it not resulted in her death, had hurt her the more because he had known her since she was a child. But it was Becky who had wounded her the most, Becky who had betrayed her lifelong friendship, Becky who had been the first to denounce her.

A mere fright, a simple haunting, might suffice to redress the misdeeds done to her by the prosecutor and the judge, but Becky would require far more serious suffering to even the scale. Susannah didn't quite know how one went about a haunting, nor did she quite know how to achieve the terrible vengeance upon Becky that she so clearly needed to wreak. And, truth be told, she didn't feel particularly vengeful, or even angry. She actually felt rather lazy, and a bit voyeuristic. She felt like doing nothing more than floating languidly about the town, peeking into people's houses, seeing what they were doing.

But, she thought, she must focus. She didn't know, and hadn't thought to ask Mgbeke, if she had a limited time with which to complete her unfinished business. Perhaps, if she gave in to these dolorous feelings, the lethargy would soon overtake her, and she would at last simply fade into nothingness, losing all capacity to achieve her revenge and thus achieve her final peace. No, she thought, she must attend to what needed to be done, and put all of her energy towards it.

So, it was with great determination that she willed herself to go to the prosecutor's house. The man stood in his dining room, speaking to another man about the events of the day while enjoying a cup of tea.

"So, Jack," said the other man, a butcher by the name of Tom. "Well done today! I reckon that the governor will be quite pleased with you."

Jack nodded. "Yes, indeed he will be. He was quite clear that the practice of witchery should be stamped out completely, and today he will see that I have done my part to further God's work."

"Ayuh," said Tom. "That you did. For my part, I know me and my Mary will sleep easier at night knowing that there's one less lady dancing with the devil right in our midst." He shuddered. "To think that we've known her all her life, and that evil was in her all along! Who'd have guessed it?"

The two men shook their heads and took sips of their tea, pondering gravely the pervasive nature of evil. Susannah knew that, if she could only feel some anger, that she surely deserved to feel, she could frighten the wits out of Jack and Tom and thus disturb their placid thoughts and easy sleep for a good while to come. She could rattle the teapot in its tray; she could dash the hot tea from their cups so that it spilled all over their shirts that had been freshly pressed for the occasion of her hanging.

But Susannah did not do either of these things. Surely these two men were not to blame; they had merely believed what they were told to believe, done what they had been told to do. They were no more capable of questioning the spurious wisdom of the masses than a slug would be capable of driving a sleigh. How could Susannah hate them for simply being obedient members of society? She found that she could not hate them, and therefore could not muster up enough energy to fling their tea into their silly, slug-like faces. Indeed, she felt only a strange sort of compassion for these men who, like ants in an anthill, did not think to question their orders, but merely performed their duties like the multitudes of others just like them.

Nay, thought Sarah, she would not waste her time here. Perhaps, she would have better luck with Judge Hatton. He should have known better; he should have done something, anything, to uphold justice. Instead, he had encouraged the hysterics of the townsfolk, and had rendered her guilty before her trial had even properly begun.

But, when Susannah came to Judge Hatton's house, she found she could summon no more hatred for him than for the prosecutor. She saw him as he was at home with his family, without the façade put on by all for public interaction. She saw that, as he read from a newspaper, his brow glowered and his eyebrows bristled over a scowling mouth, as though what he read on the page angered him somehow. She saw the cantankerous way in which he grumbled at the servants, and at his wife and sons, snapping at them to hurry up with dinner, and then, contrarily, to be quiet about it. She also saw the resentment on the faces of his family and servants, and knew that they disliked him. This was an angry man, and a miserable one. No one cared for him; no one was glad when he came home. She thought with pity that he must know nothing of love and compassion, and, further, that he probably never had. How then could she expect him to be fair to her, to be compassionate to her plight, when he could scarce conceive of such notions! Again, Susannah found herself impotent in her attempt to smite her enemy. Where she needed rage, she felt only pity; where she needed anger, she felt only a detached sort of sadness at the emotionally depauperate state of Judge Hatton's life. And, so, defeated, she left the miserable judge un-smote and none the wiser that he had been haunted, however benignly and briefly, by the witch he had put to death this afternoon.

Susannah was disheartened by this second failed attempt at haunting. Perhaps, she thought, she would feel more animus if she confronted her accuser: the woman who had once been her friend but whose jealousy had led to her betrayal. Surely, but for Becky's and Adam's accusations, Susannah would still be alive. If Susannah could not wreak vengeance on the two people who deserved it most, she despaired of her soul ever finding peace. She would be doomed to float about the world in this dim fog, unseen and impotent in her failed rage, bored and oppressed by her bland emotions that refused to rouse, for all eternity.

She came upon Becky in her kitchen, busily preparing dinner. Sharp knives slashed through tough meat and hard potatoes, and a kettle of water boiled on the cast iron stove. She felt a flash of irritation at the sight of her accuser going about the mundane tasks of daily existence. She felt angry that Becky could go on with her humdrum life, while she herself was trapped in this colorless limbo. Now was her chance, thought Susannah. Now she could wreak the vengeance that she so desperately needed in order to be at rest. Pots of boiling water could be flung, to scald skin rather than potatoes; knives could be sent off course to tear through living flesh rather than meat. Susannah readied herself, and gathered what energy she could, in order to do harm to her malefactor.

But then Becky's small granddaughter came into the room. "Grandmama," said the girl, "Mama says I'm to ask you to fix my hair for supper." Becky nodded, pulled out a stool, and gestured for the little girl to sit. Once the child was settled, Becky gently brushed and braided the girl's long dark hair, just as Susannah and Becky used to do for one another. At the sight of this tableau of domestic tranquility, the little girl so innocent and trusting, the grandmother carefully attending to the needs of her grandchild, what little anger she had felt towards Becky drained away. Indeed, Susannah felt herself smiling as Becky struggled to contain the girl's unruly curls, and the child enjoyed the attention.

Susannah, after observing those who had killed her and who seemed completely remorseless (indeed, they seemed not to think of her at all), wondered why she could feel no rage.

She thought of Mgbeke's cryptic words, that her unfinished business, the thing that she needed to do in order to be at peace, might be vengeance or it might be something else entirely. She thought of how Mgbeke had said, "You are what you will be," and a realization struck her: these earthly concerns were not her cares anymore. She wondered if being trapped in a mortal body made unimportant things seem important after all, so that now that she was free of her body she was also free to be unconcerned about what was done to it. It was Susannah, the mortal creature, who was betrayed and judged unfairly and strung up in the town square, not this fleshless being that she now was. She didn't have to force herself to feel an anger that she didn't really feel; she didn't have to remember the resentments of life.

With this thought in mind a wild excitement filled her, as though all things were possible. The gray fog around her began to sparkle, and from the center of her spirit, sparks blossomed to match. Becky's granddaughter's eye was drawn to the spectacle.

The girl's eyes widened and she pointed into the corner where Susannah floated. "Look, Grandmama!" she cried, not in fear but in wonderment. "There is an angel!" Becky glanced over distractedly, but clearly saw nothing of the amazing thing that was happening in her kitchen. "Hush!" she said firmly to her granddaughter. "That's enough of your silliness. Now, sit still so I can finish your braids."

Susannah smiled kindly at the little girl, and winked in acknowledgement of their shared secret. The girl smiled back and turned away in obedience to her grandmother, and Susannah paid no more heed to the goings on of the living. Instead, she simply rejoiced in the glorious bedazzlement of her own enlightenment. Soon, there was no boundary between the lights within and those without, and Susannah was no more.

Dust by Billie Louise Jones

"Texas is a mighty fine country for men and dogs. But. it's hell on women and oxen." Mrs. Fontaine spoke as we women gathered in the trading post whilst our husbands were wagering on a fight between a bulldog and a badger. Mrs. F. is from Louisiana. I had not known till we went in for trade day that there was another native of Louisiana in this western part of Texas. We embraced like long lost kin. Mrs. F's visage reveals inner strength now that the pennants of beauty are in tatters – or perhaps a beautiful countenance has been engraved with lines of sternness by the vicissitudes of life. Shall I experience such a transformation?

Our homesteads lie at such distances that days – nay, weeks, perhaps months – go by without my seeing another soul save my husband and children. Time has no markers. I longed for this trip. The post could not possess the music, society, gaiety, and art of the old home; but at least there would be company. I met a woman of my own kind; yet we struggled to speak. Our mouths were rusty. With so much on our souls, we spoke of ways to put up corn and tomatoes. Ah, the body must be nourished to support the soul.

Mr. Morgan, my dearest Alfred, brought us to this desert to build anew. War changed our fate irrevocably; but though the Cause be lost, we are not lost. I shall think of this land, not as a desert, but as a bare slate waiting to be written upon.

The wind piled loose, dry brush over the door. Dust seeped through cracks in the walls and window frames. It is unaccustomed labor for my dearest Mr. Morgan to clear the yard of debris and for me to sweep up pans of dust. Yet we must not let ourselves down. We must keep our courage polished.

Sabrina Cuomo Morgan rubbed a place clear on the dusty attic window and held the old journal up to the light. Not a Victorian red morocco diary with a gilt clasp, but a plain record book that a farm wife might afford. She reflexively thought that the quality of the paper was better than a similar record book of today. The ink was faded but still legible. Sabrina admired the exquisite penmanship.

Out the window, there was nothing but miles and miles of Texas, flat and brown under the sun. Even so, Sabrina put on her makeup and styled her hair. She must not let herself down. She was a tall, slender woman with a fine-boned face, not beautiful but once gamin, now dusted with fine lines. Dark eyes under arched brows still appeared to gaze in wonder at whatever was before her. Crouched in old designer jeans among decades of cobwebs and dust, she sorted through a brass bound Victorian steamer trunk. Her mind shuffled memories.

"It was for the adventure!" she had exclaimed.

Her wondering gaze traveled around Sonny Bryant's and then back to Al Morgan: what an adventure for a girl from Manhattan to be eating barbecued ribs on the hood of a car in the parking lot around Sonny Bryant's cook shack – all those Cadillacs and pickups, executives and construction workers eating the same food!

"Friends said, You can't leave New York, New York is the city, the only other place that's even possible is the Coast! As if the Sun Belt wasn't happening. The Fifth Avenue stores finally realized that, yes, there is something happening out there, a new sophistication, money, art and restaurants and new ideas, a demand for quality goods; and they're opening chains. When Steins offered me the chance to manage home décor in the new store here, I jumped at it. Dallas and Houston are the most exciting cities in the US today. This is where things are starting. I love this feeling of being in at the beginning and riding the wave. Everything is just soaring up, up, up like all these wonderful new glass skyscrapers. People have suddenly got money and want to enjoy it and create a lifestyle. I'm thinking of starting my own decorating business."

"It's the trend," Al Morgan replied enthusiastically. He was a rangy young man who just had his first blow dry hair styling, and he was still conscious of the lock of hair brushed across his forehead. He had an open face, big nose, sun-streaked hair, a new type of man for her to find attractive: a man in a tailored suit and expensive cowboy boots. She had not then wondered what he saw in a Yankee girl.

He told her he came from West Texas, but names like "Lubbock" and "Odessa" formed no pictures in her mind. "We lived on the same farm for five generations. When they hit oil back in the Twenties, it changed everything. We had the only land that didn't have any oil in it. Farming was dirt poor back then, but Grandpa had more ambition than to be a farmer. He started a business that supplied the oil companies. Oil changed all our lives down to my generation. We didn't have oil, but I'm an oil executive. I started up an independent firm of geology consultants. I'm outta West Texas!"

When Al first took Sabrina to West Texas, after they were married, she got him to take her driving. She said, "I saw some art photographs that made this country look beautiful. Black and white with shadow effects. It looked so...immense and magnificent. Now, I see that outside the frame there was just...more and more...of the same thing."

"Are you saying the camera lies?" Al retorted. And laughed.

That was before the oil bust.

Now that they were back, to stay, Sabrina was too dismayed by the bleak landscape and the distances between everywhere to make a joke. Al's father had given up the house in town, so the old homeplace was where they had to go. The house grew at angles to itself as each generation added rooms. Somewhere in the core was the original cabin.

Sabrina meant to make the best of things. Courage, she reflected, is as much stoicism as gallantry. She became excited when she thought about going up to the attic. She pictured solid oak and walnut that had made way for contemporary vinyl finish. It would be something to fix things up, create an ambience that would make the house a place of refuge, not defeat. However, all the good things had slipped away over the years.

She did find the steamer trunk full of books, something no one had wanted. She sorted through them in hopes of first editions– Dickens, Eliot, Trollope– in beautiful bindings. Elizabeth Wetherell, August Jane Evans Wilson, Mrs. Southworth, Mrs. Stephens, Mrs. Wood, Mary Kyle Dallas. Victorian middle-brow, she supposed.

She found a sketchbook. Watercolors and drawings of West Texas; some scenes were clearly of the old Morgan farm. The artist apparently stopped in the middle of sketching a flurry of tumbleweeds. Most of the pad was blank. Sabrina found the record book and opened it.

The trunk would be a decorative feature. The old bindings would look ornamental on a shelf. She took the record book, sketchbook, and a writing case downstairs with her.

Wind whistles through the house. A loose shingle bangs almost rhythmically.

BANG bang bang BANG.

The dust is even in my dreams now. It fills my veins....

"She's my greatgrandmaw. I never knew her. There's a picture in here somewheres."

Mr. Morgan took a suitcase out of a closet and rummaged in it. Al's father, always taciturn, had turned glum. Sabrina's questions lit a little spark. "Paw said she had to stay for awhile in a state hospital. Her mind. But he said she was the gentlest soul he ever knew."

It was an oval photograph of an old woman who looked straight out at her descendants, the serious gaze of Nineteenth Century portrait photography. Her cheeks and lips were sunk in on her toothless mouth. She wore a ribbon-trimmed cap, and enough of her trunk showed so that Sabrina could see the rigid corseting. When Sabrina checked the dates, she was shocked that at the time of the picture Victoria Morgan was younger than Sabrina was now. All of a sudden, she ached inside as if she were full of tears.

"The Old South thought a heap of education," Mr. Morgan continued. "'Course things were different out here. She tried to school the young 'uns herself. But she give up on it."

Al did not look away from the Cowboys game on TV when his father and wife came back into the family room. Of course, there was no need for company manners. This room, where a wall had been knocked down between kitchen and dining room, was the only part of the house truly lived in. It was organized around the television.

"It's like a one room cabin again," Sabrina remarked shortly after they moved back.

"It's what we got," Al muttered sourly.

He used to enjoy her quips.

Mr. Morgan dropped down on the sofa with his son. They had a tray of football snacks between them. Sabrina looked from one profile to the other, seeing how Al would age. He now wore a Cancun souvenir cap over his bald spot.

Sabrina sat off to the side with Victoria's picture and journal.

They were in West Texas, to stay, because the oil economy had crashed. She could not understand how this happened. Interior decorating was one of the first things to go when money got tight for people, so she had to close her business. Al's business downsized then went into Chapter 11. He was an experienced manager, but there was nothing much for men in their fifties. When things came back, it would be for younger men. The Morgan oil company supply business was still holding on, the only one left where there had been many. They went back so Al could run the business. Maybe he could keep it going, and it was not too far to drive into town.

There was nothing for Sabrina to do but go to work for the Welfare when the State had an opening. The lifestyle they enjoyed was gone. It would not come back.

Mr. Morgan nailed battens between the boards today. Perhaps this will keep the dust out of the house. It is wicked of me to think of dust, of the never-ending housecleaning, when the purpose is to keep us warm and alive through winter. The signs are that we will have another of those dreadful blue blizzards out of the North, which almost bury the house. Never can I forget when the mounds of snow melted last spring, and the mounds were the carcasses of frozen cattle.

My dearest Alfred is so worn from his labors that after supper all he can do is take a medicinal pull from the jug and fall into bed.

I sit by the fire patching a quilt.

Flickering firelight is mesmerizing. It always draws my mind back to the old days. How we used to talk! When we were courting, Father would come out on the porch with his watch in his hand. Mr. Morgan declared we must marry so that we could finish our conversations!

How strange that we are alone together in this desert, yet seem to speak and to take pleasure in each other's company less than when we lived in society.

Sabrina arranged a tablescape on Victoria's trunk, using some of her own grandmother's lace. She propped Victoria's sketchbook on some of the old books and placed her writing case and journal and grouped some Civil War era ink bottles and a pen. She liked to look at her work.

Out the window, wind rolled surface dirt and dry brush straight across the landscape as far as she could see. In a dust storm, some of it always got in no matter how they tried to seal the air conditioners and window frames. She could see no dust cloud from a car on the road all the way back to where the earth bent into the sky.

Her husband was out among the men. Again; they had hunting, fishing, stock car races, diversions even in this — Sabrina thought Victoria's word — desert.

There was not much they could do together, other than drive in for a movie, or find a country western roadhouse that would not frighten Sabrina.

Growing apart in the heartland was an unforeseen consequence of the oil bust.

There had been pain in their marriage. At one time, Sabrina had thought of leaving him; but they – Sabrina – had mended the broken places. They had a good lifestyle together. They had a house neither could afford alone, charmingly decorated by Sabrina; an exciting circle of friends; businesses that keyed each of them into whatever was happening in Dallas; clubs, causes, museum memberships and receptions; clothes and trips and toys; connections, interests, and activities that supplemented each other. With all of that gone, what remained? Sabrina held the question just below the part of her mind that formed feelings into words, so that it could not be asked, could not be answered, for it led to another question. How much were the closest relationships composed of circumstances?

Sabrina felt withered. She was bony now, and there was no reason to put on her makeup and style her hair.

Journal entries sparse of late. When day is done, bed a haven, sleep a grateful release. Remember– must stuff new mattress.

My character is weak. I must berate myself constantly in order to perform my duties. This morning I was slow to arise even though I knew I must fry pork chops and potatoes and fix an apple pie. Mr. M.'s breakfast was not on the table when he awoke. I have no excuse.

No longer can I feel that we moved West to build anew. We are in exile from a country that no longer exists. Therefore we cannot turn back. I wonder if our forebears who crossed the sea from the British Isles faced only forward, as we have been taught, desiring only the opportunity for a better life in a newer world. For think – if desperate circumstances drove them to migrate, their hearts must have held as much grief as hope. Did they not face backward also? Leave half their souls behind? Ah, well, they came to a green and fertile land of the greatest natural beauty. The fragrance of pine trees on the night air haunts my memory.

I did not dust for the past two days. My plea, the spring wash. I must watch the fire under the iron pot in back of the house. The wind could blow one spark into a conflagration. Dust stands on the sills and in the cupboards. Dust has gotten into my head. Perhaps I breathed it in, or it may have seeped gradually through my skin. I can feel it lying at the base of my skull. I must hold my head very carefully, for any sudden movement might stir up a dust storm and blow it through my eyes. Mr. M. would see it then. I dare not tell my dearest Alfred and grieve him so. I bear all in silence.

It is wicked of me to spend time on my journal. Even these few moments should be put to use. Make more starch tomorrow.

This trip was different.

Until they ran too short of money, Sabrina had gone to New York every year, to visit her family, to see what was new in interior decoration, to take in all the art and entertainment available. This time, without Al noticing, she got a portfolio together and took it with her.

Sabrina felt like herself again, able to respond spontaneously, all in one piece without having to hold part of herself in reserve. Her hair was done in a new style; and her suit, bright pink trimmed with navy braid, had not been worn in so long it felt new. She had ballet and theater tickets in her purse.

Over the years, the number of people she was close to had dwindled, of course. Bella D'Attolico, Sabrina's twin, thirty pounds heavier, was an art teacher and Brooklyn Heights housewife; traces of her East Village ethnic bohemian days turned up on her pantsuits and shirtwaists. Gerald Montrose, in Sabrina's class at Parsons, now renovated SoHo lofts; he had traveled from French berets and neck scarves to the Ralph Lauren rough wear look.

They strolled across Fifty Seventh Street to Carnegie Hall. Sabrina was excited by the bustle of traffic and the brisk pace of people with things to do and places to go. The shop windows offered only the finest authenticated antiques. Customers were seldom seen through the windows, but the shops never went out of business.

"There must be someone who keeps these places going," Bella said."I don't know them. You guys tell me."

Gerald snorted."Whoever they are, they never go down to SoHo."

Sabrina had known such people in Dallas, but that was over.

After the concert, they went to one of the West Side provincial French restaurants.Tex-Mex was the new fashion in Manhattan, but French was a treat for Sabrina.

"One thing I've always loved about New York is the way you can manage any lifestyle," Sabrina said. "The Beautiful People go to the theater and French restaurants. We can, too, even if it's not Le Grenouille."

Bella and Gerald smiled.

After they ordered and the cabernet and bread came, Sabrina said, "What jobs are available?"

Bella and Gerald momentarily lost their poise.

"Leaving Al?" Bella said.

"Leaving West Texas."

She had not exactly thought it out. The trip was to see what was there. If nothing were settled in her mind, she could still do anything.

As it happened, there was no immediate demand for a fifty year old decorator from out there. If she thought of some other job as a stopgap until she found a position, then she had no skills, no contacts, no experience.

Canal Street; a small tornado of trash and grit whipped down the sidewalk. Eyes stinging, Sabrina hurried down the subway steps. She scanned the car for a seat where the graffiti was thoroughly dry and unfolded the Times and the Village Voice to the apartment ads. She had been to the City personnel office to leave an application for Department of Social Services caseworker. The Welfare was a traditional day job for aspirants to anything in

New York City. She figured starting salary against rent and expenses in parts of town where she might consider living, and there seemed nothing left for all the things that meant New York to her. Gerald told her people now had roommates in one room apartments.

In Bella's Venetian mirror, she saw black specks all over her face; street grit.

That night, Bella sat on her bed and said, "I love your visits because I can see New York through your eyes. It brings back the thrill."

Mr. Morgan offered me such insult as I never dreamed a husband might wreak on a wife, the creature he vowed before God to protect and cherish. My heart is broken. I cannot go away, for there is no place left to go to. I must abide with my shame and grief. My only pride will be enclosing my pain within my heart, where the world may never see it. I shed tears only on these pages. No matter what, I shall bear myself in such a way that Mr. M. will know that he is always my dearest Alfred.

Sabrina stopped the car at a random spot on a dirt farm road and trudged over the field with her sketchbook and watercolors under one arm, a folding canvas chair under the other. A broad-brimmed straw hat shaded her face. She searched for little things in the endless plains, for subtleties of color and texture.

This was it. She'd had her good time and lost it. Better than never having it at all. Now I understand country music, she said to herself, and why even the fiddles wail in grief.

If life gave little choice in one's circumstances, still one could choose how to behave in those circumstances. A woman could keep herself going, live in her mind. Creativity did not depend on any locale. Books and ideas were company in themselves.

How many pictures had been painted of thunder clouds rolling over the Alps, seas storm-tossed or seas holding power in abeyance, mighty falls and rivers? A dust storm was as powerful a force of nature as anything else.

The dust.....

The dust.....

Closing Time by Matthew McKiernan

It was half an hour to closing time. Frank wasn't looking forward to wiping the tables, but at least it would get him moving. No one had come in for hours and Frank wondered if he should close early. The doors to Frank's Cheese Steak joint swung open and a man stepped inside. He was dressed in dark blue jeans and wore a leather brown jacket covered in sawdust. The man was pencil thin and had a crow like face. The hair on his head was a mixture of orange and gray. His eyes were bloodshot red and anyone could tell that this guy was on something. He took a seat at the table directly across from the counter and glanced at the light blue cash register.

Frank stood behind the counter. He was exhausted. If he took better care of himself, maybe he would not feel half-dead all the time. Frank was 62 years old, a fat greasy looking man with a couple of gray hairs on his mostly bald head. It was a cold fall night and Frank wasn't happy that the rest of the staff had already gone home and left him alone with this man.

Frank coughed a deep cough, the kind that hurts. The patron ignored Frank's agony as he coughed some more, until finally he was done. Suddenly the man got up from the table and approached him. Frank had dealt with drugged-out losers before. If they paid the bill and left all the other customers alone, he treated them like everybody else. But if they made a ruckus and refused to leave, he threatened to call the cops. If that didn't work, he had a sawed off shotgun beneath the counter. The sight of old Betty would even make a man stoned out of his mind flee.

Hopefully, tonight Frank wouldn't have to take the old girl out. The man with the sawdust covered jacket got up and tapped on the counter. "What kind of grub do you got here?"

Frank sighed and scratched his jowls. "There's a menu on the table."

"I can't read."

"Oh . . . well we have sandwiches, cheese steaks, cheese fries, hamburgers, and ice cream."

"I'll have a ton of cheese fries with a nice cold beer."

"If you could read you'd have seen our sign that says we don't serve alcohol or allow people to come here with it."

The patron scoffed at this. "What the fuck is your deal, dude?"

Frank sighed and rubbed his temple. "I'm a recovering alcoholic so I can't have that poison anywhere around me."

"That can't be good for business."

"I make do."

The truth was that Frank was a violent drunk. His drinking had cost him dearly. It wasn't until two years ago, after he assaulted his landlady and put her in the hospital, that he went stone cold sober and couldn't stand the sight of a drink since. Frank sighed. "Are you still going to order a drink?"

"I'll have a Diet Coke."

Frank served up the fries and soda. The man poured a huge amount of salt and ketchup on his fries and scoffed them down. He ate them like a starving dog, never taking his eyes off Frank. He only took a break from gorging himself to drink down his soda. "You don't recognize me, do you?"

Frank shook his head. The man sighed. "My name is Philip. Does that ring any bells?"

"I don't know you from dirt."

Philip got up and made his way towards the counter. There was a jar full of red and green lollipops by the cash register. Philip plucked one out, stuck it into his mouth, and then spat it out. Frank felt a tingle spike up his spine. "I think you should pay for your meal and leave." Frank said.

Philip reached behind his pants. "That's it. I've had enough of your bullshit." He whipped out a silver plated revolver while Frank yanked out old Betty. As out of shape as he was, his reflexes were never better. Frank and Philip stood with their guns pointed at each other's heads with fingers on the triggers ready blow each other apart. Frank's hands were shaking like crazy, while Philip didn't break a sweat. He just smiled. "Looks like we got us a good old fashioned Mexican standoff."

"Look, we ain't got no safe. All that's here is the 73 dollars in the cash register. You can take it all. It's not worth dying over."

Philip laughed a dark and deep laugh. "This isn't about fucking money you fat prick, this about making things right!"

Philip reached into his left pocket with his free hand and pulled out a tape recorder. He placed it on the counter and turned it on. He ran his hand over his face and gave a deep sigh. "You're going to confess what you did. Then we're going call the fuzz here so they can hear it!"

Frank's heart was pounding in his chest so fast that he was damn sure he was about to have a heart attack. It wouldn't be his first, but he feared it would be his last. "What are you talking about? I never saw you before today."

"Chicago, forty years ago, ring any bells?"

"I was always so high and drunk back then, I don't even remember the name of the college I went to."

Philip sneered and shook his head in sheer disbelief. Tears were starting to flow from the edge of his eyes. Frank could tell this man hated him. He had hurt many people in his alcohol-fueled days, but he had no memory of this man or if he had ever harmed him. Frank tried to recall what had happened. "Honestly, I don't remember doing anything bad to you."

"That's a lie and you know it! As drunk as you were, there's no way in hell you can forget what you did to me and my brother!"

"Your brother . . . I . . . ."

Philip cut Frank off. "My brother and I sold crack on the streets, not an honest living, but we never hurt nobody. You, in a drunken rage accused us of ripping you off and attacked us. My brother pulled out his piece, but it jammed. So we took you on fist to fist; you were a fucking savage. You broke my brother's neck, grabbed his gun, and then nearly beat me to death with it."

Philip sobbed; Frank had never seen a man cry so painfully. "I didn't die though; just ended up in a coma for six months and woke up ruined! You're the reason I can't read, drive a car, or get "it" up anymore. I'm a mess. I just wander from town to town, like a leaf flying around in the wind, doing whatever work I can find. That is, until I arrived here last week and saw you sweeping outside. Then I knew there was a God! After 40 years of agony, he had delivered you to me!"

"You got the wrong guy!"

"You may have packed on the pounds, but I still recognize you, Frank. Your face is burned into my memory."

Frank shook his head. He wanted to dismiss Philip as mad, but the truth was that he didn't know. So much of his life was a blur, but he wasn't a killer. He couldn't have done something so horrible. Frank took the deepest breath of his life. "Getting me to confess by the point of a gun won't hold up in court."

"It will make the boys in blue look back into it. They may exhume my brother's body. If there's still flesh on his neck, your fingerprints and DNA will be right there."

"No it won't because I didn't do it!"

"Your gonna confess now or I'm going to shoot you dead!"

Frank could have confessed or tried to say something else. Instead, words left him and he tried to beat Philip to the lucky shot. They fired at the same time. Frank blew Philip's skull apart. Blood and brain matter scattered everywhere as Philip soared across the bar and crashed into the wall. Frank hit the floor like a bag of bricks, a bullet buried in his sternum. Frank coughed up blood and tried to get up. His cell phone had run out of juice two hours ago and he didn't think he would make it to the phone in the back. He needed to get on the street outside and shout for help.

Frank managed to get back up on his feet, but instantly tumbled right back down. Blood filled his mouth and gushed down his chest. At that moment, Frank remembered that one day back in college he had woken up with blood all over his body. When he realized it wasn't his, he cleaned himself up in the shower and told himself it was blood from a stray animal he killed. He had kept drinking when his subconscious suggested that narrative wasn't true and after a while, he forgot all about it.

But Frank remembered all of it now. Philip had been dead right. Frank sobbed. He had destroyed Philip's life and had now taken it. Frank realized that he couldn't move, and he couldn't even breathe. Even though he hadn't taken a drink in two years, his alcoholism finally ended up costing him his life. Now he was going to die, all alone at closing time.

Place of Safety by Lesley Middleton

She opens her eyes and looks about. She is in bed but it is not her bed. The room does not look familiar and yet she feels as though she might have been here before. She tries to sit up but can't seem to move.

"Help me. Can you help me?" The words come out as a whisper, barely reaching the closed door. She needs to go to the bathroom but she can't remember where it is.

She closes her eyes.

"Cup of tea, Eleanor." The voice intrudes on her dream. Eleanor opens her eyes. A cup of tea would be nice. She tries to reach the cup on the bedside table but it's too far away.

"Can you help me?" But the woman who brought the tea has gone.

Has she been asleep again? She always feels tired nowadays. She never used to feel so tired before she came to this place. Now she can barely stay awake. She looks around her. The place is full of old people. What is she doing in a place full of old people? What time is it? It must be time to go home. Her eyes close again.

"Come on Eleanor. It's time for some lunch."

She hears the voice as if from a far distance and tries to open her eyes. It's a young voice. Is it her sister?

"Eleanor come on, wake up." A man's voice now.

Strong hands grip her under her arms and hoist her onto her feet. She feels herself being spun in a circle and then the hands force her back down into a sitting position. Now she is moving. Where are they taking her? Her eyes close again.

"Here we are Eleanor. Lunch."

With a struggle she opens her eyes. She is sitting at a table with three old women. Who are they? Why is she sitting with them? She doesn't know them.

Her plate has two quarters of a sandwich on it. She peels back a corner to see what is between the bread. It looks like egg mixed up with mayonnaise. She doesn't like mayonnaise. She's never liked mayonnaise. Why are they giving her mayonnaise to eat? It will make her ill; it always does.

One of the old women is grinning at her. She looks like an old witch. A string of saliva dribbles from her mouth. She points a crooked finger towards Eleanor's plate. Eleanor recoils from the long dirty fingernail.

"Come on, Eleanor. You've got to eat something." A young girl is crouching down next to her. She picks up one of the sandwich quarters and offers it to Eleanor, who shakes her head.

"Don't be difficult, Eleanor." The young woman sighs and replaces the uneaten sandwich on Eleanor's plate. "No dessert if you don't eat your first course."

She takes the plate away. Someone else comes and replaces it with a bowl of rice pudding. Another young girl pulls up a chair next to her. She picks up a spoon and tries to feed a mouthful of the mixture to Eleanor. Eleanor turns her head away.

"Eleanor, you must eat," the girl says. She tries again. Eleanor's mouth stays firmly closed. The girl gives up and moves away.

Eleanor watches as the three old crones are wheeled away from the table. She looks across the room. There are dozens of tables, all with old people sitting at them. Is it a canteen or a cafeteria or maybe a restaurant? Perhaps, she should ask to see a menu.

Suddenly, she feels herself moving backwards. She clings to the table; she mustn't fall.

"Let go of the table, Eleanor," a sharp voice commands her. An arm appears from behind and her frail wrist is gripped by a strong hand and firmly placed in her lap.

"No, leave me alone. I mustn't fall."

"Don't be silly, Grandma. You is sitting in a wheelchair. You isn't going to fall." The woman's laugh bellows across the room and heads turn to witness the incident. "Now you is going to look at the television for a bit. See an old film with Fred Astaire and Ginger Rogers. You is one lucky old lady. I wish I could just sit and watch TV all afternoon."

"I need the bathroom first," pleads Eleanor, clinging to the armrests as she is wheeled out of the dining room.

"Sorry, dear. I haven't got time just now. You've got a pad on though so don't worry."

They come to a sudden stop in the lounge. Eleanor's chair looks inviting. She knows which it is; the cushion with her name on it rests against the chair back. But the wheelchair is reversed into a space on the other side of the room.

"No, I sit over there," Eleanor explains.

"You is staying in your chair for now, dearie. You'll get a bit of sun here." The attendant is opening the blinds at the patio doors behind Eleanor's chair.

Eleanor looks at the television screen. The light reflecting from the window obscures the picture but she can hear the music. It takes her mind back to her own dancing days; with Joe. She wipes the tears away. Joe will be back soon, after the war. He promised.

The afternoon wears on. Eleanor wants to sleep but she's so uncomfortable in the wheelchair, and she really needs the bathroom. She can feel the sun scorching the back of her scalp. She tries to raise a hand to cover her head but can't manage it. She leans over sideways, trying to evade the burning rays.

"Please help me. Can somebody help me?"

She can hear laughter in the corridor. Young voices; male and female. Shrieks of delight and hilarity. She tries again to make someone hear. "Please, I need help." The film has ended. No-one seems to notice. A sit-com comes on. All Eleanor can hear is laughter; laughter all around her. Are they laughing at her?

A trolley is wheeled into the room. A cup of tea is put down on the table beside her but she can't reach it. As the girl comes back with a biscuit, Eleanor whispers to her.

"Can you help me? I need the bathroom."

"Not while I'm doing the teas," says the girl, a look of disgust on her face. "I'll get someone."

"Not thirsty, Eleanor?" says the young man who is collecting the tea cups. "Please," says Eleanor, "I need to go to the bathroom." She'd rather not be taken there by a man but she's too desperate to care any longer.

"Just give me a minute, dear."

Suddenly, she doesn't need the bathroom any more. She doesn't know whether to feel relieved or ashamed.

One of the nurses comes to check the cannula in the back of Eleanor's hand.

"It's hurting me, dear," says Eleanor. "Can you take it out?"

"No, Eleanor. I can't do that. We need to make sure you're getting enough fluids." She inserts something into the injection port and immediately Eleanor starts to feel sleepy again.

The nurse pats her hand in approval. She wouldn't want to put her own mother in here, but at least Eleanor is in a place of safety.

Finding the Key by Priscilla Cook

I looked everywhere trying to find him. Up the Jersey Shore and down through the Florida Everglades, then further south, stringing along the island chain until I ran out of continent. I searched until I reached the last place I could hope to find him. Perpetually clutching a dog-eared copy of *The Old Man and the Sea*, the stalwart vagabond in the deeply creased yellow rain slicker who had always been there to guide me through life's storms could only be in one place. I should have made the connection from the get-go. I should have started there. But then my mind isn't what it used to be.

Thirteen dollars and a legion of lazy, heat-beat, furniture-adorning cats later, I still hadn't found my father. A rainbow of tourists blurred around me as I gasped my way through the syrupy side streets back to Duval. I darted inside yet another Key West schlock shop, grateful for the reverberating hum of the antique air conditioner perched precariously above the door. I rounded a barrel of starfish corpses and slipped in behind the front window display. Peering out through a pod of glass dolphin wind chimes, I caught a glimpse of the familiar black fan windows on the bar across the street. Afternoon patrons waddled in and out like overfed pigeons through the white louvered doors, thrown open to a non-existent breeze. Partially hidden by the lemony clapboard exterior, I could just make out the distinctive curve of the dark wooden bar and the crescent shaped stools that spanned its perimeter.

The distance to my last hope loomed before me, the final few yards to the other side seeming infinite. I tried picturing myself walking in and sitting down, finding what I had come for, but the vision wouldn't come. I glanced down at my swollen feet with their creamy tufts of off-season flesh, pillowing through the crisscrossed leather of the sandal straps, like doughy biscuits trying to escape from their refrigerated paper can.

It seemed impossible.

But then so had dragging myself off of the cold tile of my bathroom floor and onto an airplane and across the country. The moment I had forced myself to accept that the suffering wasn't going away, and it was going to get worse if I didn't do something about it, an invisible bridge had appeared.

There was no good reason why it couldn't happen twice.

I swung the door of the gift shop open and inhaled sharply as the thickness of the afternoon hit me, the bell above the door dinging behind me like a knockout at a fight. As the heat pressed against me from all sides, I hovered in the shadows of the sidewalk palms, their feathery silhouettes mere mirages of coolness.

This is what I came here for.

Doubling my fists, I headed into the street. Heat shimmers rose up around me like oil slick landmines as I weaved my way between them to the cacophony of cars honking and breaks squealing. I kept going, afraid to look anywhere else but the other side.

And then I was there, riveted to a dizzying pattern of coral Cuban tile that lined the entrance to the bar.

I considered running.

But as if on cue, a bell above the bar gave a loud clank, marking the start of round two. Propelled by something unconscious, I found myself marching up to the edge of the bar and hoisting myself onto one of the butt-worn stools.

A leathery blonde with a single, thick braid tossed over one shoulder like some landlocked mermaid eyed me as she slapped a damp coaster on the water ringed mahogany in front of me. "Get you somethin'?"

I felt the eyes of hundreds bore into me, but when I looked up, only the bartender was watching me. As I squirmed around on the stool, trying to get comfortable, a sharp kick in my belly reminded me that time was ticking. "Orange juice, please?"

Two cavernous dimples appeared on the woman's freckled face and she gave me a nod. "You got it, hon."

The spinning blades above barely moved the air and they were starting to make me woozy. I struggled to focus on why I was there. I unfastened my watch and laid it on the bar in front of me.

His watch.

It was the first time in a month I had taken it off. Its heavy steel face and thick glass, designed to withstand the depths of the ocean, weighed on me like never before. It was simply too much to carry anymore.

The bartender set the tall glass of juice down in front of me. "Anything else, love?"

Given the woman's age it was possible she could have known him, but he hadn't been down in the Keys in a good fifteen years.

I shook my head.

"You just holler if you need anything then."

Sipping at the tart liquid, I closed my eyes.

I'm here. Are you?

But only the din of the customers and the hum of the fans answered back.

I thought if I came here, I would find you. Or you would find me. I don't know where else to go. I don't know where else to look for you.

When I opened my eyes, he wasn't there. I knew it was a long shot, but I hadn't contemplated what I would do if I didn't find him. It had just seemed like a matter of where and when. Not if.

A strange sensation sifted through me that felt suspiciously like relief.

The acidity of the juice tore down the back of my throat as I swallowed and set the glass down. As I pushed it away from me, a bird landed on the back bar next to the cash register and perched himself on the rounded bend of a spoon handle. His face was masked in gray feathers with a tiny black spot above his right eye, and his yellow bill twitched as he cocked his head and stared at me.

"You want food, don't you?"

He fluttered his wings, then landed on the edge of the bar in front of me. Distorted by the concavity of the empty glass, his fat, feathery body looked smaller and further away. I contemplated holding the glass up to my ever-expanding belly.

He took a step toward me.

"I don't have anything for you."

He twitched his head to the side, moving his tiny black feet in a silent staccato as he took two steps forward. His eyes never left me as he made his way along the wood to the splayed watch band. He paused, beak angling down as he peered up at me, then perched himself on top of the band.

God, don't poop on it.

He cocked his feathery head, as if regarding an insult, then gave the watch face a definitive peck.

"Hey!"

He skirted around as I swatted at him. But he returned, and again, tapped his beak against the watch face, then looked up at me.

"Are you trying to tell me something?"

I chuckled out loud. *It's a bird. In a bar.*

He's a bird.

One too many animated movies and more pain than I could have ever imagined had clearly conspired to bring me to this point.

The bird is not your dad.

He wasn't there and he wasn't coming. It didn't matter how quiet I was, or how many birds I met, he was gone and he wasn't coming back. This trip was nothing more than a futile effort to find someone who couldn't be found. To assuage that awful searching compulsion I had had from the moment he passed. But the sense of urgency and the power it had over me had been unshakable. I hadn't had any other choice. Find him, get him back.

But it wasn't that simple. If just once I had managed to lift my head up out of the bowels of grief, I would have realized that if I found him, I wouldn't have gotten him back. What I would have gotten was the ultimate confirmation that I had truly lost him. I had gotten foolishly caught up in the destination when what I longed for was the journey, a trade of one purgatory for another. If I kept searching and didn't find him, there was still hope that he was out there and none of it was real, none of it had happened. It was utterly ridiculous and yet, my reality.

Talking to a bird in a bar was one thing. Contemplating for even half a second that he could be my dead father was just plain lunacy.

I slid a five across the bar, eased off the stool, and grabbed the watch. As I walked block after block towards the car, I was too busy lambasting myself to even notice the temperature.

Up the seven mile highway, I drove in paralyzed silence, unable to believe that I had come all this way, that I had spent all this money, wasted all this time. And, yet here I was, at the point I had tried mercilessly to avoid. The point when hope, too had left me and I was forced to face the reality that there was nothing left of him or the life I had known. That this gaping hole in the world couldn't be closed, that this alternate universe I had been subsisting in was unalterable and worse, inescapable.

As I struggled to focus on the road, anxiety tightened the muscles around my neck until I felt as if it would strangle me to death. The urge to flee had returned and I felt my foot bearing down on the accelerator. Miles of the most beautiful turquoise water in the world flew by me, but I never saw it. All I saw was the flat, gray pavement that was leading me faster and faster back to my own personal hell.

By the time I reached Islamorada, my head was pounding and I pulled off somewhere after mile marker 98. I was going to have to take another flight. And it would just have to be ok.

Checking into the last of six lime colored cabins hidden amidst the hammock-strung palms and rangy orange hibiscus, I dropped off my bag and followed the powdery shell path out to the resort's modest pier. My head throbbed as I sat in the shade of a makeshift tiki hut, grinding my forehead against the splintered wood of the picnic table.

I had to calm down. I couldn't let it win again. I couldn't slip back down the rabbit hole. I toed out of my sandals and inhaled, listening to the sounds of the grass roof swishing in the breeze, the pilings squeaking against the pier in the current, the sounds of the birds chirping and calling.

The birds.

I lifted my head just high enough to spot a bird, similar to the one from the bar, perched on the edge of the picnic table, staring at me. My stomach gurgled.

These things must be everywhere.

I pulled the watch from my pocket, checked the time, and laid it on the table.

The bird hopped forward, looked at me, then tapped at the face.

What is it about this damn watch?

As I squinted at my second feathered friend, watching him watch me, I noticed he didn't just look like the other one. He looked *exactly* like the other one, right down to the same black spot above his right eye. My chest squeezed and I reassured myself that I could probably pick up a local guide somewhere and find the front cover plastered with little gray-masked birds with black spots over their eyes.

He tapped again at the watch.

I brushed him away.

He hopped backward, flapped, and landed on top of a piling at the edge of the pier.

This is ridiculous. It's just a bird.

I snatched the watch and strapped it back on, glaring at him as he held his post on the piling.

But what I saw behind him stole the breath from my lungs.

In the shallows of the late afternoon, where the sky fades to tangerine and the skiffs slow to a silent stillness, I could make out the white of a mainsail being raised. It was the only movement on the horizon.

My feet were at once heavy as anchors and light as clouds as I rose and drifted towards the piling where the bird had landed. From the edge of the pier, I could see the boat's captain dutifully checking and securing the rigging as the sleek sailcloth luffed in the breeze.

My mind whirred like an eggbeater, trying to conjure up rational explanations for what I was seeing, but as hard as I tried, only two made sense. And only was even remotely plausible.

Lunacy.

The pier's peeling blue deck paint burned into soles of my bare feet as I watched him move slowly towards the bow.

I glanced down at my watch.

Five thirty-four.

A chill shot through my body. An internal alarm clock had gone off daily since the moment he had died. I shook my head. *It couldn't be.*

The bird bobbed his head, then took flight.

I squinted into the distance, trying to see, trying to focus, trying to bring things closer. But when I saw the captain untie the bow line from the mooring buoy, weakness rushed from my ankles up through my legs.

He was preparing to leave.

What I had most wanted and most feared had just materialized before me and it was about to disappear. I had to do something. I had to stop it. Only this time, there was nothing for me to do. No nurses to consult, no medicines to be administered, no chaplains to call. No arrangements to be made.

The captain kept moving as I stood there, frozen, reliving the most excruciating moment of my life. I watched helplessly as he tossed the yellow pick-up line off into the water, emotions spilling out of me like pachinko balls, invisibly spattering onto the pier before disappearing into the bay.

It was as if my life before he died had gone with him. It was as if all those years simply ceased to exist and I had started over from scratch. The stubborn independence with which I had charged through life was gone, leaving me with only vague memories of the person I used to be when he was in the world. I knew before it happened that I would never be able to comprehend how much I was going to miss him, how much it would hurt, but what I never saw coming was the destruction of my foundation. I hadn't understood how his very presence in my life had given me the confidence to be the person that I had become.

He was who I was.

As the captain stepped to the center of the boat and grabbed hold of the tiller, I felt my heart wrench. I started to pray. Not like before when I had prayed to help him through the pain, prayed to take away his fear. But I prayed like the desperate five-year old that was trapped inside a crumbling adult shell, begging not to be left behind, pleading for her world to go back to being the place she was once able to delude herself into believing was safe. I prayed as if the pain itself could stop him, could pull him back.

But as the blue and white lights of the seafood restaurant up the bay flickered on, the boat was already turning toward the horizon. Afternoon was handing off to evening. I wanted to dive into the bay after him and scream until he heard me or until my lungs filled with water and all of the pain just finally stopped. I wanted to tell him just one more time that I loved him.

As the sail billowed out and took shape in the breeze, the thoughts of all the new things that would never happen and the old things that would never happen again tore at me from all directions. Everything he would miss. Everything that we would miss.

How would I keep going?

My hand shook as it found the top of my rounded belly. This had been the only thing that had pulled me out of the darkness in the small hours of the morning when I didn't know if that was the day the panic would finally win. It was the reason I was there because it was the only part of me that wouldn't let go of hope.

I cocked my wrist and looked down. Time had continued to pass. The world had continued to spin. Everything was continuing on, with or without me.

But as I looked up, the captain turned around. I felt the fluttering of a thousand monarchs beating against my sternum.

Could it be?

And with a quick doff of his ball cap, he gave me a wave.

From that distance, it could have been to anyone along the shoreline. It could have been a symbolic gesture before getting under way, but all doubt had disappeared in that moment.

It was what I had come for.

I could never convey to him everything it meant to me, everything he had meant to me, but I reached up anyway and waved back, my arm flailing in the air as tears flooded my eyes from that bottomless well. As he turned away and embarked on that next leg of his journey, I knew in my heart what had happened. I knew that nothing had changed, but it had change everything for me.

As I watched him sail off toward the horizon in ninety degree heat, clad in that yellow rain slicker, I knew in my heart that I had found him again, right where he had been all along.

Mountain Woman by Robert Pope

Some one or two times in my life, I have had experiences clearly intended as allegorical lessons, coming just at the moment I needed them most. Such was the case a few years ago now, and the images wrought from the natural world are bold as if painted on the walls of mind and memory by some primitive unseen hand given the gift to this purpose.

As I say, this episode came at a time of great need in my life. Unbeknownst to me, my inspiration had flagged terribly somewhere along the way; failing winds left me becalmed in a barren sea. I remember working on my sermon on a Thursday night, looking over the guide and giving thought to suggested scripture and recommended approaches. I leaned heavily over a legal pad, moving a sharpened pencil above the page, ready for the moment inspiration would strike. I sat for two hours in that posture, at the end of which time a bubble of silence had formed around me. It remained all night and next morning my voice came in a throaty hiss.

"Laryngitis," I hissed at my wife. I believed I had caught some kind of bug, so I emailed my dear friend Ben. We went to seminary together but had gone in different directions after. He started an inner city mission while I got myself a church.

My wife smiled when she said, "You seem pretty happy not to have to give a sermon."

"I'm sick," I wrote on a note pad, "and I get to see Ben."

"So that's it!" she said. We laughed, mine barely breaking into sound.

My wife is my great comfort, friend and conspirator. I met her in college, we got married after graduation, and have been together step for step ever since. She came from Georgia, and I kept her in California against her parents' wishes. We manage to visit her family pretty regular, though they miss her at Christmas—not a vacation time for me. Sally is usually a small, neat, pleasant woman with short blonde hair and pale blue eyes. At this time, the difference was her belly, which had become large and round with young Clay the Second.

Ben gave an inspired talk, and Sally introduced him, a big hit because everyone liked seeing her pregnant. The special offering made it worth his time. We had dinner with members of the church at a popular restaurant, over a dozen of us around several tables pushed together, and I didn't have to say a word—the subject of many jokes.

Ben said, "God had to silence Clay for the rest of us to get a word in edgewise."

I smiled, refraining from laughter, but his words weighed on me. When my voice did not come back, I asked a member, Frank White, a retired lieutenant in the Penal System, to tell some hair-raising experiences he said confirmed his faith. He gave such a moving performance the next Sunday it made me question my abilities, in which, honestly, I had always taken pride.

When Frank spoke, I had to remove the handkerchief from my inside jacket pocket and blow my nose. I had tears in my eyes, but I don't think anyone noticed because every eye was on this lummox of a man, not a hair on his head, big white mustache and a belly to match. I watched from the balcony stairs as he stood at the door shaking hands with those leaving in a manner so warm and gentle, a wash of love hollowed me out, left me weak as a kitten.

I caught Bill Williams on his way out. He had been waiting for an opportunity to show off the choir. "Do you think you could take next Sunday," I whispered. I touched my throat to indicate the reason. A smile came on his face like sunrise. I patted his shoulder in thanks. I never heard that music though, or, if I did, it was merely a backdrop to self-questioning.

I'd visited my doctor on Monday the previous week. My wife set up the appointment. He saw nothing amiss, probably the result of seasonal allergies. He said these things hit us as we mature but did a few tests to justify his existence, sent them off to a lab. He called in a few days later to give me the word—no complications.

How ironic, I thought as I hung up. Because I had become conscious of a voice in my head, my own voice, to be sure, but filled with self-questioning. At night it took over. I couldn't sleep or change the course of my thoughts.

The Sunday of Bill William's music, after sitting silent through the evening service once more, it started in and flattened me at four in the morning. I got out of bed, went downstairs, and fell to my knees before the couch. I begged for an explanation but came to the conclusion that one of three things occurred: I had been possessed by a demon; God was trying to tell me my short time in the ministry was up; or—most frightening because most plausible—I had been afflicted with severe depression, or worse.

I tried to keep my issues from my wife. The ministry had become our livelihood and she was pregnant with our son, but she came down softly. How long she watched me weeping with my forehead on clasped hands, I don't know, but I cried out hoarsely when her hand touched my head. She got on her knees and set her hand on my wet cheek.

"Clay," she said softly, "you have to tell me what's wrong."

I shook my head and whispered, "I don't know, Sally."

I said it flatly, a statement of fact. What I said was true but strange. I searched my mind for something, anything, but silence had taken over.

"You can't keep on this way," she told me.

I could not deceive her. I watched her sweet face and nodded. I closed my eyes, and something arrived, an image: me, on my motorcycle, pack in the back, speeding up a mountain road. "Going to spend tonight in the mountains," I hissed. "Get the cobwebs out of my head."

She watched my eyes closely. "I can't go," she said, "you know that, but I can make sandwiches."

She went to the kitchen and snapped on a light. I felt like a great fool, crouching in the dark, so I got up and headed to the basement to pack equipment for the trip.

"Sweetie," she told me once I was ready, "God wants you to do this."

I nodded, but God was far from my mind. The sun was rising as I roared from home, but it did not illuminate my soul: bleakness met my eye, naked landscape raced past. I had those sandwiches in my pack but no hunger. I was empty, wanting no filling. In this state of mind, I didn't know if I would ever get back home.

At some point, I went over those awful possibilities. Possession by demon I had accepted as a possibility as part of my Convention, but as a reality for me, pure fantasy. The Symptoms, however, did not greatly differ. I had a voice in my head, but I assumed it was my own. Was it? I never experienced self-questioning so intense or self-doubt that drove me to despair.

If despair was the effect I suffered, I had never imagined it could be this debilitating. It took an effort of will to think logically. Back to causes: the loss of voice was the first symptom to manifest itself. What if this alone now plagued me: this powerful case of laryngitis? In a rare bout of wit I called my demon Larry, and my face twitched in a smile that really bothered me.

The thought that I had a demon lodged in body, mind, or soul, grew more grotesque each moment. If I played host to such a hideous thing, could I separate myself from him, or her, or it? It terrified me to entertain the possibility. Certain madness lay in that direction. Much better to think God wanted me out of the ministry and thus silenced me. At least the agency was holy, not profane. I could survive such an affliction by bowing to His will, but what would it mean to be rejected by God—who I had given my life to serve?

My wife depended on me, not to mention Clay Two on the way. Friends expected it of me; my congregation honored me as pastor—what would it mean to leave this all behind? My own wife broken-hearted, cast out in the world with no prospects, friends curious, disappointed, congregation—congregation? They would simply hire someone else. A significant part of the position was to allow one's self to be honored by strangers who cast in a sacred light the hiring process to give it dignity, but who were they? What had they to do with me?

After a brief adjustment, would they miss me, or I them?

I called them before me, a sanctuary of strangers, and when I dispelled them, they flew away like crows, cawing and flapping black wings. Depression made a better, a more bearable answer, but what if they cooperated: demonic possession, rejection by God, and depression, all come to inhabit my brain while my body clung to a motorcycle moving through this space long enough to create the illusion I had arrived at a campsite, set up a tent, unrolled a sleeping bag, and crawled inside to be swallowed by a great, long fish called sleep?

She spit me up on the shores of wakefulness at two that afternoon. I moved like a mechanical man, standing in a clearing inhabited by a tribe domiciled in three other pup tents and two big campers at the far edge. Monday afternoon of the soul, I pulled on a clean, blue t-shirt, buckled my jeans, and tightened my boot laces. I had five good hours of thinning light before me, a warm sky populated by drift-less clouds.

God, you trickster, why have you delivered me here?

I went back in the tent, got on my knees, and said my normal prayer before setting off by shank's mare, my long strides cutting time into small bits—away, away. Still, stick to the trails—a man could get lost in this high, wide country. I walked as one in a dream. The air smelled sweet and did not resist my passage through it. A bush smelled like anise, a printer's fern left its mark on the back of my hand, a lizard of gray and green disappeared through rocks. I heard the sound of water, and a flute.

I saw him sitting on a rock inside a running stream, a skinny man in ragged pants, his feet bare, torso naked showing bones, a strap around his head to keep his hair from falling in his eyes. His melody mingled with the movement of the water. I leaned against a tree.

When the music ceased, I opened my eyes and saw him watching me. I reached in my pocket and withdrew some folded bills, a five, a ten, three ones. I could not think which one to give, but at last separated the five and reached across the stream. It rustled in my fingers as he brought his face close, sniffed it, and then exposed long teeth and closed them on the bill. There he sat erect on his rock, moving his head back and forth, as if displaying the bill for an imaginary audience. I smiled at the pantomime until he opened his teeth.

The bill twitched on the breeze, on the water, and sailed away. Out came his head on that turtle neck, teeth snapping until I fed another dollar, which he released to the air and water again. Then those teeth came back. I gave them two more bills, they sailed away. He watched me with those immense brown eyes of his until I wagged the ten before his face, and, with a flick of my wrist, flung it where the others had gone.

He lifted the flute to his lips, breathed, and began to play once more.

In my right mind, I would have laughed, but fear came over me. I strode away, his music coming after me like dangerous blue ribbon, until I put some distance between us. That stream widened and split and joined another, clear and fast and cold, before it disappeared in trees, but I heard more water up ahead so picked up my pace until I stood beside a waterfall from higher up the mountain, melting snows falling down a face of stone. On an impulse, I began to climb the rocks, wet and slippery where the water splashed. Further up, I stood on dry stone and looked to a higher ledge, and crawled ahead, grasping the rocky face in my hands as I climbed with the sensation of leaning backwards over empty air that a climber often gets.

I stood on wet, protruding stones to reach sharp angles of the ledge that I had seen below and pulled myself up until I got my knees in position to lean forward and fall on my chest. My arms shook with the effort expended. When I had my strength back, I sat up cross-legged and took off my shirt to feel the sun on my back. I stood at last and looked up the remaining stone to the top of the waterfall, cool droplets on my chest and shoulders.

I noticed something near the falling water, glinting in the sun as I approached—a hunting knife. I looked into the forest where the rocky cliff edge ended, across the water, up and down the face of stone. Seeing no one anywhere, I picked up the knife and held it in my hand, looking down the distance I had come. I sat once more to meditate, the space of half an hour.

Rather than climb down, I edged into the forest beside the falls, footsteps falling lightly on the reddish floor covered in soft needles. The air smelled of pine as I came over the top of a rounded hill, where a faint trail presented itself, which I followed in the sunlight, rising once again as I walked. At one strange point, my skin crawled, someone watching me. To my left, stones and brush, pines; to my right, trees blocked my view—and the eyes of an enormous hawk just above my head, watching as I took in its cocoa-tinted breast, streaked with darker brown, the powerful and feathered legs, the talons clutching at the branch. I stared at the hooked beak, the steady eyes, feathers shocked back over his head.

Awestruck, I couldn't move, not until I realized he stared at me as well. My heart rattled as I pressed on, glancing back when I heard the dive. He rose from rocks that had been on my left with a snake writhing in his talons, flying so low above my head I could have reached to grab the twisting length of black he carried off—if I had wanted, which I didn't.

I had felt the privilege to have seen him in the tree and then above me like a symbol of God's power on a pale blue sky. I interrupted him at the hunt but could not but see the chance meeting as a further blessing. My heart expanded. I felt large as I rounded the trail and saw ahead yet another of God's creatures— a naked woman in my path.

I couldn't take in so much at once. I kept walking toward her, as if I lost my senses when the hawk passed overhead. Perhaps I had. When it dawned on me it was a naked woman, I stopped. My arms came up on either side, like floating to the surface. A transformation then began—my scalp crawled, my ears rose up, my body cocked itself to act.

The woman swung her head around to look at me. I felt a wave of relief as I realized it was a small one, no bigger than my wife, unshaven anywhere it mattered. Then a second thing occurred- I saw another creature, a human being, large and bearded, appearing on the path beyond the woman and me.

I set my hand beside my mouth and shouted, "Woman!" I was as shocked as him to hear my voice. He stopped and mimicked my original response, arms rising, walking stick in one hand, and then he commenced to wave his arms, growl and shout, flailing the stick above his head. What I had thought a small, disinterested woman stood up straight.

She had been pre-occupied, as it turned out, but now I saw she was quite a bit taller than my wife, or myself, her hair cropped short as if with a knife. I began to quiver in my loins while the strange man danced and bellowed and threatened. I did not move until the woman stepped toward me, making a menacing sound in her throat I had never imagined in my worst nightmare.

I was aware I had a sizeable knife on my person, but I flung it away, in case she saw it too. I raised my hands, palms outward, frozen to the spot. I all but said, "I come in peace!"

I knew more of such mountain women than I supposed. Every bit of knowledge flashed through my mind, images glimpsed, stories heard, the myths and legends, films I had seen. They climbed trees, ran as fast as any man. None of it did the slightest good as she started after me, the path of least resistance, I suppose.

I fled the path, grabbing trees as I ran, clearer of mind than I had been in weeks. I ducked and feinted, penetrating a dense tangle of manzanita, hard, red branches tugging at my shirt, and then bouncing back at me as I climbed through. I no longer knew whether the woman pursued, but I could not stop to make certain. My body was pure action, bone and muscle, sinew, nerve. I broke onto what seemed an open path or clearing that ended sharply over empty air.

I slid against my boots to stop myself. I saw the gorge below, the rushing river and the rocks, twenty, thirty feet, or was it yards? The drop-off looked immense. I spun round to see the woman behind me on the path, coming through the brush at me—but why? What was the sense of this? What had she to gain? I turned and leaped.

Not for nothing, I reflected, had I spent those summers as life guard, gone through life saving classes, the water safety instructor course—I could find a way to land that wouldn't kill me. That was my hope, barely expressed, but my eyes watered so I could hardly see. I screamed all the way down, a sound that startled me, nothing I had heard before.

Dear Lord, save me, I said, or thought, or screamed before I plunged into cold water swirling and bubbling around me, banged the bottom on my feet, brought my knees to my chest and grabbed them tightly as I could. Oh, I stayed down longer than expected, and when I burst up through I gasped for breath and slapped my arms at the surface. Pain seared through my head as I looked up to see the woman at the edge of the cliff above, dirt and rocks falling from her feet. I thought she might come after me yet, but she swung her head and worked or stretched her mouth in an ugly manner intended only to humiliate.

Then, she disappeared, went back to being an indifferent woman. I never saw nor hope to see her ever again. I dragged myself from the water, shaking on the bank, fearing I might fly out of myself at any moment. I'm not sure how long I lay there, but I did have sunburn, next day.

When I tried to stand, my right leg wouldn't have it. A cooperative branch lapped at the edge of the gorge, and I helped myself to his aid. When I stood, surveying the environment, I realized I had landed in a beautiful spot. The river rushed in one side, filled the deceptively passive gorge, rushed out faster down the other side. Water was so clear I saw brown trout floating in the midst, above their angled shadows on the bottom. Silence surrounded me. A hawk flew overhead. I was alive, in this or any other world.

I wished I had the sandwiches Sally made for me, but I would have to earn them by getting back again. I was not a boy scout for nothing, I told myself. I didn't think my leg was broken or I couldn't feel it yet. The world was huge. It was immense. It went out in all directions. I sang as I hiked out, a song my mother loved:

Have thine own way, Lord! Have thine own way!
Thou art the potter, I am the clay.

The Garden of St. Luke's Parish
by Michael Estabrook

"When the kids move out I'd like to move to the city. What do you think? Wouldn't you love to live in the city?"

I look over my coffee mug, squint my eyes and swallow. "No, no I wouldn't. What are you talking about?"

We're visiting our good friends of twenty years, who recently moved into crowded New York City from New Jersey, the Garden State. They bought a loft in Greenwich Village. It's a beautiful place.

"I'd like to live in the city."

"What?" I can't believe she's beginning such a silly conversation. "Oh, really? And how do you know you'd like to live in the city? You've never lived in a city anywhere near the size of New York. What are you talking about?"

This discussion is exasperating me already, and we've barely begun. Why do people always think it's better, somehow, more pure or fulfilling somehow, to live in the damn city. What's wrong with the country? What's wrong with fresh air and sunshine? What's wrong with seeing the sky and feeling the earth beneath your feet? I don't get it.

"But I still know I'd love it," she continues, all smily and looking pretty this morning. "Wouldn't it be great, so much to do, everything right there at your fingertips."

I put my mug down on the thick-glass table between us. I look around our friends' loft. It's a nice loft, spacious, airy, tall ceilings, hard polished dark brown wooden floors. It only cost them half a million dollars, and they got a deal. We still have two kids to get through college, and I'm the only one with a full-time job.

We're visiting for the weekend, and it's Sunday morning. Yesterday, we took an extensive tour of The Village, saw where all the famous folks lived over the years - John Barrymore, Edna St. Vincent Millay, Bob Dylan, Edgar Alan Poe, some painters I never heard of, and an assortment of politicians. And we went into countless art galleries, too. I don't have any money to buy art, but it was fun looking anyway.

"No," I shake my head again, "it wouldn't be great." We live in a suburb a half hour outside of Boston, close enough certainly, to enjoy all the city has to offer. My wife is just exuberant right now, I think, about being in New York. That's why she's talking about living here. We love New York, it is a wonderful place, but a place to visit, in my opinion, not a place to live, for me at least.

"What would you do here all the time? Why would you want to live here? What are you talking about?"

"It's convenient, so convenient. Art galleries close by, magazine stores, theaters, banks, pizza parlors, all kinds of restaurants, everything's here, so close-by, within walking distance. Isn't that great, everything so convenient? I mean, if you need," she shrugs, "a loaf of bread at three in the morning you just walk down to the corner store and get it."

I laugh, "That's ridiculous! That's not justification for living in the city. Who the hell needs a loaf of bread at three in the morning? Jesus, what are you talking about?" This is funny, really it is.

"Well, OK, but look at last night. We just walked down the block and saw a great play." We saw *Gross Indecency*, all about the three trials of Oscar Wilde, the first famous gay person, I suppose, to come out of the closet, publicly.

"Yes, that was wonderful, no doubt about that. But why do you have to live here to go to a play?"

"Because then we could do it all the time."

"Oh, OK," I say, but I think she's losing her mind. I'm tired of being made to feel guilty because I have no desire to live in the city. It's as if city living is what we should all be aspiring to and if you don't there's something wrong with you. You need to be explaining yourself or defending your choice of not living in the city. It's all so stupid, such a stupid conflict, like preferring the winter over the summer or liking red more than blue.

"You know, I love visiting the city and would like to do it more, but I can't see myself living here, all the time."

Lynn comes out from the nether end of the loft and joins us for a coffee. "Did you two sleep all right?" she asks.

"Yes, fine, it was great," says Pat.

I nod and continue, "I simply cannot envision myself living in the city, can't see myself looking out at the street every day, stepping out onto the sidewalk every day. I'm not saying it's bad, not making a judgment here of any kind. I'm only saying that it doesn't seem right for me."

"I understand," says Lynn, "it's not for everybody."

"Right, exactly. See Pat, it's not for everybody."

"Yeah, but I would like to try it. I could live here the rest of my life."

I shake my head again, "Why? You've never lived in a big city, what are you talking about? It would be a big change to how you've lived your whole life."

Yesterday, we walked over and sat on a bench in the St. Luke's Parish Garden. It was so calm and peaceful in there. People were relieved to be around bushes and trees, to actually walk on the earth.

"There's no land around you to speak of, no trees or bushes or lakes or mountains."

I glance over at Lynn. I don't want to offend her, she's a city person now. But she's not offended. She's nodding and petting the cat. She recognizes, I suppose, that there's the city and there's the country. There needn't be a conflict of any kind really. Some people like chocolate ice cream and others like vanilla.

"But why are you so against it?" my wife presses on. My wife is always pressing on.

"I've mentioned a lot of reasons."

"But what's the real reason?"

I sigh. See, I think, there's something wrong with me because I don't want to live in the city. The city is what I should be aspiring to. I'm sorry, but I think that's backwards. Who the hell wants to be so damned busy all the time? The city never sleeps, yes I know, but that's the problem. The city should get some sleep, Jesus.

"The real reason," I say slowly, "is that I don't want to know there are millions of people essentially within walking distance all around me every single minute of every single day. I don't want to have to walk all the time on asphalt and concrete. I like walking on dirt and on grass, I like seeing the trees and the birds in our backyard. I don't like this city living perhaps because it is too convenient, and too busy. I think that's it. It's too busy."

"Too busy?"

"Yes, too busy. I find myself getting more contemplative the older I get. I don't want to be busy and productive," I make quotation marks in the air with my fingers around the word productive, "every damn minute of every damn day. It's nice being closer to nature, it's calmer than here."

She pauses, "I admit I miss seeing the sky. I mean, you can't see the blue of the sky through all the tall buildings."

"My point exactly, Ha! It's unnatural, living in the city. You never step on the earth. You can't see the sky. It's like living on a concrete and metallic spaceship hurtling headlong through the cold void and endless emptiness of space."

I glance at Lynn again. She's smiling. Good old Lynn, she's not getting into this one.

It's now my wife's turn to shake her head. "I wouldn't go that far. I'd still like to live here. If we had the money and could do it right, I'd live here."

"OK, no need to argue about this any longer. Different people like different things, that's the beauty of the human experience. And you're still a young and attractive woman. I would hate for you not to live your dream because of me. There's still plenty of time for you to find a man who you can live with in the city." And I have a smirky look on my face.

But she doesn't smirk back, or make a little laugh like she normally would. Instead, she sips her coffee and gazes longingly though the window into the busy street.

Fairy Tale of Dublin by Tomas O'hArgadain

"Merry Christmas," sang a bell-ringing Santa Claus outside Brown Thomas department store, in Grafton Street, Dublin. I shifted my weight from one foot to another, stamping my feet in a pathetic attempt to keep warm. Sporadic blows into my cupped hands caused breath to escape in mini fog-like gusts. Shop dummies, lavishly dressed in cosy, expensive furs, sneered at me from the huge window.

Santa leaned over to me and whispered, "Listen, pal, move on or I'll get security." Stale beer dripped from every word.

I did not have to be told twice. Bitter cold ripped through my threadbare track-suit, the icy chill biting through my bones. *I'll have to find a place for tonight. I dread another night in that hovel,* I thought; as misery consumed me up, inside.

From nowhere, a middle-aged woman bumped into me. Her precise, posh accent belied her plain attire of duffle-coat and faded jeans.

"I beg you a pardon, young man. My fault as I'm late for work." She smiled warmly, and somehow her balmy, brown eyes bewitched me.

Those enchanting eyes scrutinised my six-foot, skinny frame. Awkwardness resulted and my appearance suddenly became important. I managed to push the half- broken zip of my track-suit top upwards, in order to cover the hole in my sweater, as if this somehow made me more presentable. But I also felt those smiling, warm eyes dousing me in sunshine, could not be judgmental.

"OK, no damage," I managed to mumble. Her scrutiny brought embarrassment but not annoyance. She was about to say something else, so I hurried onwards. For some unknown reason, I knew we would meet again.

Up ahead, a large, open alcove at the front of a television shop struck me as an ideal place to get shelter for the night. *Good, no security shutters in the alcove. I'll collect my stuff later and bed here for tonight,* I thought, cheered up somewhat.

Inside the busy shop, wafting heat welcomed me and tickled my week-old stubble. Plasma screens adorned the walls. They were alive with different programme channels on different screens, 'Secret Millionaire,' a re-run of 'Friends,' and one particular TV even had the volume raised. This TV attracted a lot of gift-burdened, tut-tutting customers. Curiosity and the absence of security men drew me over. I listened.

A TV presenter questioned a government minister, "Minister, this budget has impacted badly on the disabled, lone parents and homeless people by the savage reductions in social protection. How do you justify attacking the most vulnerable in our society?"

"Well, this was a difficult budget, but necessary in these times of economic crisis," replied the Minister, sounding a tad too mournful, with his face etched in serious concern. He brushed imaginary dust from his silk suit. His gold signet ring, with a beautiful, crested bloodstone, reminded me of my wife's similar gift to me. Regretfully, I sold the ring to 'Fats' Burke.

I fell into remorseful reflection: *Sorry, Mandy, I let drink money take precedence over everything ... even anniversary gifts. Oh, Mandy ... I'm sorry I let you down.*

"But let's look at the positives; mortgage interest tax relief has been raised." The minister became more upbeat.

A bit late for me, I thought. *Recession and negative equity separated me from my wife and family; it also cost me my home, business and dignity.* A shop security man interrupted my thoughts and roughly escorted me to the door. Outside, evening darkness joined the stinging wind. A street choir sang the words of John Lennon:

**"A very merry Christmas and a happy New Year
Let's hope it's a good one without any fear."**

On spotting me, the choir conductor moved the collection box nearer to him. With pursed lips, I shook my head from side to side. I wanted to climb inside his head and run a tape of my life, a good, crime-free life. Show him a proud, well-off Dubliner, who once gloried in her multi-faceted splendour, dined in her finest eateries, followed her sporting heroes across the globe and boasted about the best city in the world to whoever would listen. But now the *other* side of Dublin revealed itself to me. I sighed, and decided to return to my fleapit squat.

Outside the abandoned building, the apparent absence of my unwanted, drug–addicted and recent fellow squatters brought enormous relief. Door slightly ajar, I put my foot against the bottom rim and pushed; this caused an indent in the decaying timber. It opened. A screeching rat got caught between door and floor, and then freed itself, its tiny body proving more durable than the crumbling door. Frantic scratching and scurrying sounds followed. Rusty hinges squeaked, adding a further jarring note.

Inside, the room stank. A combination of odours loitered in the semi-darkness: urine blended with widespread grime and reeking damp. This created a sharp, pungent pong that lingered; it forced me to cover my mouth with the sleeve of my track-suit top. A large, faeces-caked, double mattress dominated the floor, the worst of the smell settled there, almost like all the sweat, urine and grime had been soaked up and savoured. My sleeping bag lay twisted on top of the filth. I bundled it up and put it in a rucksack alongside the precious cans of beer. A freezing, fluctuating burst of wind blasted in through the broken window and flicked the pages of my magazine. Used syringes and dried blood pointing to past conflicts, lay scattered around. I pocketed the magazine and left that habitat of hopelessness.

Later that evening, I returned to the TV shop. Luckily, the sheltered alcove remained unoccupied. Bono's words, from 'Do they know it's Christmas?' blared from a passing taxi:

"Well tonight thank God it's them instead of you."

Sitting on my cardboard and sleeping bag, I gulped down my beer. Soon, I had a visitor.

"Hi, remember me?" She had added trendy, new sneakers to her duffle-coat and jeans. I gratefully accepted a carton-cup of coffee and a sandwich.

"Yeah, I remember. And thanks for the grub." I wrapped my hands around the hot carton, relishing the heat and easing my numbness.

"I'm Shirley."

"Tony."

"The magazine ... em ... *Better Gyms*." She nodded to my magazine on the ground. "Is it just reading material? Or do you have an interest?"

"Both, I suppose. I owned a small gym once. A good business ... but now ..." I shrugged and swapped the coffee for a large swig of beer.

"I might be able to help you." She sat down on the cardboard. "Have you heard of the 'Secret Millionaire' television programme?"

"Think so. Don't watch much TV."

She smiled. "Briefly, a bunch of multi-millionaires go undercover and become volunteer charity workers. They assess various charitable organisations and see if they can offer practical advice, support ... or whatever."

"So, let me get this straight, Shirley. I don't mean to be rude, but you're a millionaire ... a secret millionaire ... sitting on cardboard, in the freezing cold, talking to the likes of me?"

"Don't put yourself down like that."

"I don't see any TV cameras."

"No, not this time. Listen, I understand your scepticism. We don't normally operate this way. But, I saw something in you today ... something different from the rest. Call it a hunch. And I've made a lot of money from hunches."

"How did you know I was here?"

"I followed you here. I knew you'd be back tonight. You're not the first homeless person I fed in this spot." She stood up and rubbed her legs. "However, you're the first one I revealed so much to." She handed me a mobile phone. "I got this for you earlier on today. There are a couple of my contact numbers on it and plenty of credit." She smiled a shining smile; it exuded confidence and put me at ease. "I feel I can trust you, Tony. Remember, I can give you the leg up you need. We'll keep in touch." She waved goodbye. I nodded.

Nice one, I thought, examining the phone. *A camera and video phone. I should get a good few bob for this from Fats. I* opened another can of beer and swallowed half of it in one greedy gulp. *But what about my fresh start and leg up? She trusts me, for fuck's sake.* A few more cans of beer obscured the conflicting thoughts, and I fell into a drunken sleep.

A lurid, graphic nightmare followed. This horror show recurred for a long time after; it has also stuck in my memory - probably forever.

The dream started pleasantly enough, but it quickly turned into stomach-churning terror. I swam in a ludicrously clean, flowing, swirling river—almost like a giant Jacuzzi. From a distance, Shirley swam towards me. As she neared, everything changed: the water became stagnant and turned a filthy, brownish colour. Soon, we stood and faced each other in the neck-high, rat-infested river. An invisible vice-grip ensnared me, reinforcing helplessness and immobility.

Her soft eyes suddenly turned blazing, angry red. The lighthouse beacon eyes emitted fiery beams of light. Swarms of bloodied worms burst through her cheeks, wriggling and climbing over each other, in a surreal, slimy race. A remote, contemptuous laughter could be heard from somewhere. A rat's head erupted from her festering mouth. The hairy rodent bared its pointed, polluted yellow teeth, drooling with saliva. I struggled to scream, but paralysis prevented me. The mocking mirth intensified. A gushing, sallow waterfall burned my face.

I awoke to two sniggering men spraying my face with their urine.

"You scumbag junkie," one of them roared. I curled up like a baby and cried. And cried. And cried. They kicked me and then staggered drunkenly onwards. A river of tears and exhaustive self-pity soon brought sleep.

Later, a revving bin lorry and chirpy, bin men banter awakened me to the new day. I packed and left.

By early morning, I arrived at the day-care centre, down near the Dublin quays. Despite the early hour, the long, snaking queue had reached Connolly Lane. A zombie march of new and old poor trudged tiredly towards a waiting, free breakfast. They were a colourful alliance of economic refugees and the people poverty always possessed. Various accents abounded: working and middle class Dublin, country brogue, African and East European. I spotted Fats Burke, he wormed his way through the queue, buying and selling 'God knows what.' I patted the phone in my rucksack and awaited Fats.

A few minutes later, a phone rang loudly to the tune of Mariah Carey's **'All I want for Christmas is you.'**

> **"I don't want a lot for Christmas**
> **There's just one thing I need**
> **I don't care about the presents**
> **Underneath the Christmas tree"**

Nobody answered. I looked at the fellow beside me and showed my eyes to heaven. He gave me a weird look. The tune continued:

> **"I just want you for my own**
> **More than you could ever know**
> **Make my wish come true**
> **All I want for Christmas is you"**

People turned and stared at me. I sucked air through my teeth, realising the offending phone belonged to Shirley. Fats also noticed and waddled towards me. Hurriedly, pressing the little, green phone icon, I answered.

"Hello?"

"Tony, Shirley here. Listen, I'm in the Gresham Hotel, O'Connell St. Do you know it?"

"Yeah."

"Good. My team have a room. You can have a shower, shave, fresh clothes … and a hot breakfast, of course. Interested?"

Warring thoughts wracked my brain: *Shirley's mobile's worth at least two weeks drink money, and drink gets rid of pain. A "fresh start "requires detox … and detox means plenty of fucking pain. But then again, if I accept help maybe Mandy might come back. Maybe. God, I need to quench this thirst.*

"Story bud? Are yeh sellin'?" Fats interjected, pointing his stubby finger at my phone.

I took a deep breath and made the best decision of my life. "No," I replied. Fats shrugged.

"Sorry, Shirley, I didn't mean you. I'll see you in 20 minutes."

Ten months later, after a successful detox programme, I have my own apartment and a job as a gym trainer. Also, for the first time in two years, I've a date to meet my wife next Wednesday. Fingers crossed, this coming Christmas might be a memorable one, in this city I love, warts and all.

Prisoners of War By J Saler Drees

The light from the holograms brightened the otherwise dark room. Orville sat in the center of the room among an array of robot dismantlings: metal limbs with wires protruding, microchips of various shapes and sizes strewn over the tile, boxes full of motherboards, old hard drives and outdated video cards from past projects. In the center of the tech pieces was a near built robot, his own creation of mixed parts, with only the head missing. Her limbs, torso, and breasts were all intact, the outer layers soft like a baby dolls, pliable like putty. Orville had carefully folded the rubber cloth over the wire veins and metal bones. He smoothed out the creases, made sure no lines showed. His hands moved over the frame with precision, the grace of piano player's fingers hitting all the right notes.

As his fingers fiddled with wires, he turned to glance at a hologram that shined out of the surface of a map. A blue dot moved along a grid. The blue dot represented the delivery drone with his package. Twenty-three miles away. About another twenty minutes to wait.

He ignored the other ten screens showing 3-d angles of machines working at the drone factory. It was his job to monitor the machines and make sure they were running smoothly. He could do this in the safety of his dwelling, a windowless shelter, one of many in the building. Only small vents lined the top of the walls before the ceiling met in order to let air in.

After checking the blue dot on the hologram map, Orville looked over at another hologram screen where the light flickered out a woman with mahogany skin and slicked back black hair. She was an indie reporter named Harmony who owned an individual drone that she flew around filming various footage. She was streaming on her Meesite from her dwelling, and even without corporate sponsors, her fame had grown. And she was the woman Orville swelled for.

"People have gone days without their food or sanitary products delivered to them," she said. "Imagine a whole day without food or toilet paper. And with the holidays coming up we want to make sure every delivery makes it safe on time. Shooting down drones not only increases the price of products but also of the delivery itself."

Orville was familiar with the drone issue. Even though he worked for the drone industry he did not own a drone. He didn't feel the need to see through a drones eyes like many others did, flying their drones about the world while they sat at home. Orville only needed drones for his packages and thus he supported the movement to arm them. If anyone shot down his ordered cargo he couldn't fathom what he would do.

Harmony continued, "New drones need to be created with every delivery interference and citizens can't afford such expenses during the holidays. We want to show our families we care but how can we when we can't afford these outrageous prices due to the hoodlums who shoot our cargo carriers?"

"You'll look like Harmony, my Belle," Orville promised the robot as he folded another sieve of rubber material over the robot's metal arm. Harmony's face, the way she talked, her eyebrows moving up and down and overbite slightly protruding over her lower jaw gave her an air of innocence. But her breasts heaving in the low cut shirt told otherwise. Her voice was molasses, sweet and slow, and Orville liked to imagine her talking to only him. He liked to imagine touching her breasts, holding her. He had hugged his pillow once, pretending it was her waist, but women weren't stuffed with foam. Then he grabbed two grapefruits, fresh delivered that day, and squeezed so hard that the rinds split and sour juice squirted into his eyes. No, her juices wouldn't be sour.

In desperation, he petted the moss of one of his house plants that lined the upper shelf by the air vents, imagining it was pubic hair that he would part and there would be his prize, but all he found was dirt. From the porn girls who posed in their rooms naked and sent out their holograms he knew that dirt was not the prize. It was a hole and in that hole was what, a soul? A soul in those hologram holes, untouchable, the women in walls beyond, in their own rooms, forever single.

He realized that organics and holograms didn't give climax, so he began ordering robot parts old and used, since that's what he could afford. Yet, it didn't matter. His robot, his Belle, would save him. Soon, she would be complete and he'd no longer be alone. So tired of being alone.

A loud grating buzzer sounded. Orville jumped. The fourth camera at the factory was highlighted red on Hologram 7. Machine Z05 had stopped moving.

"Why now?" Orville asked, pulling himself away from Belle. He sat down in his chair at the Base, his workstation. After four passwords, a finger test, voice over and eye examination, Orville entered the mainframe where he connected to Machine Z05's database and began punching in codes. Usually, he was able to override a glitch from his home system. However, nothing worked. The machine still remained jammed, its arm outstretched in the middle of the conveyor belt, shutting down the entire production of the drone propellers.

The sound of a ref's whistle blasted shrilly from the Base speakers. The ringtone for supervisor incoming. Orville switched on the main screen and a hologram shot out of a large scowling face, unshaven. Supervisor Hardy Tom. Several blocks over he sat alone in his own dwelling, sporting relics of history, a baseball cap on his head even though physical sports were of the past and sunglasses even though he was indoors. His mouth sucked out the tobacco juice tucked away in his bulging lower lip.

Hardy spit in a can before saying, "Section ten is not moving. Why is Z05 still down?"

Orville typed in more codes, the interior of Z05 popped into a window on the hologram. He zoomed into the highlighted compartment and saw that the gears apparently were overheating. Odd, since he had just preformed a spectral analysis a week ago on its various parts and none indicated signs of wear.

"Somehow gear A150 is causing friction, creating overheating," Orville replied.

Hardy crammed more tobacco in his protruding lower lip. "For the love of God, you need to go down there and loosen the gear."

Orville licked his lips. "Go to the factory? Can't you send the maintenance robot?"

"Oh hell, you know that robot is currently out of commission."

"We still don't have a replacement?"

"Not for your section, so you're out of tech maintenance," Hardy spat. "Hail Mary and go down there to fix it."

Orville closed his eyes, dizzy, sweating. Slick wet drops leaked out of his pores, smelled oily, felt slimy even though his dwelling was always set at seventy degrees. Images from past news clips showing shredded limbs, blood stained faces, resurrected in his mind.

"What if I get bombed?"

"Sweet Lord. You have armor. Wear it." Hardy spat into an off screen container. The sound of the spit hitting more spit made Orville's ears feel waxy.

"I can't withstand a large explosion."

"You asking to get fired? There are many others who would die for your job and be willing to get paid less for it."

Orville sucked in his breath. He couldn't afford to lose his job. Not when he had Belle to take care off. She still needed add-ons like hair, eyes and skin tone. She would need the latest upgrades and maybe one day she would even be able to become pregnant, carry a baby inside her plastic womb. But eggs were not cheap and neither was a surrogate robot. Plus, the continual updates on security were increasing in price monthly. He couldn't protect Belle if he couldn't pay for security.

"So is that what you want? To be jobless?" Hardy asked.

Orville shook his head. "I'm on it. I'm going now."

"Thank Saint Mary Mother of God." Hardy snickered and the screen went blank.

The blue dot on the map was five minutes away. He had to wait at least five minutes. The thought of going out there, outside into that dangerous world made him stiff. He hadn't been out of his dwelling for six months, which was normal. Most people never ventured out anymore. To go outside was a death sentence.

Could he really go out there? Where soon, the mailmen of drones would be armed.

"Shit, Belle, I don't know what to do," he said from his chair over to the headless robot who stood motionless at the center of the room.

Artificial birds chirped from the speakers. His mother's ring tone.

Orville leaned over the Base and flicked on the call. A hologram of his mother's face popped up. Her pinched nose and shriveled prune lips were tight.

"You see the news?" she asked from her dwelling across the city.

"Mom, I can't talk long."

She cut him off. "The delivery drones have guns."

"Yes, the company I work for is starting the new model in ninety days."

"You knew about this?" his mother's voice rose.

Orville's eyes leaked fluid. Being inside for so long he began to notice parts of his body acting up. He wiped his eyes with the back of his hand, and watched the blue dot on the map. It came closer and closer to the highlighted square. His home. And yet he'd have to go outside, soon. He couldn't prolong it much longer without Hardy calling back.

"Listen, I need to go. I have to go out there."

"What? Go where? Outside? You can't do that!" His mother shrieked and blew her nose on a silk handkerchief. A faint light from his hologram in her room indicated chinaware, porcelain dolls, ivory horns on shelves behind her. Heirlooms of the past. Even his name was a cry for past times. Times his mother never knew, but liked to imagine.

"I must." Orville leaned his head on the back of the chair. "One of the machines stopped working."

Her face of pixilated light moved closer to Orville, every wrinkle exposed, their lines pulsing with age. Her eyes gleamed watery, wild, frightened. He reached out, his hand going through the hologram, but he pretended he felt her papery skin on her forehead, her dried out hair.

"You'll get shot out there or kidnapped or worse."

"Mom, listen, today I don't have time to talk. I don't want to go out there any more than you want me to."

"Oh dear, Orville, Oh dear. My only baby being sacrificed out there in that war zone for what? The factory? Preposterous. Don't let them make you," his mother said. Her room went dark. The china and dolls become invisible. Must be another blackout in her area.

Orville looked at the blue dot again. Minutes away.

"I'll call you tomorrow," he said.

"Wait, Orville." The lights blinked back onto her face bunched up, turned pink, shrinking in on itself, making her appear smaller. She was going to cry. "I fear I'll never hug you again. Actually I know this."

Orville gulped saliva that tasted like ash. He shuddered. "Don't do this now, Mom."

He glanced over at Belle, the unfinished robot standing amidst many parts.

"Orville," she begged. "Don't do it. Don't go out there. Your job isn't worth your life."

"Sorry, Mom." He clicked the hologram off, feeling guilty. Usually, he wouldn't dare ignore her, afraid if he did, she would go away forever. But the package was almost at his door, would be in the room with him while his mother was in another room, another dwelling by herself across the city, really only a mile, but a mile too long shaping loneliness into a stone, wedged in the way.

I fear I'll never hug you again. She was right. But who wanted to admit that?

Belle stood headless and waiting.

The alarm system sounded and Orville checked his security camera, watching the delivery drone drop off his package at the base of the building at a scanning station. First the package was screened for explosives, poisons, dangerous animals before being vacuumed up and shot out in front of an iron gate outside his dwelling. The gate lifted and the delivery slid into his room.

Orville tore the box, flung foam and padding about the tiled floor till he got to another box. He hoisted the box up gently, placing it on the futon bed and kneeled before it. With meticulous care, he unfolded the flaps and reached in, lifting up a sleek silver blue skull, void of facial features. Holes for the eyes, nose and mouth punctured into the face. The skull spiked rays of blue about the room. He cradled the skull close to his chest, feeling the cold, heavy smoothness of it.

"Belle," he cooed, stroking the metallic cap. "You're here at last and now I have to go. Out there. But for you I will come back, and you'll be completed."

Soon the skull would be attached to the body. Soon Orville would power her up, connect her to the internet and download information into her empty mind: house cleaning aps, cooking aps, gaming aps, joke aps, lover aps, bondage aps, and he would program each ap to his liking. She'd be most attracted to pasty men with flabby arms and stick legs. His receding hairline, graying beard and sagging eyelids, her preference. The hologram women he dated never came back, seeking other men in other dwellings to hologram chat with. But Belle wouldn't care how he looked. She would bake him the best chocolate brandy cheesecake. Something he could actually taste. The other women, distances away could never provide something tangible, something to touch, to taste, to feel deep in his core. But Belle, he could feel. She would know how to make him happy.

The ref whistle blew through the speakers again. Orville scrambled back to the Base and Hardy blinked on. Orville cradled Belle's skull in his lap.

"Lord God Almighty, why are you not at the factory? Z05 is still not running."

"I'm getting ready to leave now," Orville said, out of breath. He closed his eyes. The dread, the footage of that world beyond the safe walls of his dwelling, pressed on his skull.

"What's in your lap?" came Hardy's voice. Orville opened his eyes to see Hardy's squinting, hologram face looking at him.

Then he leaned back and laughed. "Sweet baby Jesus. You bought yourself a Mimi? You know Mimi's break down all the time, right? Haven't you read the reviews?"

Orville placed his hands over the skull, sheltering her from further scrutiny. "She's not a Mimi."

"Right, whatever," Hardy smirked. "Now get your ass up and go to the factory. Our production rate is especially important this month. All eyes are on us with the new model coming out so don't make me fire you."

"Not wasting another minute," Orville assured him as the hologram snuffed out.

Delicately placing Belle's skull on the futon, Orville then reached for his gear in the closet. After clicking on his headset, he thrust the helmet over his head, snapped on the radar goggles, suctioned an oxygen mask over his mouth, strapped a bullet proof vest over his chest, and over that a flame resistant jump suit. He pulled on his boots, clasped the metal buckles shut and then slung a rifle over his shoulder along with magazine clips, shoved a pistol into his holster and hooked grenades to his belt.

The fear of the outside hung heavy over him. He tried to remember the last time he'd left his dwelling. It had been to go visit his mother, but the news of bombings hadn't left his ears. He turned and went back to his safe haven, his dwelling of steel and iron bolts among all the other dwellings with the same safety features.

Every year, it was more difficult for him to leave the confinement of his home. Drone news flickered in his mind with scenes of crumbling buildings, people running blind, blood squirting from eyes and ears and noses torn off, limbs soldered, babies limp in mother's arms, squeezing out every horror, making it ooze into the air.

Orville took a deep breath. He looked back at Belle's skull resting on his futon, glowing the bluish hue.

"I'll return," he whispered into his oxygen mask.

He opened his front iron door to an empty hall and walked down to the elevator. Its doors slid open with a loud scraping sound, hurting his ears, but he willed himself to move onward. It clanked and rumbled down to the first floor and its doors creaked open, revealing just a few feet away the main entrance to the outside world, a black narrow door rising up to the ceiling, giving off a sense of foreboding.

Once directly in front of the door, Orville paused, envisioned the worst out there. Sonorous clashing ruptured into his mind, and shrieks echoed as bodies thudded to the pavement, thump, thump, thump, like heartbeats. He could even hear the blood pulsing out of gashes, hear last breathes squeezing out of chest cavities and trash bobbing along in the copper water that spilled into the gutters. But that wasn't here. That was on the drone news elsewhere, right?

He counted to ten and then pushed the door open, stepping out into the empty steel world. A loud buzzing filled the sky as drones whizzed past on their flight paths to deliver packages of oranges, juice, boxes of cereal, cans of soup, coffee, clothes, toiletries, computer parts, robot parts, all from factories delivered to secure front doors. No pedestrians walked on the sidewalk. No cars drove by on the road. Black shiny buildings with no windows lined the streets, only small slit vents could be seen that brought in the oxygen to the dwellers within. The air smelled of fizzing wires, like electricity falling down from the sky. The sun burned a ghoulish ochre through the goggles, hurting his eyes.

Once outside, he took a step, then another and another. The drones swarmed back and forth. Some were camera drones no doubt taking footage, some were personal drones out spying. What if someone realized he was outside and came to attack him? Despite the armor, he walked faster, rifle extended out before him, index finger on the trigger. The factory was only five blocks away but even if it was one block, venturing beyond one's secure apartment dwelling was a foolish endeavor.

Orville's skin tingled. Anyone could shoot him. Even personal drones were rigged.

Decades ago, it started with attacks in public places. Suicide bombers and machine gun attacks at schools and malls. Soon security was everywhere. People were searched before even entering a grocery store. But then even the security lines were getting bombed. Soon if someone walked down the street they could be sniped. More and more civilians bought their own weapons for protection and the fear escalated.

The radar goggles flashed red before Orville's eyes. Somebody was approaching him. Through the lenses he stared ahead at the steel buildings reaching up. The factory was only one more block over, the smoke stacks stuck their heads in the sky, belching gray pillows of smoke out of their throats. The only movement he saw were the drones and even they looked like endless crisscross patchworks against the dimming sky.

Then he saw her, emerging out of the haze. She wore no helmet, no mask, no armor, no boots. She held no guns. Instead her face was fully visible, sandy skin, strong and taut, raven hair bouncing over her shoulders. She wore a navy blue button down dress with pink flowers dotting it. He only knew this because he zoomed his goggle's vision on her. Her feet were bare, toes bloodied and dirt streaked.

She could have a bomb under her dress. Why else was she unarmed? Why else was she unafraid? She was ready to take her life and his. One final attempt at the end. If he shot her, she would explode. He held off on the gun, lifting it up onto his shoulder, showing he wouldn't hurt her. That's not what she wanted though. She wanted to die. Orville was certain.

His feet tingled, itching to run. But she may chase him and his armor weighed heavy over his trembling limbs. She may throw a grenade at him behind his back. She looked fit enough to outrun him.

The two stared at each other. Her hands were down to her sides and slowly she lifted her right hand to the center of her body and then outstretched it, extending the elbow, revealing soft flesh there in the crook against the sandy skin. Her palm faced out toward him, seeming to beckon him with offering.

Orville shifted the rifle off his shoulder, pointing it back on the woman. Corners of her eyes lifted, mouth opened, revealing teeth, as lips curved up. Her smile eclipsed Orville's rationale thinking, made him want to tear off his helmet, rip off his goggles and oxygen mask, and hurry to her, pressing his mouth on her mouth. Her smile ate him, he felt consumed into her, unable to look away.

There they stood, the two of them, only a few yards a part, with no walls in between and for a moment Orville felt frozen, as though all outer sound stopped, the drones buzzing overhead, the smoke gurgling into the sky from smoke stacks, the steel buildings full of dwelling compartments, all hushed quiet. In that moment as he stood paralyzed before the woman's bare face, his mind became sick with longing to touch her. He reminded himself Belle was waiting at home for him, that the Z05 needed to start running again, but his fingertips on the trigger burned, wanting another human, to feel tender skin against the palm of his hand. To kiss that skin, smell it, tuck it into his heart. The hologram women, even the rubber skin of Belle, couldn't fulfill this void. He had forgotten what it was like to feel a real person. A live person, a woman. He had to have her, this woman in the blue dress dotted with flowers.

He would take care of her. He would love her.

His voice sounded through the speaker on his mouth piece, "Are you lost?"

The woman cocked her head to one side, her smile fading, much to his dismay, although he understood she probably was afraid. He lowered his rifle.

"Why are you out here?" he asked. He stepped toward her, rifle still lowered. "I won't hurt you."

Her eyes darted back and forth and she shook her head, her arm still up, showing the exposed sandy flesh which ignited within him inexplicable desire for her. She seemed in danger and he had to save her, feel that flesh, her hand in his. He'd tear off his gloves and feel her skin. Kiss those fingers, taste her salt and iron.

"I want to help you," he said, slowly bending down, his eyes still fixed on her through his goggles as he set the rifle upon the ground. The logical side of him was screaming, abort, abort. You'll lose your job and possibly your life. This has to be a trap.

But the woman, her button down navy dress with those pink flowers looked so innocent, so helpless and confused. His radar wasn't firing off any warning of imminent danger. He straightened himself, hands empty, rifle on the concrete.

The ref whistle blasted in his headpiece along with the message flashing "Urgent." Hardy Tom was undoubtedly angry the machines were still paused. Orville tried to hit ignore but as he lifted his hand up to his headset, the woman charged toward him.

"Stop!" Orville called out, his legs moving, jolting backward.

Suddenly, a bright light flashed, the woman's face before him split apart, but he saw no blood, no flesh, only a sun. A sun in a distant memory reawakened. A force rammed Orville in the chest, solid and debilitating. His body shot backward, hitting against the steel wall of a building, knocking the wind out of him and his vision grayed, the world around him looked like it was behind a mesh screen, the sharp angles of the buildings momentarily soft.

He couldn't move. Some invisible force like gravity seemed to press him against the wall. Closing his eyes, he thought of Belle back in his dwelling, waiting for him.

Author Information

Gary Beck

Gary Beck has spent most of his adult life as a theater director, and as an art dealer when he couldn't make a living in theater. He has 11 published chapbooks. His poetry collections include: Days of Destruction (Skive Press), Expectations (Rogue Scholars Press). Dawn in Cities, Assault on Nature, Songs of a Clerk, Civilized Ways, Displays (Winter Goose Publishing). Fault Lines, Perceptions, Tremors and Perturbations will be published by Winter Goose Publishing. Conditioned Response (Nazar Look). Resonance (Dreaming Big Publications). His novels include: Extreme Change (Cogwheel Press) Acts of Defiance (Artema Press). Flawed Connections (Black Rose Writing). Call to Valor will be published by Gnome on Pigs Productions. His short story collection, A Glimpse of Youth (Sweatshoppe Publications). Now I Accuse and other stories will be published by Winter Goose Publishing. His original plays and translations of Moliere, Aristophanes and Sophocles have been produced Off Broadway. His poetry, fiction and essays have appeared in hundreds of literary magazines. He currently lives in New York City.

Katarina Boudreaux

Katarina Boudreaux is a writer, musician, composer, tango dancer, and teacher -- a shaper of word, sound, and mind. She returned to New Orleans after circuitous journeying. New work is forthcoming in HARK and YAY!LA. www.katarinaboudreaux.com

Arthur Carey

Arthur Carey is a former newspaper reporter, editor, and journalism instructor who lives in the San Francisco Bay Area. He is a member of the California Writers Club. His fiction has appeared in print and

Internet publications, including Pedestal, Funny Times, Defenestration, Perihelion, Eclectic Flash, and Writers' Journal. His short stories, novella, and humor novel, "The Gender War," are available at Amazon.com.

Priscilla Cook

As a Seattle area native, Priscilla Cook enjoys writing about the blustery, coastal northwest, but frequently trades in the monocloud for tropical breezes in more sun-soaked locales. In addition to writing short story and novel-length mainstream fiction and romance, she dabbles in Haiku and has been published in several editions of Modern Haiku. She is a member of both the Pacific Northwest Writers Association and Romance Writers of America, and holds an MBA from Washington State University.

Melodie Corrigall

Melodie Corrigall is an eclectic Canadian writer whose work has appeared in *Litro UK, Foliate Art, Emerald Bolts, Earthen Journal, Still Crazy, Six Minute Magazine, Halfway Down the Stairs* and *The Write Place at the Write Time* (www.melodiecorrigall.com).

William Doreski

William Doreski lives in Peterborough, New Hampshire. His latest book is *City of Palms* (AA Press, 2012). He has published three critical studies, including *Robert Lowell's Shifting Colors*. His fiction, essays, poetry, and reviews have appeared in many journals, including *Massachusetts Review, Notre Dame Review, Worcester Review, The Alembic, New England Quarterly, Harvard Review, Modern Philology, Antioch Review, Natural Bridge*. He won the 2010 *Aesthetica* poetry award.

J Saler Drees

J Saler Drees lives in San Diego CA, and when not reading and writing, enjoys bicycling around the city as well as working with children.

Michael Estabrook

Michael Estabrook is a recently retired child-of-the-sixties baby boomer freed finally after working 40 years for "The Man" and sometimes "The Woman." No more useless meetings under fluorescent lights in stuffy windowless rooms. Now he's able to devote serious time to making better poems and stories when he's not, of course, trying to satisfy his wife's legendary Honey-Do List.

S. P. Hannaway

S. P. Hannaway is fairly new to writing short fiction. His first short story appeared in *Litro Online* in 2014. Since then his stories have featured in *Dream Catcher*, *The Sonder Review*, *Gravel* and *Brittle Star*. He's completed the Short Story Writing course and the Writers' Workshop course, both at City University. He's worked as an actor for a number of years and lives in London.

Tomas O'hArdagain

Tomas O'hArgadain is a freelance writer and blogger. Dublin born and bred, Tomas loves writing and especially enjoys writing about his native city, whether fictional or non-fictional. His non-fictional blogs about Dublin can be found on the popular Dublin website, 360dublincity.com. He believes, like the famous Charlie Chaplin, that: "A day without laughter is a day wasted." Tomas strives to see the funny side of life, and also endeavours to maintain a social conscience.

Matthew Harrison

Matthew Harrison has had more than fifty stories accepted by venues such as Every Day Fiction, Infective Ink, On the Premises, White Stag and Elohi Gadugi.

Kate Hodges

Kate Hodges is a teacher turned student - writer, trading a middle school science lab in the US, for the uni library in Scotland. Growing up she wanted to be Ramona Quimby, Dawn Schafer, and Sarah, Plain and Tall. She has a literary crush on Gilbert Blythe. She still believes you can tell a lot about a person based on their favourite Wakefield twin. She is on a quest is to both bake a perfect pie crust and to win a pub quiz.

Billie Louise Jones

Billie Louise Jones was born in Louisiana and raised in Texas, She has lived in Shreveport, Dallas, New York City, New Orleans, Austin, and Hot Springs. Each of these places has its own character. She has been published in some literary magazines and anthologies.

Allen Kopp

Allen Kopp lives in St. Louis, Missouri, USA. He has had over a hundred short stories appearing in such diverse publications as *Grey Wolfe Publishing, Simone Press, A Twist of Noir, Bartleby-Snopes, Penmen Review, Short Story America, Danse Macabre, Skive Magazine, Churn Thy Butter, KY Story, Quail Bell Magazine, State of Imagination, Gaia's Misfits Fantasy Anthology, Back Hair Advocate, Wilde Oats Magazine,* and many others. His Internet home is at: www.literaryfictions.com

Paul Lamb

Paul Lamb lives near Kansas City but escapes to the Missouri Ozarks whenever he finds the chance. His stories have appeared in Aethlon, Bartleby Snopes,The Little Patuxent Review, Danse

Macabre, The Platte Valley Review, The Nassau Review, and others. He blogs about his writing and other oddments at Lucky Rabbit's Foot. He rarely strays far from his laptop, unless he's out running, which he's been doing a lot lately.

http://www.paullamb.wordpress.com

Thomas Larsen

Thomas Larsen have been a fiction writer for twenty years and my work has appeared in Best American Mystery Stories, Newsday, New Millennium Writings, and Puerto del Sol. My novels INTO THE FIRE and FLAWED are available through Amazon.

Ken Leland

Ken Leland won the Carleton University Creative Writing Contest, *Passages*, for 2015 and his debut historical novel *'1812 The Land Between Flowing Waters,'* was published by Fireship Press in 2013. Three of the author's short stories are included in the 2012, 2013 and 2015 anthologies published by Inwood Indiana (Prolific Press) and a fourth has been accepted for publication.

Matthew McKiernan

Matthew McKiernan was born in Cranford New Jersey in 1990 and moved to Yardley, Pennsylvania in 1994. He graduated from LaSalle University in 2013 with a BA in English and History. He received his MFA in Creative writing at Rosemont College in May 2016. His first short story, "A Leap of Faith" was published in "Skive Magazine" in November 2013. He is currently editing his Science Fiction Novel,"Human" which he hopes to publish in the near future.

Stephen McQuiggan

Stephen McQuiggan was the original author of the bible; he vowed never to write again after the publishers removed the dinosaurs and the spectacular alien abduction ending from the final edit. His first novel, *A Pig's View Of Heaven*, is available now from Grinning Skull Press.

Jim Meirose

Jim Meirose's work has appeared in numerous magazines and journals, including Blueline, Ohio Edit, Bartleby Snopes, Innovate, the Fiddlehead, Witness, Alaska Quarterly review, and Xavier Review, and has been nominated for several awards. Two collections of his short work have been published, and a novel, "Mount Everest" was just released by Montag Press. Four more novels are under contract with Montag for 2016 release: one never before published and three which had gone out of print from other houses. More information is available at www.jimmeirose.com

Lesley Middleton

Having retired from teaching, Lesley found she had time to resurrect her ambition to become a writer. Initially she thought freelance journalism might be interesting and challenging but it wasn't long before realisation dawned: writing fiction is much more fun! She writes mostly short stories and flash fiction. Several of her short stories have appeared in anthologies recently and two more are due to be published later this year.

John Mueter

John Mueter is a pianist, composer, educator and writer. His short fiction has appeared in many journals including the American Athenaeum, Lowestoft Chronicle, Halfway Down the Stairs, Bibliotheca Alexandrina, Simone Press Publishing, and the Bethlehem Writer's Roundtable. He is on the faculty of the University of Kansas as opera/vocal coach.

Website: www.johnmueter.wordpress.com

Don Noel

Retired after four decades' prizewinning print and broadcast journalism in Hartford CT, Don Noel received an MFA in Creative Writing from Fairfield University in 2013. His work has so far been chosen for publication by Calliope, Shark Reef, Drunk Monkeys, The Tau, Indian River Review, Midnight Circus, Oracle, Clare Literary Magazine and The Raven's Perch.

Columbkill Noonan

Columbkill Noonan has an M.S. in Biology, and teaches Anatomy and Physiology at a university in Maryland. She writes historical fiction with a supernatural slant. In her spare time, Columbkill enjoys hiking, aerial yoga, and riding her horse, Mittens. To learn more about Columbkill, and to hear breaking news about her all of her latest works, please feel free to visit her at-www.facebook.com/ColumbkillNoonan. She's been published by Mystery and Horror, LLC Publishers, Running Press, Strange Musings Press and Schlock! Webzine.

David Perlmutter

David Perlmutter is a freelance writer based in Winnipeg, Manitoba, Canada. The holder of an MA degree from the Universities of Manitoba and Winnipeg, and a lifelong animation fan, he has published short fiction in a variety of genres for various magazines and anthologies, as well as essays on his favorite topics for similar publishers, including most recently SFF World.com. He is the author of America Toons In: A History of Television Animation (McFarland and Co.), The Singular Adventures Of Jefferson Ball (Chupa Cabra House), The Pups (Booklocker.com), Certain Private Conversations and Other Stories (Aurora Publishing), Orthicon; or, the History of a Bad Idea (Linkville Press, forthcoming) and Nothing About Us Without Us: The Adventures of the Cartoon Republican Army (Dreaming Big Productions, forthcoming.)

Rob Pope

Robert Pope has published a novel (*Jack's Universe*) and a collection of stories (*Private Acts*), as well as many stories and personal essays in journals, including *The Alaska Quarterly Review, The Kenyon Review,* and *The Conium Review*. He teaches at The University of Akron.

Gillian Rioja

Gillian Rioja was born in Manchester but has lived half her life in La Rioja, the wine region of Spain. A few years ago she joined a local writing group and has had stories published in Spanish magazines. However, she realised that to truly express herself she needed to write in her mother tongue, English. She has just finished a distance-learning MSc in creative writing with the University of Edinburgh, and recent stories have appeared in Structo and Avis. She writes speculative fiction as well as slice-of-live stories which often focus on British people living in Spain.

Fariel Shafee

The author has worked in scientific fields, but enjoys writing and art. She has published prose and poetry in various online and print magazines. http://fariels.tripod.com

Victoria-Elizabeth Whittaker

Victoria-Elizabeth is a writer who was brought up along the central coast of California and the northern shores of Lake Michigan, but finds herself living, inexplicably, within the southern suburbs of New Jersey, where she translates French symbolist poetry and writes fanciful speculative fiction. Her stories have appeared and are forthcoming in The Writing Disorder and Ealaìn. She is currently at work on her second novel.

Made in the USA
Columbia, SC
24 July 2017